ASH WEDNESDAY

BY A.C BILLEDEAUX

Ink Smith Publishing

www.ink-smith.com

Printed in the U.S.A

Cover. Image created by: SBXDesign.

ISBN: 978-1-939156-18-1

Ink Smith Publishing

P.O Box 1086

Glendora CA

ASH WEDNESDAY

Are you ready for the fight of your life?

AC Bullen x

Prologue

At the world's end, a hero did not rise. So the people set out to make one.

It was already referred to as the "ruins of Chicago" sixteen days after the war was over. The United States had not surrendered—the worst devastation in the world had fallen upon those that refused surrender—but it didn't matter. Nothing was spared. Not Chicago, not New York City, not Los Angeles. Nothing. Once upon a time, they had all stood invincible.

Now they didn't.

What was left of the population—those that had not fled during the evacuation, burned in the fire, died of starvation, fear, hopelessness, or whatever it was that had killed so many—were camped in the hospital tents that the Red Cross had left behind when they'd abandoned them. They were the last. A handful of survivors, men with wives and children, carrying burdens that made them hostile and uncompromising.

Pilot Archer sat at his son's sick bed, elbows resting on the sheets, head propped up in his hands. He'd been sitting like that, in a sort of meditative prayer, almost since the day he'd arrived. Back when the fires were still burning in the city, when dark never really fell, and he'd carried the unconscious boy to safety.

It made no difference at all. The boy was delirious with fever and that was when he was awake. Pilot's son woke very little.

Across the room, the others sat in a circle of folding chairs. They were not leaders, not one, since the leaders of the city had died with Chicago. Months ago. But they were all survivors. They had earned their place to sit on this strange, belligerent council. They had earned the right to have their voices heard.

The problem was that, sixteen days after the war—and the world—had ended, they still couldn't figure out what exactly they wanted to say.

Jonathan Haze, a former school board representative and a father of four, frowned. "But if we leave, where do we go? Some of us-"

"-have families," another man interrupted. He chewed at his thumbnail absently, a fixation left over from a cigarette habit that he'd been unable to rid himself of even in the face of the apocalypse. "We know. For God's sake. We know."

There was a grumble from the others, who functioned mostly as a mob rather than any single person. Haze ignored them. Just outside the council's circle, two children sat cross-legged, playing a game that involved whispering words into each other's ears until one of them laughed.

The girl leaned in, pressed her lips to the boy's cheek, and blew. No words, she just blew hot air into his ear. The boy laughed, squirming away from her.

Haze swatted at a fly. "And yet, we have to do something."

The council blinked at him. They had been over this. It was not a question of whether or not something had to be done. Everyone in the circle knew something had to be done. It was the matter of deciding what, exactly, that something should be.

"A last stand," someone suggested. Again. "Fight for our country."

Behind him, Pilot groaned. "What country?" he demanded.

Haze ignored him.

The others on the council did not.

"What do you mean, 'what country?' The United States of America. *Our* country."

Pilot stood. The screech of his chair against the metal of the sick bed gave the council a start. “And if we fought for our country, who would we be fighting against? What would we be fighting for?”

Someone sighed. “He’s right.”

The council grumbled. Of course he was right. Everyone knew that.

But still, something had to be done.

“We have to save our world!”

The children giggled in the corner. The mob turned quiet.

“What world?” someone retorted bitterly.

Pilot kicked the leg of his chair. It folded and crumbled, suddenly, to the ground. The clatter echoed uncomfortably in the silence that followed.

It was the silence that finally drew Haze's attention. "You'll wake your son," he said coolly.

Like a magnet, all eyes went to the boy.

Pilot Archer's son did not stir.

So Pilot strode to the circle and took the seat that had been left empty for him. He brushed his hands along the sleeves of his tattered black jacket, wiping soot from the fabric but leaving stains in its wake. Then he looked up at this council—perhaps the last of its kind—and smiled.

"I have another way."

OLD TESTAMENT

Chapter 1

The boys in Pilot's Coliseum usually made an effort not to talk to one another.

Fights in the arena came regularly—every ten days like clockwork—but it might as well have been a daily affair. You never knew when a friend, or at least a guy you'd shared a bunk with for the last two months, would suddenly die.

And if they didn't die, there was still the chance they'd kill someone else you knew. It was better not to know anyone, that way it didn't matter when they finally, inevitably, met their match.

So it wasn't unusual that the boys living in the locker room that served as a dorm didn't bother to say anything when Red sat up, suddenly, and choked back a sobbing scream.

His leg hurt like hell.

His leg had been hurting like hell for more than a week. That was what happened when someone stuck you with a knife.

But Micah was dead and Red was not. He slipped his fingers under his pillow, reaching back to wrap his hand around the hilt of Micah's knife. The metal was cool under his palm, but it wasn't enough to ease the throbbing in his head. Last night, he'd been drowning in a fevered sweat. He hadn't slept. He'd barely closed his eyes. It didn't matter, though. Red had another fight today.

And Pilot's fighters did not feel pain.

Red eased his right leg off the bed and settled it against the cement floor. So far so good. He checked his weight, then stood up. Eyes flickered open around the room; Red could feel them watching him.

The boys in the Coliseum usually made an effort not to talk to each other, sure, but they were still curious.

His bunkmate, Alec, gave a low whistle. Red looked up, neutral smile fitted on his face, and Alec touched his fingers to his forehead in a mock salute.

Red raised an eyebrow.

Alec shrugged. "Hell, man, I would not want to be the one fighting you today."

"You look like a train wreck," one of the other boys offered.

Red crouched, pretending he didn't feel the sudden stiffness in his right leg, and pulled out a long-sleeved, red cotton shirt from beneath his blankets. He tugged it over his head. Most of the other boys, all accustomed to the ache in the shoulders and sudden sweaty palms right before a fight, had the good sense not to wake up to watch Red go through the routine.

He might have been one of the best, but he was not the only one.

Red had been a fighter in Pilot's Coliseum for almost a year and a half. Before that, he'd been nothing more than a rat. A scavenger. Sometimes it was for food, sometimes for security, sometimes for anything at all. Anything that was not already dead or dying.

That was right after the war ended, or at least after the bombs stopped. Red had never been sure when the war had actually ended. Either way, by that time his parents had been gone—not even buried. Just dead, dead and then abandoned—long enough that Red knew starvation better than their faces. He knew what it was to be rabid, delirious, desperate. He still had nightmares, sometimes, of that long, fevered trek towards nothing.

And Pilot had saved him from that.

Pilot had saved all of these boys from that.

Ignoring the jibe about the train-wreck, Red snatched his new knife from the bed and tossed the thing between his hands a few times. The weight felt the same, as always, no matter which hand he used. He rolled the weapon along his palms. Maybe he would be left-handed today. It was good to have options.

He glanced up at Alec, nodding farewell, and flinched when Alec touched his own cheek in sympathy. Red had forgotten about the black eye. He tugged his fingers through his dark hair, hoping he didn't look like he'd gotten the worse deal out of that train wreck.

***

There was little left, at the end of the world, which people were really willing to turn out for. Nobody watched movies anymore. People didn't talk idly like they used to, not unless it was family and sometimes not even then. Better to save room only for the kind of person you could really count on. And there weren't a whole lot of people like that left walking around.

So mostly people just kept to themselves.

The greatest exception—maybe the only exception—were the fights. For a day of atrocity in the Coliseum, they turned out by the hundreds. Red had never been in a fight where the stadium *wasn't* full. That was part of the thrill of the thing: knowing everyone was watching, knowing that half the people up there knew how you walked, how you threw a punch, how you handled a knife, even better than you knew it yourself.

Today was no different.

They went crazy when Red sauntered into the arena. His hands were in his jean pockets, like always. The crowd loved the way the knife was tucked in the back of his pants, like it was a gun, and the way he moved in the arena—slow and graceful. They loved that he didn't give a shit about any of this.

And if they really believed it, well then, it was no more than Red had expected from a mass of scared, lonely, angry people. What else were they supposed to believe in? There weren't any heroes left.

Might as well worship a star.

When Bret came out of the other gate, about 30 yards to Red's left, the upward swinging started a breeze across the sand. For a moment, the arena was washed with dust, the gust of wind rushing in speckles of sand across Red's face and through his hair. He closed his eyes but didn't move.

Bret must have flinched, or covered his face, because there was an uproar in the crowd. Red heard his own name, screamed, and then echoed across the stadium like a whispered chant. He blinked the dust out of his eyes, waited with hands still in pockets as Bret made his official entrance onto the arena. The crowd was not impressed. Hissing charged through the stadium on their lips.

Red smirked.

In the center circle, now, Bret presented his dagger. He'd been gripping it in his right hand already, but held it out in front of him now, running his thumb along the dull edge and then looking up into the amphitheater for a reaction. He was rewarded with a spattering of cheers.

Only amateurs checked to see if the world was watching.

Red knew they always were.

He reached behind him, pulled the knife out of his waistband. The practice pattern he made, first with his right hand and then with his left, was not for show. He was testing the loyalty of the thing, deciding once and for all which hand should bear its weight.

The mob exploded in crazed, tense anticipation anyway.

Red decided on his right hand.

***

Circling each other was too cliché, but Red always thought this moment—before the voice boomed over the speaker, inspiring the crowd to rise to its feet—was awkward if he didn't. There weren't a lot of other options. He could raise his weapon threateningly at his opponent, or do one of those stupid fist pumps towards the crowd and get the energy rising on his own. But it was bad form, in the arena, to deride the opponent. More often than not, mockery was the surest means of losing a fight.

Besides, Red had an image to maintain. And he tried to keep his self-inflated ego out of it.

A low, cheaply amplified voice boomed from above them—around them, underneath them, it was hard to tell which direction it came from in this strangely acoustic arena. "Ladies and gentleman! Boys and girls! Are you ready for the fight of your lives?"

This was what the announcer always said.

Red thought it wasn't very inspiring, but apparently the crowd disagreed. He felt them rise to their feet in one, rushing moment of tension that spiraled wind across the gritty floor of the arena.

Bret did not flinch this time.

Red dug his heels back, checking his stance. The announcer laughed into the microphone.

"Out of the gold gate, a special double-feature from your very own Red Ferris!"

Another round of cheering brought a small smile to Red's face. He was thinking of the stiff, aching pain in his right leg and was glad that no one—least of all Bret—could see that his smile was hollow. He hurt like hell. His grip on the knife tightened.

The announcer went on. "And, coming back to make good on his two-month winning streak, Bret Tanner!"

The microphone man always said it like that. Like any of them *didn't* have a winning streak.

"So place your bets, find your seats, and let's get this thing started!"

Red rolled his weight up onto the balls of his feet; Bret darted forward in a short, rushed spurt that settled into a comfortable jog to close the distance between them.

One of the fighters always had to do this—turn a large arena into a small fighting space—and the one who did the running usually endeared themselves to the crowd.

And if the mob loved you, so did Pilot. If Pilot loved you, you usually didn't have to fight on a bad leg.

The thought of crossing that distance made Red nauseous. He twitched his knife hand. He walked towards Bret, met him in the center of the arena with the same saunter that he'd started with. Bret, in engaging distance now, was hot and wild. His eyes were delirious with a rush that any Coliseum fighter would be familiar with—it was the primal thrill, the one that emptied empathy out of your system in a cold flash of confidence. It was the reminder, the fuel, the promise that the kill was something to be proud of.

Bret was still young to the Coliseum. He was young enough to need to turn the savagery on for the arena.

A veteran wouldn't know how to turn it off if he wanted to.

When Bret slashed upward, Red stepped clear. The blow should have landed square in his right shoulder, maybe even carved a new scar across his chest, but Red was walking and collected. Bret was hot and rushed and burning for the kill. In his defense, Bret turned at the last minute, trying to catch his opponent before he escaped completely.

But Red wasn't running. He dropped low and half-spun as he moved and he caught skin with his knife just below Bret's left knee, crippling the guy with his sudden speed. Bret crumbled, despite his best effort to hold his stance with only his right leg. His hands hit the ground. Suddenly Red was there again, in front of him.

The crowd saw Bret tumble, gave a soft start, and then screamed triumphantly when Red appeared again. In a move akin to rising out of the ashes of dust and grit on the arena floor, Red stood like a phoenix above his opponent. Reborn.

To the audience, it was clear that the fight was over.

On the arena floor, Bret was on his hands and knees, scrambling for traction. Only a handful of seconds since he'd been on his feet, but more than Bret could afford to lose. Red saw him realize this. He saw the muscles in Bret's left leg go limp. He knew that the fear would be rushing back into Bret's face now, that his eyes would go wide, pallor become light and pale. But Red found that he didn't really care whether or not he saw the look on the guy's face when he died.

He really didn't give a damn about this kid.

What he gave a damn about, he suddenly realized, was the fact that Pilot had made him fight today. After he'd just gone into the arena ten days ago, after he'd given the man a hell of a brawl—two hours in the arena was more than most of the veterans could give for Pilot's show—and killed Micah with the guy's own knife. He'd deserved a month off. Maybe two.

He was Pilot's golden boy. Special occasions only.

This shit was for amateurs. It should have been someone else's dirty work.

So he caught the back of Bret's collar, slid his hand up so he had a firm grasp of his hair too. It was surgical, precise, this maneuver. There was no thought, no show. Red was cleaning up a mess.

What's more, he was cleaning up a mess that wasn't even his. He kneed Bret, hard, in that spot just under the chin. The kid went limp, unconscious, in Red's hands. Red didn't even look down. He glanced at the stadium seats, dispassion obscuring his inexpressive face. Enough was enough. He leaned in and rotated his arms, gripping the soft, indented spot on each side of Bret's slack jaw with firm fingers.

And then he snapped his neck.

First, silence. Then the mob roared.

Chapter 2

Red steadied himself against the concrete wall outside the south gate. He used both of the provided antibacterial wipes to get the blood off of his hands, pausing to work the stains carefully out of his shirt. It had been a pretty clean kill this time, but Red didn't like anything lingering and sometimes he scrubbed even when there was nothing there. Just in case.

Above, the stadium was emptying. Red could hear them, rushing to gather their belongings and scuffle out of the big entrance columns. He knew they could not see him, even if the younger children stuck their small faces between the barred area behind Entrance C, as they sometimes did.

Some of the newbies would stroll over after a fight to bask in the glory of being a fighter. They'd accept the thanks, play at fearlessness, and revel in the idea that they were not entirely alone. It was a newbie mistake, of course, to think that the mob really loved the fighters.

After a newbie died, the crowd still gathered to get a glimpse at the winner. They didn't care who it was.

So Red kept his distance. He kept his back against the cool concrete and his weight off of his right leg, listening with his eyes closed as the muffled sound of footsteps began to fade away.

"Short fight."

Red didn't open his eyes. The voice was low, lolling against a familiar southern lilt. Not like Red's easy vowels, but molasses heavy. Deep South. There was only one Coliseum resident with a thicker drawl than his own.

Red said, "I was making up for last week."

He heard Elijah scuff a boot as he passed in front of Red to stand in the light that flooded in from the open arena floor. Red himself preferred the shadows. Especially today, when he was so goddamned hot that he couldn't kneel without getting dizzy. But he knew most of the other guys craved the light. On the nicest afternoons, the Coliseum was littered with human lizards—splayed across the stadium seats, sleeping in the late sun, and dreaming about a time when someone cared what happened to them.

"It's a talent," Elijah said, "to be able to turn it off and on like you do."

Red didn't say anything.

Elijah chuckled. "I think I'll aim to just stay alive."

"That's fair," Red replied. He opened his eyes. Stillness had settled into the bleachers above them. The mob was gone. Gingerly, Red pushed himself away from the wall. "Does that mean you're fighting next week?"

Elijah was almost a head taller than Red, but ganglier. He had this way of looking down at people that was entirely unbefitting of his frame. A veteran, of course, but not one in Red's league. Elijah had been here the better part of a year.

No one had lived in Pilot's Coliseum as long as Red.

Still, Elijah was a force in the arena and a fiend with a saber, if the rumors were true. He grinned at Red. "Yeah. They haven't said who I'll be fighting yet."

Red gave him a nod and turned away.

"Headed up to see your girl again?" Elijah asked. His voice was casual.

It was nothing. It was a joke.

But it was enough to make Red turn back to face him.

Elijah was grinning still. He could not know that something feral had rolled over in Red's stomach, that Micah's knife was still hot against his hip, or that Elijah himself had just said something very stupid. Elijah had been the one to find the girl, after all, and he'd been nice enough to tell Red about it. The boys in Pilot's Coliseum didn't talk much.

Elijah couldn't have known. So Red kept his expression carefully blank. He didn't say anything, but Elijah's smirk wavered. There was a weighted silence and then Red stuffed his hands in his pockets, nodded once more, and left.

***

New Chicago was divided into five districts, one for each of the men who'd built it. Ironically, Pilot's Coliseum was actually a football stadium. It was the smallest of the districts but was still the heart of New Chicago-- now that the true center of Chicago and all that it had been was gone--and was governed by Pilot alone. The fighters were housed in the locker rooms, twenty bunked together. Red slept in the home team's lockers. Though fighting often occurred between the locker rooms, Pilot didn't like to encourage camaraderie, so one just as often found himself fighting a bunkmate as someone from the other dorm.

Food in the Coliseum was provided by the audience, who paid a substantial tribute each time they came to see a show. The boys took turns, along with volunteers from the small surrounding neighborhoods, at policing the stadium. It was an easy job and you got an extra set of rations for your trouble.

There was no fighting outside of the arena. That was the only real rule. And for the most part, the boys upheld it. The only alternative was leaving.

And the boys at the Coliseum knew better than most that leaving wasn't really an option.

Entrances C, D, and E were open to the public to filter through on fight days as they made their way, packed, to the stadium seating. In the old days, the entrances had been numbered gates, not lettered. Most of those were destroyed, though, and the debris was dangerous. The confusion had gotten a fighter trapped behind one of the west gates and he'd suffocated to death, so Pilot put an end to it. Everyone used the lettered names for the entrances now. It was atop Entrance D that the press boxes sat. No one used them anymore. All the windows were boarded up except for one, where a set of metal bars had been installed instead.

And sometimes, if you looked up at just the right moment, you'd see something move at the window, maybe a strand of strawberry hair. Then, of course, you'd know Red's secret.

There was a girl in the box above Entrance D and Red was in love with her.

***

Red pressed his hand against the doorway as he passed through, hesitating in the shadows with the setting sun at his back. It was sticky hot in the box suite, made worse by boarded up windows and little breeze. The sudden darkness blinded him.

Lila Sinclair saw him first.

"You're okay. Please tell me you're okay," she said. He heard the clatter of chain against chain, masking the sound of her footsteps, and then suddenly she was there. Bright eyes. Small face, small frame, with long red hair that turned her pale skin to snow.

But it was the way she moved, always, that caught his attention. The shock of the silence. There were few in the arena that could walk as she did, with unbound energy.

Even with the chains wrapped around her ankles, leaving discolored bruises against the tops of her feet.

The light at Red's back cast strange, shapely stripes across her face. She tipped her head, cheeks flushed. "Tell me you're okay, Red," she repeated. He felt her thumb against his cheekbone—his black eye—and he reached up to intertwine their fingers, pulling her hand away.

"I'm fine."

She searched him with bright eyes. Then, she dropped his hand and retreated back to her corner of the room.

The chains followed her, rusted gold in her dark prison, and only her pale skin glowed in the grey light. "I was worried," she said, "after you had to fight Micah. And then again today, with your leg-"

"There was no reason to worry," Red interrupted.

Lila turned suddenly, red strands of hair catching her lips. "Someone has to. And you never do."

"Well that is just not true. I'm still alive, aren't I?"

Lila made a face. "That is not consoling."

Then Red laughed, because he couldn't help himself. She was a beacon in the dark room, and he loved the way she smiled, the way her eyes lit up when she saw him, the way her whole being transformed. He loved the way she made him feel. Satisfied.

Lila misinterpreted his reaction. "Do not laugh at me, Jared Ferris. I hate the fights."

Her voice was taunting, but her bright eyes were reproachful. Red knew she worried. He knew that she couldn't do anything but look out her window and watch him take a knife to another boy's throat. He knew she hated every minute of it and sometimes he was sure that she hated him—just a little—for it.

He crossed the room and took her hands in his. He pressed them to his cheek. "I'm fine. I really am. See for yourself."

Her fingers were cool against his skin. She brushed her thumb across his chin, but let her hand fall. It was hot in her box, hotter still when she stepped closer. Her face had that strange, discolored sheen of an early illness.

But she wasn't sick. Lila was strong.

She pursed her lips. "And your leg?"

Red almost lied again, but she was close enough that he could smell the mint in her hair and he suddenly changed his mind. "It's getting there."

Lila searched his face with her bright eyes.

"Honestly. I even walk without a limp now."

That satisfied her. Lila settled back onto her heels, putting space between them. For a second, only the echo of her chains against the floor filled the silence.

Then Red raised his eyebrows. “So can I wish you happy birthday now?”

Lila started. “What?”

Outside, there was a rumble of thunder. The brutish heat eased, briefly, against the force of a sudden breeze. Maybe it would storm.

“Don’t tell me you forgot,” Red said.

Lila’s eyes widened. She shook her head. “It’s not my birthday. It’s…”

Red waited.

But Lila was already counting off weeks in her head. She paled. “Oh my God. It is.”

If it had been cloudy before, than the storm only made matters worse. Lila’s face shadowed; the humidity melted from the room. The warmth went with it. She looked, just for a moment, unmistakably sad. Her eyes dropped to her hands, where she’d intertwined her fingers.

And then Red couldn’t see her face. He reached out, but she suddenly looked up again and gave a strained smile. “I didn’t realize it had been so long.”

He hadn’t meant it like that.

“Lila-”

She inhaled, interrupting him. “So what did you get me?”

She knew what he’d gotten her. It was the gift he brought every time he visited, any time he could. But now it didn’t feel like enough, because she was so sad and trying so hard to pretend she wasn’t.

Lila had never looked so small.

“Well, there’s the obvious,” Red said. He dug into his jacket pocket and pulled out a handful of mint leaves. The smell of them had been rubbing off on his clothes all afternoon, so she must have known as soon as he’d come in. Not to mention the fact that mint leaves were the only thing that grew within a mile of Pilot’s Coliseum.

But it was tradition.

Eleven months and twenty seven days ago, Elijah had appeared at Red’s bunk in the middle of the afternoon. He’d made a confession: that there was a girl locked up at the top of the Coliseum and that he himself had gone to take a look. 'Pilot's pet' was what he'd called Lila that day.

Red had gone to see. The first time he'd come, Lila didn't speak to him. She looked at him with her bright eyes, but stayed where she was on the floor, under her window. She had her fingers interlaced between her ankles and the chains to keep them from scraping at her skin and making her bleed.

By the time she'd spoken to him, she'd given up that habit. There were still traces of blood on the chain, the floor, and her jeans as evidence of those first awful days. But that was also the first time Red had brought the mint leaves.

And in exchange, she'd told him her name.

Now, Lila took the gift in her cupped hands, rolling the leaves between her fingers. "Of course," she said, smiling a little easier. She untied the string at her neck and handed it to Red, who strung the new leaves to join the others. When he gestured, Lila turned around and he put it around her neck again, tying at the nape as she held her hair aside.

"You don't have to spend another birthday here," he said quietly. He finished tying the necklace, but didn't step away. Lila leaned back, resting her weight against him.

"But where would I go?" she asked. It was an old argument.

"You wouldn't be alone. We'd figure it out."

Lila scoffed. "Sure. And then we'd both starve. This is how you survive, Red. These fights feed you, they keep you safe, and warm. You can't get that anywhere else."

"You don't know that."

But the truth was that Lila knew it better than he did. She'd come from the suburbs, the old Chicago, and she had no intention of going back. Red didn't know why. He was pretty sure she had a family, out there somewhere. Not that she talked about it. They'd known each other for a whole year, and she'd never brought up the past. Not once.

But Red didn't blame her. He didn't like to talk about Louisville either. Sleeping dogs were best left alone.

"It's fine here," Lila said. She stepped away from Red and her rusted chains clattered. "At least I'm safe. There's a lot to be thankful for."

As utterly unconvincing as *that* was, Red let it alone. It was her birthday.

"I've got another present for you."

There was a crack of thunder and a rush of lightning right on top of it. Lila jumped. She giggled softly, her voice drowned out by the patter of rain against the roof. Then she turned and Red could see her face, flush and hopeful.

"Oh?"

It was easy to distract her, to keep her ghosts at bay. It was harder not to blurt out that she was beautiful, that he would take her away in an instant, if only she'd let him. That he loved her.

But she was right. She was safe here; they both were. For now.

So instead he just shrugged. "Well I'm not scheduled to fight again until the Russian roulette."

Lila hesitated. "That's not for another month, right?"

"Thirty days."

And finally, finally, she smiled the way that he loved. It lit up her whole face, burned in her eyes like an unquenchable fire. "I get you for all that time?"

For as long as you want, he wanted to say. He only smirked. "Every day."

***

Alec met Red as he passed out of the tunnel under Section E and back into the wide hallway that circled the outside of the stadium. He looked pale.

"Did you hear?" At his blank look, Alec added, "About Elijah's next fight?"

Red shrugged. "It's against some newbie."

There was a beat of silence and Red hesitated, looking at Alec sidelong. "Isn't it?"

Alec cleared his throat. "Peter got scrubbed from the list."

"So who's in?" As if he needed to ask.

Anyone could see what the answer would be, by the look on Alec's face. "Me."

Red's expression stayed neutral, but only just barely.

It wasn't that Alec was a bad fighter. In fact, after Red, he'd been here the longest of anyone. Not inconsequential in a hand-to-hand fight, either. But back when they had first met—Alec fresh off the streets of the new world and Red barely five months at the Coliseum—that hadn't been apparent. Those were the days when they'd looked after each other. They'd shared victories and fears. Their secrets.

Sometimes even their weaknesses. So Alec knew about Lila.

And Red knew that Alec had asthma.

Usually it didn't matter. Alec was calm in the arena, calm and ruthless. He had an inhaler that he hadn't used in almost a year at the Coliseum. But then again, Pilot usually used him as a showcase, pitting him against the newbies to weed out the ones that would never last.

Elijah was not new and he would not be easily weeded out.

When Red didn't say anything, Alec pulled at the collar of his dark T-shirt, blanching. "The style hasn't been announced, so I've still got a chance. But…"

"But we haven't had a throwback fight in weeks," Red finished for him. Pilot liked to rotate through fight themes, and the last time he'd put the boys in the arena with full metal shields and broadswords, the fight had pulled one of the biggest crowds the Coliseum had ever seen. None of which was a good sign for Alec.

"Yeah. Exactly."

Red glanced at Alec. His tall form was cut short by his lowered head, the way it always was—Alec was the kind of person who stayed out of your way and then came down suddenly like a hammer in the arena. It was one of the reasons Pilot treated him so well. There were few people who could make a statement like Alec.

But seeing him today, Red remembered that it hadn't always been like that. In his first weeks at the Coliseum, Pilot had reamed him, fight after fight, trying to get him killed. Alec didn't look like much, when he didn't want to. He was tall, but he could hide it; he was big, but that didn't always mean something. He could pack a punch. But you wouldn't know it by looking at him.

Though he'd never told Red as much, he was pretty sure Alec had learned that particular skill from his asshole of a father.

At the time, Red hadn't thought much about Pilot's actions. He, too, had been in the arena a lot. The newbies always were. It was the only way to clear the weak ones out. Besides, veteran-to-veteran made a better fight, drew a greater crowd, and fed everyone much more contentedly. It was business.

So why did it feel like a betrayal today?

"Look," Red said, stuffing his hands into his pockets and shoving the broken gate between Section E and D open with his shoulder. "I've got to get my rations from the office, but if you want to come, I'll run sword drills with you."

Alec hesitated, then shook his blonde hair out of his face and went through the gate Red was still holding open. "You sure?"

Of course he wasn't sure. There were only a handful of guys that could handle a broadsword at all and certainly none the way Red could. If he taught Alec, even if he never matched him, that wouldn't be true anymore. The secret would be out, and Red would be the weaker for it.

But a long time ago—a whole lifetime ago, it felt like—Red had done something irrevocable. He'd let Alec in. They were both so new, then, that Red hadn't known any better.

Sometimes he still didn't know any better.

"I've got to pass on my knowledge while I still can," Red said.

Alec snorted. "Does that make me your apprentice, Master Red?"

Grinning, Red shoved Alec with one hand. He made a face.

They rounded the corner and the hallway opened up suddenly on a big entryway. On the wall between each opening to the stadium bleachers, the long ticket booth was still set up. The waning light fell in shafts along the windows, so the booth had to be lit by a kerosene lamp and the two boys manning it were both at the center window, pouring over a book with a flashlight.

Red cleared his throat and the boys looked up, the youngest flushing pink. They were newbies, almost certainly.

Alec crossed the room in long strides—he was taller than Red—and leaned against the counter, peering down at the book from the other side of the barrier. "What've you got there?"

The shortest boy flushed even brighter. "Nothing."

Red sighed, putting both elbows on the counter and raising his eyebrows. He considered each boy in turn, but finally settled for the one who had spoken. He'd closed the book abruptly, calling attention—with a sudden thud—back to himself.

"All books are supposed to be turned into Pilot," Red said, almost verbatim from the regulations they'd all memorized within their first week at the Coliseum.

If Alec gave a soft, involuntary chuckle, the newbies were too scared to notice.

"We were going to," the other said, "but Pet-"

The first boy nudged him. "Don't tell them my name!"

Alec smirked.

"-but it was a present from his mom, so we were just…waiting," the second boy finished uncertainly.

Red shrugged. "Whatever. I'm here for my rations."

The first boy looked relieved. He retreated to the far wall, picking up a box labeled 'Winner 81', and hoisted it up onto the counter. "You've got to fill this out," he said, pushing a form under the barrier without looking at Red.

Alec leaned forward until his forehead almost touched the glass. "How long have you guys been at the Coliseum?"

"Six fights," the second boy said quickly. He sounded almost ashamed.

Alec considered him. "You been in any of them yet?"

The second boy swallowed, but it was the first, the shorter of the two, who spoke. "I have."

Red hesitated at the bottom of the form. A note had been scribbled across the signature line. "Half-rations," he read aloud.

The boys behind the counter froze. Alec turned, snatching the paper up to look at it for himself. Red didn't move.

"You're supposed to see Pilot," Alec said quietly.

Red exhaled, shaking his head. "What the *fuck* is going on today?" he asked.

No one answered him.

Alec tucked the form into his back pocket. He nodded once to the boys at the ticket booth and then turned his back on them. Red hesitated a moment longer, tucking his box of rations under his arm.

“Be careful about reading Poe this time of night,” he said finally. “This place has a lot in common with the House of Usher.”

The older boy grinned. When Red crossed the room to catch Alec, the younger boy’s voice called after him. “You were brilliant in the arena this morning.”

Not good enough.

Red glanced over his shoulder and grimaced. “You mind telling Pilot that for me?”

The boys laughed because they thought he was joking. They knew he was Pilot’s golden boy.

But Red wasn’t joking. Pilot was the only person that had ever protected him. Pilot had saved him from ghosts of a life that had haunted him for hundreds of lonely miles. The things he did for Pilot now—they were nothing compared to the things he’d done before. To live. Red would give almost anything to be sure that he’d never have to go back to that.

Maybe the boys in the booth were too new to understand. Maybe they didn’t know how lucky they were to have been saved. Maybe it took time.

But one day they would know. They’d see what Pilot had done for them.

And then they’d know how bitter it tasted, to know he’d let the man down.

Chapter 3

Alec waited outside.

Pilot, when he was at the Coliseum, worked in the coaching box for the home team. He had a house somewhere, everyone knew, but no one asked. None of the fighters really saw much of Pilot, after their first few weeks at the Coliseum. The place ran under this pressing urgency that Pilot saw everything, but it mostly functioned without him.

He'd been waiting for Red. He looked up from his desk when Red knocked on the open door.

"Good. Please come in." Pilot didn't get up, but he did flip his notebook shut and set it carefully aside, pen laid atop. The desk was neat, like the office, and like Pilot himself. He had on black slacks, dirtied but not tattered, and a grey vest over a rolled up white dress shirt. Hot, for October in the Coliseum.

Nevertheless, he looked comfortable, much more comfortable than Red felt. He made Red feel underdressed. Maybe even ill-prepared. And something else. Pilot was thinner, shorter, older than Red. He was sitting, Red was standing. And Red had Micah's knife, always, in the back of his jeans.

But still Red felt small.

"Please sit down," Pilot said. He clasped his hands on his desk before him and looked at Red expectantly.

Red sat down.

"I'm concerned," Pilot said. His voice sounded sincere. He leaned in and lowered his voice. "I worry about you."

Red looked down. "I'm sorry about the fight."

Cocking his head, Pilot smiled pityingly. "I could see you were upset about going into the arena today."

"I shouldn't have been scheduled again." Red was surprised by the hardness in his voice. He wasn't angry. He was just disappointed—with Pilot,, with himself, with the poor fool he'd killed this morning. But he was glad he said it aloud, because it was true.

And it reminded him how he had felt in the arena, when everything had been so clear. He had been angry then. He had been *furious*. It had been wonderful.

Pilot nodded, drawing Red's eyes back up to his face. "You're right," Pilot said. "There was a mistake in the lineup and it was approved without my knowledge. You must have known you weren't required to do both fights."

Red scrubbed his face with his hands. "What?"

"Why didn't you come to me? I would have fixed it."

The surprise was clear on Red's face. He knew it was. The surprise and the relief. "Really?"

"Of course."

Pilot reached over and patted Red's hand where it rested on the table. And Red felt safe.

Then Pilot leaned back in his chair and sighed. "But Red, I can't have you undermining a fight just because you are upset about something. That's not professional."

Red crossed his arms. "I know. I'm sorry."

"The arena is not an outlet for your personal life. You have to learn that. The arena is your job, and I expect your best at all times."

Red closed his eyes, nodding. He knew that. He knew that he was lucky to be here, where there was food and shelter and this man sitting in front of him, this man who had gone to great lengths to rescue the boys at his Coliseum from the wrath of the new world.

Red knew this because he'd been out there, and he was terrified of going back.

"It won't happen again."

Pilot nodded. "And I believe you. The half-rations will get you through the next two weeks, and you're scheduled to fight the Russian roulette. You'll get double rations then, assuming you prove what I know you will."

And somehow, even though it was a punishment and Pilot was condemning him for not putting on a show, of all things, Red left the room feeling like he was being given another chance. He left feeling like he had to prove that Pilot was right, he could be a better person, a better fighter, a more worthy investment.

Because this was business.

***

He spent the rest of the night training with Alec, so it wasn't until late the next morning that Red made his way up to see Lila again. He was feeling better; the muscles in his leg didn't burn as badly. He felt reborn, the way he always did after a good fight.

Alec wasn't any better with a sword for their efforts, but Red hadn't expected that. It would take more than one session, not to mention a whole separate series of drills, before Alec would be able to swing the thing without that fatal shift of unbalanced weight. There was still time.

And if it didn't work, then at least Red had tried. He hoped it would be enough.

It was hot again today, and humid, but the sky was clear. When Red crossed the bleachers in Section E, he wasn't alone. There were a handful of guys lying on the seats, eyes closed. On the arena floor, some of the newbies were practicing, but mostly they were sitting in the sand, sloth-like in the heat.

Red climbed the stairs. He didn't turn around when he reached the top, even though he heard the clatter of metal against metal. Someone else had arrived, testing the weight of a sword for the next fight. Elijah was probably down there.

Red didn't want to see him.

He pulled open the door to the box suites, and almost yanked the hinge off as he went. He'd forgotten how bad the door was getting. It was crippled, a victim to decay. Everything was.

Red scrubbed his face with his hands and moved to pull off his long cotton shirt—he had a t-shirt under it—but stopped up short. There were voices in the next room.

"You're a good girl, you know that."

Red used the wall as a guide through the darkness, quietly moving into the doorway. Lila was at her window, standing still with her hands gripping the window frame at her back. At her feet, a man was wrapping the chains back around her ankles, locking them with the key that he held between his teeth like a cigarette as he worked.

He was bigger than Red had expected. Lila had told him, of course, that there was a man. He took her out, twice a day, to use a portable toilet at the entrance of Section E and eat her daily ration of food. She never ate in her cell, so the food wouldn't attract rats. It was why the room was so clean. Why she was so clean.

She always told him the man wasn't a problem. She said he didn't do anything but what he was supposed to. She said he didn't talk to her.

But he was talking to her now.

The man stood up slowly, hands on his thighs as he pushed himself off the ground. He was big, certainly, but not in good shape. He would have been no match for Red. The man coughed, and stepped forward, so his face was inches from Lila's.

"Go on," he said. "Test the chain. Got to make sure it's locked up tight."

Lila backed away, three small steps, until her back was pressed to the window. The chains ached and clattered.

The man smiled. "Good." He took another step forward, this time closing the space between them. For one, awful moment, Red couldn't see Lila. He pushed off the wall, thoughtless and seething.

She had turned ghostly white. Shuddering, lips pressed firmly together. She kept her eyes closed.

Red saw the man's hands rush across her body.

And he exploded.

Soundless. Savage.

He was a Coliseum fighter, for God's sake, and this man was a fool if he thought he could hurt the girl that Red loved. He would slit the man's neck before he could take another breath. Simple as that.

But Lila saw him first.

Her bright eyes widened—guilty but frightened. Not afraid of this guard, the man with his rough hands and waddling voice, but afraid of Red. She did not want to watch another fight today. And so she begged him.

She wanted him to wait. She wanted him to leave it alone. She wanted him to hide.

Like a coward.

He took another step forward. But at the same time, the man stepped back.

"You really are a good girl."

Lila squeezed her eyes shut, turning away to the window.

The man shrugged. He turned around, but Red had retreated back to the shadows. Micah's knife was still heavy in his hand; he turned it round and round, rolling the hilt along his palm, deciding.

He could bleed this man right here.

But he didn't.

The man left.

Red stayed in the shadows. He counted to fifty, slowly, as he watched Lila with her back to him, hands splayed on the windowsill.

Then he spoke. "You lied to me."

"It's nothing," she said. She didn't turn around.

"Has he hurt you?"

"No."

Red went to her. When she didn't move, he leaned against the wall at her side. "Lila."

"He hasn't done anything. I swear." Her hands were shaking. She clasped them together, stepping away from the window.

Red reached out to her, then changed his mind. At his movement, Lila looked over suddenly, her face ashen.

"Why didn't you tell me?"

She crossed her arms. "I can handle it."

"But you don't have to," Red said. He reached out again and this time actually took her hand.

Lila resisted. "It doesn't change anything. We're still safer here."

"*You're* not."

Lila scowled. "I told you. He hasn't done anything to me. I'm fine."

Red cupped her hand with both of his, trying to quell the way it was shaking. She wouldn't look at him again. "But if he does. Will you tell me then?"

She pulled her hand away. "I'm okay. It's okay. I can deal with this."

Red was torn. He wanted to hold her. He wanted to gather her in his arms until she stopped shaking and that awful, sick expression on her face melted away. He wanted to make her safe. On the other hand, he wanted to kill that man. He wanted to take him to the arena floor and slit his throat. He wanted to stand over the body and revel in the awe of the crowd.

He would be proud of that kill.

And most of all, he wanted to take Lila away from here.

Then he remembered the rations.

"We couldn't leave now anyway," he said aloud. Lila finally turned to face him again. He ran his hands through his hair. "Pilot only gave me half of my rations until the next fight. We wouldn't survive on that."

Lila looked at him with her bright eyes. "It doesn't matter. We don't have to leave now. Nothing's wrong."

Red let Lila convince him. He knew she wasn't safe here. He knew that she hated the fights, that at any moment Pilot could make her disappear again, and that he was helpless to protect her. But he let her convince him anyway.

He wasn't ready to leave the Coliseum. He didn't know where they would go or how they would get there. And he wasn't ready to face that wasteland yet. The last time he'd crossed it, the passage had nearly killed him.

Red sighed. How was it that all roads led back to Louisville?

"I can't believe Pilot's punishing you for that fight," Lila said.

Red shrugged. "It was a bad fight. I could have done better."

"And you really think you should be punished for it? Not for killing another human being, but for doing it too *fast*?"

Lila was hot. She was still angry about what had just happened. She was angry that Red was trying to protect her again. She didn't like that he had to protect her at all. Not to mention the fight. He knew that she watched his fights closer than the others.

She had told him once that if he dared to die on her, he'd have to do it knowing she'd seen.

Red smiled wanly.

"Okay," Lila said. "We don't have to talk about it. I'm sorry. It's been a bad day."

Red took a step closer.

Lila sighed. "If my birthday was yesterday, then tomorrow is officially the anniversary of my arrival."

Red didn't know this story. He said nothing.

"I didn't tell you because I didn't want you to feel sorry for me," Lila went on. She hesitated, then went on in a rush. "But…I'm stronger than you think I am."

"Lila-"

She shook her head. "No. Listen. I mean it. You don't know what it was like. I can take this." Her expression frightened him. "This is nothing."

Red took a step forward.

"After-" But the words died on her lips.

"After what?" Red prompted. His voice was neutral. It surprised him.

There was a fire in his gut that was going to burn him alive.

Lila swallowed. "After everything else."

Too many surprises for one day. Too many. "What are you talking about?"

"Do you know how I got here?"

"Pilot," Red replied uncertainly.

Lila sighed and for a second, there was just silence. She turned to her window. Then, quietly: "But didn't you ever wonder how I came to be with Pilot?"

Red didn't say anything. Of course he'd wondered. It was Lila.

But it was Lila, so he'd never asked.

He watched her lift her head to the ceiling, her hair tumbling over her shoulders, away from her face. Nothing in her expression at all—just blankness and fire. Foreign.

Broken.

Then she looked at him and it was gone. She was just Lila. Whatever he didn't understand about her was again firmly bottled up and buried deep.

Her words were silent as a prayer. "My parents sold me to him."

"Lila-" Red was already reaching for her. His fingertips brushed her skin and she pulled away. The look on her face was like ice.

"Let me get it out," she said, low.

Red put his hands up in surrender. She turned her back on him.

"My house is—it was on the South Side, near Kenwood," Lila said. "Far enough from downtown that we thought we would be safe. It was just another war, after all, in some other country. We thought we were invincible. My God, we were so stupid. Even after DC got hit, it wasn't real. New York City. Los Angeles. One after another, we didn't even flinch."

A sigh.

"Then they came for Chicago. The sirens went off. And we thought we were lucky."

She gave a strange, dry laugh. "Maybe we were. It could have been nuclear."

Instead, Chicago had gotten carpeted. Twice. For nine days, it had rained fire from the sky. Red knew because he'd seen it on television.

Just before the mushroom cloud erupted over Indianapolis.

There wasn't much in the way of TV after that.

"Do you know what I did? I watched the city burn through a window. A *window*. The world was ending, and we didn't even care. Nobody panicked. Nobody left. It was like we all thought that everything was just going to go back to the way it was. Maybe next week, or next month. We all just sat down and waited."

Lila closed her eyes. "We didn't even know the war was over until the first influenza outbreak."

There had been diseases across the country in the first months. Everything that had been irrelevant before was deadly now, wave after wave after wave, and there was no stopping it. Everyone had been sick, and everything had died.

"My family survived that. We survived the break-ins and the robberies, and the night when the lights finally turned off and never turned on again. I thought we would get by."

Red moved closer, and Lila looked at the floor. "But then the food ran out, and the water stopped running. People died. A *lot* of people. People I knew. And one day, my parents decided they couldn't take care of me anymore. If there were three mouths to feed, we'd all starve."

Lila stopped. She inhaled slowly and when Red touched her, she flinched. She wrapped her arms around herself.

"So they decided to get rid of me. I think they were just going to send me away, but then Pilot came through town. He had food."

This time, when Lila stopped, she closed her eyes. Her hair cascaded across her face, a sheet of fire.

"They sold me to him," she whispered, "for a meal a day."

Hatred, unexpected and violent, seized Red.

But then Lila gasped, stifling a sob, and slammed her fist against the bars of her window. "Weren't they supposed to love me?"

Red touched her cheek. Lila pulled away, putting her back to him. “But they didn’t. They sent me with Pilot, who locked me up here in a box, because no one cared about me enough to stop him.”

He wanted to reach out. He wanted to tell her that she didn’t need them. She didn’t need anyone. She was perfect.

But he didn’t know how to tell her that. He didn’t know how to tell her how scared he was, all the time. Her fearlessness was the only thing that made him strong.

He could not be without her.

"I missed the draft,” he said suddenly. Lila turned around. “Wasn't eighteen yet. By the time they changed the rules and I registered, they weren't calling in troops anymore. We thought we'd gotten through the worst. It was the end of that summer, September I think. They were telling us to celebrate, because it was almost over."

He closed his eyes. "Then DC got hit."

The panic had come next. The riots. The burning effigies. The bombs and everything that came with them. The dead.

Lila's features softened. "I remember."

Red looked away. "We were living outside of Louisville. God, it was so hot that summer. There were these storms in the sky, this heat lightning that went on for days at a time. Everything was so heavy down there. Everything was dying.”

“What happened?”

“It wasn't a long walk to the Coliseum, not as long as some of the other boys living here.”

It had taken almost a fortnight. In the newly formed desert, there had been days when he hadn’t eaten anything. Dust storms had rolled over the Mississippi River every other day. He’d stolen a knife off of a dead girl’s body. By the time he’d finally gotten away from the water, he’d held up two families at gunpoint. On the nights he went without sleep, he’d hallucinate.

He’d dreamt about his mother every night. He’d dreamt her body was being torn apart by dogs, by wolves, by his neighbors. He dreamt it because he’d seen it happen to other people, other bodies, other loved ones.

“But it was enough,” he said.

"When did your parents-"

"One right after the other, three weeks after the war was over."

"Pneumonia?" Lila asked quietly.

Red lifted his face to her, uncertain what he wanted her to see in his numb expression. "Typhoid."

Then Lila came to him and kissed his cheek. She rested her head against his chest. “I’m so sorry.”

Red closed his eyes, wrapping his arms around her. “Me too.”

Chapter 4

It was an effort not to sigh when Alec's blade came tumbling down again. Red rotated mid-swing, letting gravity take the brunt of his own sword's weight so he could drop it as well.

"Sorry," Alec said in the suddenly silence. He was panting.

Red leaned forward, palms on his thighs, to catch his breath. It turned out that fighting was much harder when he was trying *not* to hurt his opponent. He flashed Alec a smile that he didn't feel and stood up.

"It's fine. Let's run it again."

Alec nodded, but when he reached down to grab his weapon, he stumbled. His left hand grasped the hilt of the sword but his body overextended, toppling him. Red caught his arm before he fell.

"You alright?" Red asked. Alec didn't respond, sagging against Red's hand. Red let him slide down to the floor, back against the wall. This time, when he inhaled, Red heard him wheeze. "Shit. Where's your inhaler?"

Alec gripped Red's wrist, stopping him from pulling away. Shaking his head, he coughed. "Just…give me a minute."

So Red slumped down unceremoniously next to him.

Alec leaned back, closing his eyes as he rested his head on the wall. Red listened to him breathe.

"You okay?"

When Alec didn't answer, Red turned to him. Alec's face was pale, a sheen of sweat turning his already washed-out complexion into something alarming. But he smiled wanly.

"You look like death."

Alec exhaled forcibly and rolled his head back to look at the ceiling. "There are benefits to that."

"Oh?"

Alec grinned, coughing, and then sighed. "Maybe Elijah will think I caught the plague."

Red rolled his eyes and reached over Alec to pull the broadsword into his lap. He'd never spent much time with heavy weapons before, but despite Alec's lack of improvement, Red found himself enjoying the thing. Nothing had a satisfying, slow arc in its swing like a broadsword. True, his loyalty lay with Micah's knife on the ground beside him, but Red had never been a one-weapon kind of guy.

Actually, he'd never met a blade he didn't like.

Alec groaned. "Damn thing just likes you more. It's not my fault."

"That's absolutely the problem," Red replied, cocking a small smile. "But if we go another round or two, maybe it'll see just how much of a man you are and change its mind."

Alec glared. "You saying I don't fight like a man?"

"God no," Red returned, getting to his feet and holding the hilt of the sword out for Alec. "When you dropped the sword and it almost landed on my foot? Sheer terror."

Chapter 5

It had been a mistake to wait until morning. But he'd been working with Alec all day, and his leg had been so badly abused by the end of it that he couldn't have managed the stairs even if he'd tried. The recently healed wound had nearly reopened in the strain of the fight and Red had crumbled on the field, almost into Alec's ill-placed sword.

Lila hadn't been expecting him yesterday. He'd warned her this might happen. But still, he should have gone.

Because now Red could hear her crying.

He had never heard Lila cry before.

Red ran.

She was in her corner, ankles crossed and bound as always, the savage red scars just visible against her light skin. Her knees were tucked up to her chest and her back was against the wall. She did not look at him.

"Lila, what's wrong?"

He could see that she was shaking, shivering even though it was always so hot in this cage. She kept her face turned away, looking out the barred window where he could not see. Red crossed the room in two easy strides, reaching out to touch her arm.

Lila cried, low, and stumbled to her feet. She tripped on the chain, gripping the wall at her back for support, her head hung and eyes on the floor. Putting space between them. *Terrified.*

"Lila," Red whispered, bewildered. "Please."

She looked up at him cautiously, both hands splayed against the wall behind her. She was shaking, the bruises along her forearms purpling. Red saw these, but did not wonder what they meant. It was the bruises along her neck and collarbone that caught his attention. It was the wide, empty terror in her eyes and the way she smelled like sweat and fear.

He stared at her.

There was nothing in her expression but those wide eyes. Tears running down her face, clinging to her eyelashes, but she made no sound. Red wasn't even sure that she could see him.

And then she collapsed, suddenly, shaking and crying and clinging to him.

Red helped her to the ground, drawing her body close to his. She shivered, balling her hands under her chin, letting him guide her head to his chest. They sat like that, Lila curled up against Red as he leaned against the wall, watching the door, for a long time.

It was only after Lila had fallen asleep that Red understood.

The bruises stretched the length of her back, and in the waning light he could see them turning blue and purple underneath her thin shirt. At her collar, the bruises were worse, leaving red welts like a noose around her neck. There was a distinct thumbprint, a dark mark, that turned to shadow against her pale complexion.

He saw now that her wrists had been bound too, her skin rubbed raw by a restraint. Probably rope. The residue of it left her soft skin marred and bloody. Something rolled over in the pit of Red's stomach, an uncomfortable tension in his chest that made him nauseous and angry.

Lila shuddered in her sleep, flinching away from a nightmare. Abruptly, the sickening churn in Red's stomach was gone. It did not matter what had been done here, only that he could make it right. He was careful not to touch the wounds as he ran his hands through her hair, trying to sooth her.

But there were so many wounds.

And she was so small.

There was a commotion below them; the arena was open to practice fights again. Lila squeezed her eyes shut, rolled so she could bury her face in his shirt. Her shirt gathered at her waist, exposing only a thin line of hot skin.

It was enough. He saw the bruises at the waist of her jeans. The nausea returned; brutal and sudden. Gently, he tugged her shirt away from the wounds, knowing what he would see. Horrified despite that.

Her stomach was ripped and raw, scarred with blood and bruised all along her ribcage and low at her hips. He remembered the restraints—the ones she wore now and others, on her wrist, leaving their sadistic evidence behind—and imagined something that he did not want to imagine.

Lila in a corner, dragged to her feet. Lila whispering, pleading. A man laughing, humorless and unrelenting. Lila fighting with her hands, and with her teeth after her hands were bound. Lila crying out, screaming at first but then only gasping against his touch as she was suddenly, horrifically, unendurably a witness to the granting of her wish: that she would not be alone in her cage.

A hatred, a heat flash, passed through Red's body. He wanted his knife. Maybe two. Not that he needed a knife to make the scars that he was planning for the man who had done this.

What he really wanted was a bat.

He didn't touch Lila, too hot with anger to put his fingertips to her bruised skin, but she flinched anyway. Something must have changed in his posture because suddenly she was up, like she knew what he was thinking, like she felt his hatred and had turned it to fear. Still shaking, she couldn't get a grip on the floor to draw herself away from him, but she tried anyway. She put palm to the cold wood and bit her lip against the pain that washed across her face. Her left thumb touched the red scars on her right wrist. She gasped.

"Please," she whispered. Her eyes on the floor, bangs falling into her face, crying. Drowning. "Go…go home."

Red didn't move. He was going to kill the man slowly. Start with the knife strikes he'd learned in the arena—the ones that crippled, not killed—and then move on to the better stuff. He had heard that a grown man could stand several rounds with a brand.

He'd like to try that.

"Lila," he said and reached up to brush the back of his fingers against her cheek. Lila let her head be tipped up by the gentle tug of his hand. Her eyes were clearer, her cheeks red and scarred with tears. But she was looking at him. Seeing him.

"Stay with me," Red said.

Lila watched him, eyes wide. Her lips barely moved when she whispered, "I'm so scared."

"Stay with me," Red repeated, although what he meant this time was anyone's guess.

She tensed when his hand moved to rest on her shoulder—and Red burned against that desperate ache in the pit of his stomach, wishing he could make good on the phantom pressure of that man's skin on his blade—but consented to be led again into Red's warm arms. She rested the back of her head against his chest, his legs on either side of her, watching the doorway.

Below them, a newbie fight had apparently gathered attention. There were scattered cheers every few seconds, a palpable sort of sweat in the air that always reminded Red of the taste of dust on the tongue after a particularly hard kill. Screaming exploded, as always, but it was only a muffled echo in the cage, dusty and hollow.

Of little relevance way up here.

Lila drew one of his hands up to her chin, shared its warmth. He felt the tender way she moved against him, trying to make herself as small as possible. Her skin was hot, pale. She held her breath when she closed her eyes, warding off a lingering fear that Red could not protect her from.

Below them, he felt the sudden familiar silence rush across the Coliseum. One fighter was about to best the other. It was *his* moment, the one that fueled every other minute of each fight. Everything he did was to reach that moment of perfect existence. Empty. Strong. Unendurable. It was the moment that everything made sense; it was just him alone in the arena, the only authentic person among the thousands that screamed his name.

But it wasn't the same in Lila's cage as when Red was on the arena. Up here, it was just another kind of quiet. Almost disappointing.

Lila intertwined her hand with his empty one.

Outside there was rain.

Chapter 6

Things got worse before they got better. Lila started having nightmares, the kind that lingered on for hours after she'd woken. She slept fitfully, when she slept at all, and every time she nodded off, she'd jerk awake with a barely concealed cry. Red could not appease her. Red could not touch her. She withdrew into herself and would not even look at him, except in careful, sidelong glances.

And in those moments, her eyes were wide and wild and delirious, like she was suffering from some long, fevered delirium that kept sanity just out of reach.

But she never sent him away.

Instead, Red sat on the other side of her cell. They talked, not about anything in particular, and certainly not about anything important. They didn't talk about Lila. Instead, Red made her laugh with gentle, soft words that coaxed color back into her cheeks. He did not try to touch her and he never said out loud how that vacant horror in her eyes made his stomach churn, made him want to take his knife to every man in this damned stadium.

But, slowly, Lila came back around.

Then, one afternoon when he'd fallen asleep in her hot, humid cell, she said his name. He opened his eyes, yawned.

"Red," she said again. He caught her gaze.

Her eyes weren't bright, exactly. There was something frantic in her expression still.

"Will you-" she started, stopped. Afraid all the time. Her fingers flitted to her stomach and something flashed across her face, not quite stifled.

Red would give anything to take away that fear.

She looked up at him again. Her face was desperate but her voice was calm. "Will you teach me to fight?"

And so it was the Lila Sinclair finally embraced their sad new world.

Chapter 7

After most of the boys in the Coliseum had cleared out of the plastic folding chairs and tables that filled the open space in front of Entrance C, Red waited. It wasn't a cafeteria exactly, as everyone was responsible for managing their rations as they saw fit, but most people ate here because it was convenient. The tables were always set up and just because the world ended didn't mean people didn't like to eat lunch around the same time each day.

So by two o'clock, they were mostly gone. Red fell asleep on top of one of the tables.

He was woken by a hand on his forearm.

Alec stood next to him.

"My fight's in two weeks. Assuming I survive, the rations could feed three people for a week, maybe two."

Red closed his eyes. “After the roulette, I’ll get enough to take us another month at least.”

“So the night after the roulette, then.”

Red could hear the restraint in Alec’s voice. He opened his eyes and reached into his pocket, digging out a switchblade. He handed it to Alec. “You’ll survive the fight.”

“And you?”

Red grinned. “I always survive.”

Alec nodded once, then lowered his voice and glanced over his shoulder. “What about the key?”

“The guy’s in Pilot’s pay. Which means Pilot has a key.”

Red saw Alec’s face fall. He saw the fear. “And you’ll get it?”

“I’ll kill him for it, if I have to. I won’t leave without her.”

Alec tensed, then nodded.

Chapter 8

The first few days were easy. Lila had to learn to be still first, after all. She had to learn to balance her weight properly, to gauge a reaction, to get to know the strength of her own body and then—later—Red's knife. In the beginning, the fighter had to learn strength. There wasn't a lot of moving involved in strength.

Which was why it came as a surprise, on the afternoon that Red taught Lila her first practice pattern, when her chain suddenly became part of the exercise.

The pattern was a simple one. It was mostly in the feet and designed to teach a fighter to protect his core even while moving. The attack was the only moment a fighter should be defenseless, and even then, for as short an amount of time as possible. It was a lesson he'd learned in Louisville.

Back when street fighting was still done out on the street.

With Lila though, it did not go as planned. She swung through the knife work, a little wider than Red would have liked and leaving herself more unprotected than was really best, but satisfactorily nonetheless. It was the turn that caught her off-guard. She took a step forward with her left foot and pivoted, rocking her weight forward and lunging at the same moment to catch her invisible opponent at the soft spot behind the knee. It was Red's favorite strike: simple and quick.

Except for today.

Red heard the clatter of her chain as soon as she stepped forward. He recognized the error immediately, but Lila was already committed to the pivot before she realized her mistake. Her right step faltered, the chain yanked her weight backwards. It was snaked between her left and right foot in an almost-figure-eight, a loss no matter which direction she moved. Lila dropped the knife, stumbled forward, trying to regain her balance before the weight of the metal dragged her down.

It didn't really work.

Lila landed clumsily on her hands and knees. Her red hair fell over her face, a fiery curtain. She blew at it, obstinate, looking every bit like a six-year-old having a temper tantrum.

Red smirked. "Smooth," he said.

Lila huffed.

Then, suddenly, she rolled onto the balls of her feet and was up again. Her eyes were bright, mischievous. The chain was wrapped around her right wrist. Loose and intentional. Red's brows wrinkled, he took a step back.

Not fast enough.

She was quick this time, prepared for the weight of the chain at her elbow and using it to propel herself forward. Suddenly she was in front of him, her palm on his head to keep the metal from hitting him as she let it tumble down his back. A flick of her wrist—and a flicker of pain at its weight—and she tightened the slack.

She'd trapped him. Before he'd had a chance to move, before he'd even really realized she was coming. Caught.

For a second, they stood face to face, wrapped in her heavy metal chains. Sound, muffled and indistinct, echoed around them. Her breathing, though, was loud and sweet in his ear. He studied her face. Her eyes widened.

Then she laughed.

"Caught you," she sang.

Red grimaced.

He was trying not to grin like a fool.

***

The days had all started to look like one another. Red filled them with much of the same. He spent the mornings working with Alec, trying to improve his grip, his stance, the way he worked with his weight. Sometime last week, his fight had officially been declared a throwback, and their exercises got more intense.

He spent the afternoons with Lila, trying to make her smile, trying to protect her, and inadvertently teaching her the best ways to use her speed, her weight, and her energy against heavier, more combative opponents.

Days rushed by. Became weeks. Took all the time they had left and crushed it into one long, hot autumn of practice drills and quiet, earnest, repeated lessons. It just went on, day after day after day.

Until eventually, they ran out of time.

And Red had to face the problem that while Lila was getting quite competent, Alec was not. *Would* not.

Ever.

"Hold, hold," Red repeated quietly. Alec was steady, both hands fisted at the hilt of the sword. Red counted to twenty in his head. Then, "Okay. Now right only."

Maintaining his stance, Alec slowly let his left hand drop.

"Steady…"

Then, abruptly, Red leaped at him. Alec spun out the way, drawing his blade in a sharp vertical arc just like he was supposed to. But it wasn't fast enough. Alec was never fast enough.

Was Red the only one who never had trouble with the swing? If there was one perfect moment on the arena, it was the first offensive strike. No sense of self-preservation, no concern for what the opponent might do. Just *swing*, hard and fast. And if he was lucky, he'd get what he wanted: that *look* on their face.

Terror.

As it was, Red pivoted and used his forearm as a brace against Alec's elbow, getting underneath the swing and stopping the momentum. They stood, frozen, eye to eye.

Red sighed. "Again?"

Alec let the sword's tip hit the ground as he stepped back, wiping away sweat with his left hand. "Yeah. Again."

Red stepped wearily back out of range. Once Alec was again in position, he started the count. This time Alec used his left hand. It didn't help.

They went another three rounds, until Alec's arms were shaking and his breathing—though still light—sounded like a tenuous whistle. But still he stood there, waiting for Red's next attack.

Red shook his head. "Let's just call it a night. You're exhausted."

Alec let the sword hang at his side. "Yeah, okay. Thanks. I'll just go through a couple more patterns, meet up with you later."

Red hesitated. "Alec-"

"I'll just be a minute," Alec interrupted. But he didn't look at Red.

Picking up Micah's knife from the floor, Red tossed it between his hands. Once. Twice. "You'll be fine tomorrow. It'll be enough. You'll see."

Alec didn't say anything.

Red left him alone. The sound of careful breathing and the heavy swing of displaced air followed him out of the corridor.

***

Alec didn't wait for him in the morning. He was already gone when Red woke—or he may never have come back to the dormitory at all. Red wasn't sure.

Either way, Red didn't seek him out. He could have said it was because Alec didn't want to be found, because Coliseum fighters coped better on their own. It wasn't that those things weren't true. It wasn't by coincidence that all of these boys had ended up alone on Pilot's doorstep.

But there was the other reason, the bigger one, that Red wasn't really ready to face. He didn't have the first idea what to say to Alec, should he find him.

Red was a terrible liar. And he didn't want to let Alec down.

So he was still loitering in the dormitory, tying up his boots at half-past noon, when Elijah stopped at his bunk. "I've got to tell you something," he said.

Red raised his eyebrows.

Elijah sighed. "Look, I know that Pilot is hoping to get rid of both me and Alec. Alec is a hell of a fighter, and even if I survive, I probably won't be in any kind of shape to win the next one, so my number is pretty much up."

Red bent down to tie his other shoe.

"I wanted to tell you something about the girl."

Red paused.

He stood up and gestured for Elijah to follow him out into the hallway. They both had felt the attention shift in the room as soon as he'd mentioned her.

"What about her?" Red asked quietly. His expression was neutral; his voice was stony.

"I didn't find her on my own," Elijah said. He hesitated, then stepped forward suddenly and whispered, "Pilot told me."

Red jerked backward. "What?"

"It's not just that. He was the one who told me to tell you."

"Why? Why would Pilot do that?"

Elijah shrugged. "I don't know. Honestly. I have no idea what it's about. But I thought you should know. In case…"

In case this goes badly.

And suddenly Red felt like he'd been cheated, because he was struck by the thought that he didn't want either of these boys to die.

The bell rang in the hall. It meant a fighter hadn't shown up for duty yet.

Elijah searched Red's face, then turned abruptly. "See you around," he said, over his shoulder. Because he could not ask Red to wish him luck. Red couldn't give it.

Red was supposed to be hoping Elijah died in this fight.

Chapter 9

The stadium was more crowded than it had ever seemed from the arena. Red emerged from the shadows of Entrance C, carried on a wave of grimly smiling patrons who were equally tense as they were exhilarated. He did not count himself among them, and when a man nodded in his direction or a woman gave a short, acknowledging smile, Red turned his head away.

They were not people.

He would be damned if he was going to treat them like they were.

He found a seat just before the south gate—the gold gate, his gate—opened. Alec stood there, small in this huge stadium but still larger than life. He'd been fitted in leather and a light metal chest-plate. His helmet's visor had been damaged and Red knew from experience that the weight of it was completely off, making it more of a hazard than a benefit in the arena. But Alec wore it dutifully, shining in spite of himself, a beacon of hope for the mob to cling to.

And how they worshiped him.

Red did not stand when Alec entered the arena, did not clap when the gate closed achingly slow behind him. And when Elijah came out of the north gate, Red squeezed his eyes shut, dropped his head, and waited for the announcer to speak the familiar words that would transform this into something surreal, impossible, and thus survivable.

"Ladies and gentleman! Boys and girls! Are you ready for the fight of your lives?"

And for the first time in many long months, Red actually heard the announcer. He heard the words that he knew by heart and actually *understood* them. He remembered what death was—the sickness that marked the end of breathing, struggling life. And he saw what *he* was, a monster in the arena and a disease out here in the stands, watching it.

He heard the mob roar. He saw the look on their faces, the way they admired and feared and loved with a passion that was so utterly beyond him. Red saw the mob face Death—not just the concept of its existence, but the literal being of the Reaper reincarnated in the faces of two lonely, proud boys—and they *rejoiced.*

And Red admired them, because he couldn't even look.

He was going to be sick.

There was a fumble of noise as the fight began. Many stayed on their feet, most sat. Tension gripped the air. Red felt the anticipation claw at his skin and itch, unsatisfied.

For a second, the mob waited anxiously. They were prepared to be impressed.

Whatever they saw, it did not disappoint.

The announcer laughed into the microphone. "A feint that caught our Elijah by surprise, I think."

There was a grumble of assent from the crowd. Red ran his hands through his hair. He did not look up. He *could* not look up. He was terrified.

And he didn't have the faintest idea what to do with that terror.

A soft gasp rushed through the mob, as like a hive of bees they each took up the emotion of the person sitting beside them. This time, there was no word from the announcer. Red gripped his chair, closed his eyes.

Then, in his private hell, he saw Alec die.

Red's head shot up. In the arena, Alec was half-fallen, helmet dislodged somewhere in the dust, scrambling forward to grip something. His sword. It was a long piece, a two-handed blade that Alec had never really been talented with, no matter how Red tried to teach him. It was only after Alec reached the thing, leaned against it as he dragged himself to his feet, that Red realized the sword was not his.

It was Elijah's. Alec turned to face him. Elijah was on his feet already, though face drawn and white, ready to meet Alec's challenge with empty hands.

What had Alec brought into the arena? And where was it?

Alec lunged forward, a desperate stumble, not nearly fast enough. The sword shook in his grasp; it came down, out of control and frantic. Inadequate. When Elijah dodged the force of the blade and rammed his fist into Alec's unprotected jaw, Red flinched against the sound of a break that he could not hear. Alec crumpled, suddenly and indelicately. There was blood. And the sword clattered to the ground.

This time Red was on his feet with the mob.

Lila was right. He cared about the guys who lived in the Coliseum. He cared how they died, especially if it was in a gruesome, bloody mess for the sick pleasure of this new world. It was wrong. It was terrible. He didn't want this.

Or, at the very least, he didn't want this for Alec.

His first thought, irrationally, was that he was going to kill Elijah. And then the second thought, as swift and fierce as the first: he would never forgive Pilot if either of them died today.

Then, just as Alec pushed himself forcibly from the ground to meet Elijah's final, terminal lunge, Red realized that he was a fool to think he had any power over Pilot.

Alec moved unexpectedly, rolling with Elijah's blow and driving something small, metal, and precise into his throat. This time it was Elijah that crumbled to the ground.

He did not get up again.

Alec turned his unsteady, lolling gaze to the audience, blood dripping from his deformed, slack jaw. He raised his fist into the air, gripping his switchblade. Radiant in the afternoon sun. They rose, all around Red, and worshiped.

Red smiled, tasted salt, and realized he was crying.

Chapter 10

Red took the shortcut through Section D to get to Lila's box. He ran into Alec there, sitting on one of the bleachers. He was staring down at the arena, the switchblade in his hands, flicking it open, then closed. Open, then closed.

"Congratulations," Red said quietly.

Alec jerked up, whirling with wide, guilty eyes. Then he saw it was Red and he turned back to the arena. "I picked up my rations this morning."

Red looked at the arena too. "Are you okay?"

"I sort of knew him," Alec answered. The switchblade flipped open, then closed. "I've never fought someone I knew before."

"But it's done now," Red said.

For a second, neither said anything. Then Alec turned, his smile slow and wondrous. "You're right. I'm done."

***

Lila and Red had been working the same patterns all afternoon. Each was just like the one before. Lila tried to remember to keep her elbows in, her body tight, and forgot to watch Red's unarmed hand. He disarmed her. Again.

They started over. Lila focused on Red this time. She watched his movements, stayed out of reach. In her haste, she underestimated the force of his "punch". He tapped her, flat-handed, in the stomach. She rolled her eyes and took three steps backward.

Red laughed.

Lila switched the knife to her left hand. "Again," she said.

It had been a fight like any other.

Red darted forward, just out of reach when she swung out at him. He thought, suddenly, that he probably shouldn't let her practice with the actual knife anymore.

One of these times, she was going to catch him.

Then she took two steps forward, mimicking a drill she'd already mastered, and spun to catch him where he should have been. But, of course, Red was moving too. He caught her knife-arm, twisting just so she couldn't get away, and then spun them both to pin her against the wall.

Lila glared.

Red pressed his fingers against hers, urging the knife out of her hand. His body was hot against hers, arm restrained by his palm, making it impossible for her to strike again. He dragged his thumb along the soft spot of her wrist, up into her hand, forcing her fist open. When his fingers traced hers, it was an accident, but it stirred something in his chest and he ran his thumb across her palm. The knife clattered to the ground.

It had been a fight like any other. And then suddenly it wasn't.

"Lila." He said her name like it was a blessing.

She shuddered, raising her eyes to his.

"Lila."

He felt her weight shift. She rolled up onto the balls of her feet, slow and cautious. But her kiss was not.

***

Later, in the cafeteria, the blond guy who slept in the bunk across from Red grinned savagely.

"So I finally figured out what's been keeping you so busy up in section D," he said.

Red put his fork down.

The guy nodded smugly. "I heard you've got a nice piece of ass tucked away up there."

Nothing in Red's posture changed. His expression was as indifferent as it had been when the blond guy first sat down. But Alec's head jerked up.

The guy didn't notice.

"And I was just thinking," he said. "That if you don't mind sharing-"

Red turned his head towards the guy slowly, considering him with dark, narrowed eyes. He did not interrupt. Instead he just examined him. Then suddenly, nonchalantly, slipped his knife between the guy's stomach and the table, bracing his back with his knee.

The tip of the blade nicked his navel, came away with a tiny bubble of red.

"Say another word," Red said calmly, "and I will kill you."

For a second, no one moved. No one was sure what to do. The rules were clear, after all. There was no fighting outside of the arena. No exceptions.

Not even for Pilot's golden boy.

But Alec exhaled softly. "Red," he said. His voice was not reprimanding, not cautioning, not warning. His tone said nothing at all. Red's eyes flashed to his face.

"Pilot will throw you out," Alec said quietly. He did not say *what will happen to her if you're gone?* But Red understood anyway.

He closed his eyes. Then he withdrew the blade.

No one talked about Lila after that, neither outside of Red's hearing nor within it. But nothing escaped Pilot. He heard about what Red had done in the cafeteria.

And he was glad. He had been worried it would take longer.

Chapter 11

Red broke into Pilot's office alone. He could have taken Alec, he supposed, but he still wasn't sure exactly what he wanted out of this excursion and Alec's sense of self-preservation might get in his way.

If Red, say, decided to kill the man who'd raped Lila.

It was an unnecessary caution, however. The Coliseum was empty. Pilot was at home. The fighters were all asleep. And even if they weren't—what did they care what he did in his free time? They'd never cared before.

And they certainly didn't care about a girl locked up against her will. Or the key to a rusted old padlock that would set her free.

So Pilot's Coliseum lay still, as its greatest fighter slipped through its fingertips.

It was dark in the hallway. Red pushed gently on the chain-linked fence that split the locker room from Entrance C, careful not to let it rattle after he slipped through. There were two boys on duty tonight, as always, but they were walking along the perimeter. It was their job to stop trespassers from getting in, not a troublesome fighter from getting around. Besides, Red was fairly certain it was a pair of newbies from the south lockers tonight. Newbies would never bother him.

There were advantages to being Pilot's golden boy.

He passed Entrance E, ducking to stay out of the light cascading from the sky above the arena. His footsteps echoed in the hall, but otherwise it was quiet. The silence reminded him, suddenly, of Louisville in the summertime. He remembered hot, empty nights on the porch outside the house. Long days, lying back with his legs dangling over the edge and touching grass.

Chicago had no grass anymore.

Pilot's door appeared unceremoniously at the end of the hallway, where it curved off to the right and disappeared into shadows. It was dark, both in the room and in the hall, so Red didn't hesitate. He tested the doorknob, found it locked, and abruptly knocked against the tottering weight with the full force of his shoulder.

Once upon a time, it wouldn't have swung open. He'd have just gotten a nasty bruise and a good laugh at thinking he could outmatch a lock.

But this was not once upon a time. This was the weak, crumbling remnants of a world that had already ended. So the door yielded.

Red stepped inside.

The office was as uncluttered as it had been before. Papers in careful piles on the desk, a lamp that presumably didn't work still standing in the corner. The blinds were drawn on the windows, keeping out the dust as best as they could without the window panes. Red hesitated. He could practically feel Pilot's touch on this place. It was on the tabletop, the door handle, and the ugly stub of a candle perched on the desk.

But then again, Pilot's touch was on him too.

And Red was beginning to feel like that touch was ruining him.

He went to the desk. He pulled one drawer after another, careful not to displace anything, until he came up short. There was nothing there. He paused. Then he saw the cup.

It was filled with pencils—a few pens, a paperclip—but there was also a key.

Red grabbed it.

***

Alec was sitting up in his bunk when Red got back. "Did you get it?"

"I got it."

There was a moment of silence and then, inexplicably, Alec grinned. His teeth flashed in the darkness. "Tomorrow, Red."

Red touched the key in his pocket. He climbed into his bed, kicking off his boots and pulling on a sweatshirt. After he settled in, he drew the key back out and rolled it between his fingers, watching it flicker against the pale moonlight.

"It's almost over," he said quietly.

Alec made a noise like a sigh and the silence settled in. Red thought he'd fallen asleep.

Then Alec laughed, his voice barely above a whisper. "Make it a hell of a fight, man. We'll need it."

***

"Be careful," Lila said for the thousandth time.

"I'm always careful."

"That's a lie."

Red sighed. "I'll be fine. I'll deal with this, and then we'll be gone. It'll all be over. You'll be safe again."

Lila pressed her hand to his cheek. "We both will."

Red closed his eyes and drew her into his arms, relishing her warmth. Then he leaned down and kissed her.

"I have something for you," Red said, pulling away just far enough to pull the key out of his pocket. He held it up.

Lila hesitated, her eyes searching his face. Then her bright eyes lit. "Is that…mine?"

And something about the way she kissed him when he nodded, about the way she pressed his hands to her lips, about the flush of her cheeks and the warmth of her body, literally *undid* Red. He felt like he was glowing, like he would burst from this sudden, overwhelming happiness.

And all it had taken was that look on her face.

Lila took the key. "Can I…now?"

Red nodded.

She dropped to her knee, strands of her hair falling against Red's shin as she worked the key into the lock. There was a soft click, the clatter of metal, and Lila gave a cry that sounded like a swallowed sob.

Red touched her chin, drawing her face up. She stood to meet him. They stayed like that, face to face, for only a moment.

Then Lila stepped out of her chains and into his arms.

"Thank you," she whispered.

He kissed her forehead, her eyelids, her cheeks, her mouth.

Lila sighed. "You will be careful?"

Red smiled against her lips.

Then he pulled away. "Do something for me."

"Yes?"

"Don't watch this fight."

Lila stepped closer. "Red-"

"No. I mean it," Red insisted. He ran his hand down a strand of her hair. "The roulette is awful. It's supposed to make you sick. We use bats and planks. Things that make messes. Things you can't ever get out of your head."

"I have to know you're okay."

He cupped her face in his hands. "And I have to know that you don't ever see me do this. Not this. Not from me."

Lila rose onto her toes and kissed him. "Fine. I won't watch."

"Thank you."

Outside her window, the arena had already come to life. People were rustling about, settling into their seats, trying to figure the best vantage point from which to view one boy beat another to death.

Red scowled. “I have to get out of here, before the stadium gets packed. They can’t see me here.”

“You’ll come back after?” Lila asked. She already knew the answer, but he didn’t mind the way she leaned against him, stalling him longer.

“Yes. As soon as it’s over. And then we’re gone. You, me, and Alec.”

“Good.”

Red didn’t have as much trouble getting through the crowd as he’d expected. He kept his hands in his pockets and his head down, and no one recognized him. They had no idea that he was one of the fighters—one of the best fighters—in this arena. They had no idea he was a real person at all.

The hallway between the entrances was largely vacant. It was early enough that there wasn’t a line yet, slowing progress into the stadium bleachers. Red pulled off his jacket and wrapped Micah’s knife inside, passing under the archway between Entrance C and B just as a handful of boys finished their dinner.

“Hey man, good luck today,” one of them called.

Red nodded. He pulled open the door to the locker room and hesitated, glancing back.

“You know anyone else in this fight?”

The boys shook their heads.

“Good,” he said, then left them behind. At least he wouldn’t be killing anyone’s friend today.

Or, at least, anyone he knew.

Alec was at his bunk. “How’s your leg?” he asked quietly.

“Okay.”

“Anything I can do?”

Red dropped his jacket on his bed and scrubbed his face with his hands. “No. I’m fine.”

Alec sat down on Red's bed. He watched as Red carefully rolled up his right pant leg and checked the wound. It didn't need bandaging anymore, and it hadn't been hurting at all this past week.

But then again, Red hadn't been doing a lot of fighting to the death this past week.

He ran his finger across the new scar and felt nothing.

Alec raised an eyebrow and Red grinned. "No problem at all."

Then the bell rang.

"Guess you're late," Alec said.

Red shrugged. "I'm the star of the show. Let them wait."

He sat down next to Alec and put his boots on, one after another, and then stripped one t-shirt in favor of a long-sleeve cotton shirt.

"It's a little hot for that."

Red pulled at the fabric. "Just one more thing between me and somebody's weapon."

Alec rolled his eyes. "Won't do you much good against a bat."

Red ignored him, grabbing his gloves from under his pillow.

"See you on the other side," he said, and then turned to head back the way he'd come—Entrance C and the ticket office.

Alec stood, Red heard the bed creak behind him. "Come back alive, alright?"

One hand on the door, Red hesitated. Then he turned around and said, almost too quietly for Alec to have even heard him, "If I don't…"

Alec crossed his arms. "I'll take care of her, Red."

"Thank you."

****

It was a beautiful day for a fight. The gate was already open when Red got there, because the Russian roulette was different. Red hesitated in the shadows, searching the wall until he found the bat hanging there, decent sized. He grabbed it and practiced a swing with each hand. It was a little heavier than he'd like, but it would do.

The Coliseum was packed now. Red came out slowly, one hand in his pocket, the other holding the bat he had resting against his shoulder. The crowd went wild when they saw him and because the fight hadn't started yet, he had the luxury of looking at them.

The stadium was always full, anytime Red had ever seen a fight, but it was louder today. The noise amplified against the metal bleachers, rebounding across the field violently. People cheered; people jeered; people just screamed for the sake of screaming. Red thought that the noise made the heat more unbearable. He was almost dizzy from the humidity.

His three other contenders were already in the arena. They were spread out in a perfect diamond, including him, like it was a baseball game.

Red did have a bat.

The announcer's voice crackled to life. "Ladies and gentleman! Boys and girls! Are you ready for the fight of your lives?"

When the crowd roared, Red went utterly deaf. The sun bleached the dusty ground, the heat turned the air to stone, and he thought suddenly that he was going to be suffocated.

Then the announcer's horn went off.

And a year and a half of fighting experience took over.

Red took an easy step forward and swung the bat down to rest at his side, where he could maneuver better.

The kid to his left had sprinted, suddenly, across the arena. He was headed for the guy on Red's right, a fighter on the short side with a too-open stance. The runner would win that, but he was clearly a newbie, because he was afraid of Red.

He could tell because the guy had looked up, just once, after the horn had gone off. He'd gauged Red, to see if he was coming after him. And when Red had only strolled forward, his relief was unmistakable.

Which meant that the other veteran in this fight was opposite him.

There was no sign of that fighter. The runner hit the shorter guy with the full force of a 2x4 in the gut, sending him tumbling backwards. Unlucky for the runner, he'd hit the guy's center almost dead on, so he only stumbled but didn't fall.

Red wiped the sweat off his forehead.

The shorter guy used his instability to roll forward. He hit the runner across both knees with his crowbar. Red heard one of the kneecaps shatter. The runner screamed and dropped to the ground.

The crowd had not been paying attention to Red. He'd been walking toward the scuffling boys, keeping his attention open to interruption, in case the veteran made an appearance before these two killed each other. Red doubted he would, though.

It was only Red that had to prove to Pilot that he could put on a good show.

The shorter of the two clambered to his feet, clutching the crowbar and trying to recover his balance. He raised the crowbar over his head. The runner, a dark-haired boy with wide green eyes, crawled, straining, and tried to get to his feet. But he couldn't manage his left leg, which had become completely unresponsive.

The guy with the crowbar swung. Missed.

The green eyed boy looked up again, crying from the effort of rolling out of the way.

The guy raised the crowbar again.

And a bat connected with his head.

A collective gasp silenced the crowd. Then Red took two more paces and kicked the crowbar away. The guy blinked, coming conscious again just in time to feel the bat hit his abdomen.

He screamed.

Red raised the bat again. The kid curled, helpless, like the novices did when they saw it was over. They never fought to the end. And Red, suddenly, couldn't finish it. He took a half step backward. He was lightheaded. He couldn't get a grip on the bat.

Then there was a noise behind him.

He heard the silence of the mob. They could see what he could not, and they were sure he was about to die.

But they had no idea how much he wanted to live.

Taking one step forward, he crouched and swung, hard enough to spin him around and catch the kid behind him directly on the hip. It was the runner, the green-eyed boy, and he stumbled, grappling with his 2x4.

Red didn't even let him hit to ground. He switched hands, raised the bat, and swung it again. It hit the kid's head with a sickening crack. And then Red saw the force burst the veins behind his green eyes.

He turned away, but it was too late. He'd already seen the blood pool in the kid's eyes, crying ghoulishly down his face.

Red was going to be sick.

Then, again, behind him, something changed. This time Red heard it before the crowd did. Silence.

The boy he'd left at his back was dead now.

Red didn't get a chance to turn this time. He threw his arms over his head and caught the full force of some kind of bar against his left forearm. He screamed, but when he crumbled, he rolled. Someone swore behind him.

Wincing, Red got to his feet. He'd lost the bat.

The guy he faced was a little taller than him, but no bigger. He had what appeared to be a lead pipe, which he held in front of him like a batter ready to swing, and he was panting. He took a step forward, then another. Red didn't move. The crowd thought the guy was taking it slow for effect; they thought Red was making a valiant last stand.

But Red had seen something they could not.

The veteran was trying very hard not to limp.

So Red held his ground, because he needed to find a way to get behind the guy and back to his bat. And if he just ran for it, there was a very good chance this guy would not be able to catch him.

The guy took another step forward and his left leg bowed, just slightly. Red lurched forward, kicking him in the shin, and twisting the lead pipe out of his hand as he held it to his own chest.

You can't swing something if it's already in contact with its target. The guy leaned away, trying to keep his wrist from breaking, and finally released the weapon. Red shoved the arm back, hard, and heard it snap. Now they were even.

As the guy stumbled forward, Red turned to face him again. He gripped the bar in his right hand—his good hand—and waited until the guy had regained balance enough to turn, injured arm cradled with his remaining one, to find his opponent again.

Pilot would like that. Pilot loved a moment of silence before a kill.

The guy caught Red's gaze, flinched, and only then did the bar came down on him. It only took one swing, clean against his skull.

The crowd exploded. They screamed. They cheered. Red heard his own name. He heard the stadium shiver against the sheer volume of the noise. He gripped the bar tightly in his fist to keep his hand from shaking. He took a stumbling step forward and saw, suddenly, the body of the green eyed boy.

Red hadn't realized he'd cracked the kid's skull open.

He walked out of the arena, cradling his broken arm. Away from prying eyes, where Pilot would never hear about it, he crawled into a corner and threw up. He threw up until there was nothing left in his stomach.

And only then did he cry.

***

He was still there when Alec found him. His arm still hurt like hell and he clutched it to his chest. It only made the pain infinitely worse, but he had the confused, unfocused idea that if he let go, his arm would shatter.

Alec leaned against the wall next to him.

"Are you going to be okay?"

Red stared at nothing. He inhaled slowly and realized he was not crying anymore. Then he nodded.

Alec held out an antibacterial wipe.

Red wiped down his face, his mouth, his hands. He bit his lip at the searing pain in his left arm, but otherwise found himself the better for being clean. Alec offered to help when he rose, but Red ignored him, using the wall and his good hand to get up.

"Red-"

"Was it a good fight?" Red interrupted.

Something he didn't understand flashed across Alec's face, but then he nodded.

Red smiled shakily. “Good.”

“I just-” Alec stopped again. He looked at Red. Pity. Then it was gone and Red felt dizzy and sick. He probably had a concussion. Everything felt misplaced and distant.

“Are you okay?” Alec asked. “Is your head okay?”

Red reached up with his left hand to rub his temple and almost threw up again. He switched to his right. “It will be.”

Alec started to say something again. He shook his head.

“Am I okay?” Red asked him. He touched his forehead, then his abdomen. He seemed alright, but he felt missing. “I’ve got to go see Lila.”

Again that expression Red didn’t understand. Alec crossed his arms. “Pilot announced the next fight after you left.”

“So? Why does that matter?”

Alec took a step forward, like he was going to put a hand on Red’s shoulder or something, then changed his mind. “Apparently there is going to be some big fight to reveal the nation’s new ‘hero’, or so Pilot says.”

“I don’t understand why this is important.” Red kept his hand on the wall but stepped forward, expecting Alec to get out of his way. “I need to see Lila.”

At last, Alec’s expression broke. “That’s what I’m trying to tell you, Red. She’s on the list for the hero’s fight.”

“What?”

Red stumbled, almost fell on Alec, and then retreated to the stone at his back. He studied the far wall. “What?” he repeated. “What does that mean?”

“She’s gone. I checked the box. I don’t know where Pilot’s put her. He announced that the hero’s fight is going to be tomorrow. He says it’s too important for the future of the nation to wait even another day. You should have heard the crowd. They went crazy. They think it’ll be the fight of a lifetime.”

Red stared at the floor.

It seemed like they were having a conversation. There were words. Sentences, even. Alec was saying something. But it all just kept slipping out of Red’s reach.

All of it but one.

"She's on the list? Lila?"

"They really believe him. They think the winner of the next fight is going to be some kind of hero," Alec fumbled. The words were a rush. "They think one person can just put everything back to the way it was. Like Pilot just happened to find some kid who can save the world. It's-"

He was out of control.

And he was missing the point.

"Alec," Red interrupted. He looked up. "Lila is on the list? For tomorrow?"

Alec nodded.

And finally Red understood. It had all been a waste. He couldn't save anyone, not Lila, not Alec, not even himself. He hadn't won the fight. He'd *lost* it. He'd lost everything.

Lila was going to die.

Lila was going to *die*.

Red settled hard against the wall, his broken arm forgotten. The force sent blinding pain across his chest. It was like a shock of clarity. He blinked, raising his hand palm up. Stretching his fingers until he couldn't see straight, until the pain was all consuming. Until he couldn't remember his own name.

Until it wasn't even about him.

Then he looked at Alec. "Who else is on the list? Who else is fighting?"

"Lila Sinclair, Aiden Manor, Creed Tenison, and you."

"And me?"

Alec tensed. "Yes."

He waited a second. Then another. Red said nothing.

Alec's face redden. Fear was replaced by panic. "Red. Red, look at me. What are you going to do?"

But Red was not afraid. Not anymore. It wasn't about him.

"I'm going to save her."

"How?"

It didn't matter how he did it. Alec didn't understand; there was no other option. There hadn't been another option since the moment Red had walked into Lila's prison a year ago.

Pilot had made sure of that.

"You can't just play his game," Alec worked his tongue, searching for words. "This is exactly what Pilot wants you to do, Red. Don't you see that? You can't just..."

The words ran out. He reached for Red, hesitantly. The distance was too far. His arm dropped to his side. His hands were shaking.

"Do you have another idea?" Red replied. "We don't know where Lila is. The next time we'll see her, she'll be on the arena. I just happen to be one of the only other people allowed on that arena with her."

Alec looked furious. "But don't you think there's a reason that Pilot picked you? Don't you think he knows that you won't let her die?"

Red squeezed his eyes shut, rubbing his face with his hands. He felt overextended and exhausted, wound so tight that he was about to explode. "So what if he does? What does that change? If Pilot has a plan, let's see it. I'd like to see a hero. Wouldn't you?"

"There won't be a hero. There'll just be more dead kids."

Then he was defeated. Checkmated. Blocked into a corner and lashing out like a caged animal. Because Red *was* a caged animal. He was a Coliseum fighter.

Cage fighting was all they were good for.

"As long as one of those dead kids isn't Lila, then I really don't care."

Alec shook his head. "You can't save her. It doesn't work like that."

Red stared at him, expression arena-neutral, and waited for him to understand.

And then Alec did.

He took a step back. "No. You can't do that either."

"Do you have any other ideas?"

"Red, she wouldn't want this. She *doesn't* want this."

Red didn't say anything.

"You can't just give up. Not now. Don't you see-"

Alec went on, but his words didn't mean anything. He wasn't looking at Red. His eyes flitted around the corridor, restless. Still talking. He must have known that it was a waste, that he couldn't stop Red, but that didn't keep him from trying. Alec just talked, an onslaught of words that wouldn't change anything.

Because the boys in Pilot's Coliseum were not supposed to be friends. It was just that, sometimes, they were.

And Red was breaking his heart.

But it didn't matter. It couldn't matter.

"I won't let her die, Alec," Red said quietly.

This wasn't about them. It was about Lila.

And damn the rest of it to hell.

Because if he didn't draw the line right here, then where?

Alec's hands balled into fists. He didn't move. "How much control do you really think you have over that?"

Red flinched, but held his ground.

Alec was shaking. His face was a flurry of emotion. Raging, desperate, furious. Pleading.

And Red looked away.

"Red. Please."

Everything inside him turned to ash.

He went around Alec, back towards the dormitory. "I *love* her," he said, not looking, unwilling to see the expression on Alec's face. "I won't let her die."

Alec tried to say something. Red knew because he heard him choke on his words and knew that he was crying. Red didn't want to see him cry. He would lose his nerve.

"She didn't choose this, Alec. She's the only one who didn't choose."

He hesitated, just for a second. There was a stifled sob, and then Alec's voice, broken. "I won't watch you do this."

Red closed his eyes. "You don't have to."

Chapter 12

Red had been here twenty one times before. He stood in the tunnel, waiting in the shadows for the gold gate to open. He could hear the mob already. They were tense, thrilled by the sheer anticipation.

It was unheard of to see four kids kill each other two days in a row.

He'd wrapped his left shoulder in an ace bandage, tying it off across his chest so his arm hung limp at his side. Ideally, it wouldn't hurt there. Red really only hoped it wouldn't get in the way.

The fight that was to determine the world's new hero was apparently to be done with knives. Red had Micah's knife in the waistband of his pants. He kept his good hand free. There was a scuffle of noise on the arena. Red looked up, but his gate didn't open.

He was alone.

Alec had been as good as his word. There'd been no sign of him since Red had left him in front of the locker rooms yesterday. Since then, the headache had passed, the nausea had faded, but the fear remained, palpable and nearly unbearable.

He was *terrified* to go out on the arena. But he was much more scared of staying behind. So here he stood, ready to see Pilot's plan through to the end.

And so what? Pilot claimed he was creating a hero. Red was not opposed to heroes. Red didn't really care much about heroes at all.

What he needed was a miracle.

What he needed was to see Lila again, to tell her he loved her, and to tell her he was so sorry that he had been too scared to take her away before—before it was too late, before it had come to this.

If Lila Sinclair died today, it would be his fault.

And that would be one too many deaths to Red's name.

There was an explosion of noise from the crowd, and the announcer called out. "Ladies and gentleman! Boys and girls! Are you ready for the fight of your lives?"

For one, awful second, Red thought the gate wasn't going to open. He thought he was going to have to watch them kill her through the metal bars of this barrier. But then it creaked to life.

"Are you ready to make a hero?" the announcer asked.

The mob went *wild.*

For the first time in his life, Red ran out onto the arena. He couldn't wait. The crowd explode when they saw him. They saw him run and thought that meant he wanted to be a hero. They thought it meant they would get a better show. They saw him move—burning and feral—and they knew that he was powerful, that he was worthy, that he would survive. They worshiped him.

Lila was not met with such fortune.

She stumbled out of the bench area for the away team. Her red hair cascaded across her face, sharpening her features. She was barefoot, but her ankles were marred with fresh bruises. In her hand, she gripped a knife.

And Red could tell by the way she was standing that she had no intention of using it.

Silence fell like a brick across the Coliseum. The mob had never seen a girl in the arena.

Lila took a hesitant step forward and looked up, rocking back onto her heels to see the full breadth of the crowd that had come to see her die. The crowd that had come to see them *all* die. They looked back at her.

"Out of the east," the announcer suddenly cried. "Lila Sinclair!"

Then, because it was okay to see a girl killed as long as they knew her name, the crowd cheered.

Lila turned to him. "Red?" she asked. And he heard her because he could see the fear on her face. Because he knew what she would say, now, when he had failed her.

The gates opened on their contenders. The taller proved also to be larger, and he took three steps out of the gate and then broke into a charge at Red. The second opponent, out of the north gate—closer to Lila—didn't hesitate either. He already had his knife out.

And Red could see that they were working together. Someone had told them what to do. Someone had told them how to win this fight. Someone they trusted.

There was only one person that the boys in the Coliseum would ever take orders from. There was only one man that they would ever trust with their lives, because they had done it once before. They had come to his doorstep, looking for a way to survive, and he had protected them. He had trained them. He had saved them all. So they believed he had their best interests at heart. And they loved him.

Red almost laughed out loud. They had been so stupid, to think that anyone could love them. Every one of them were outcasts, himself included. They'd done terrible, savage things to the people they loved most. And they killed each other because it was easy. It was simple. It made them feel better.

They had learned to be monsters because one man had told them that he would love them more if they were. And they had believed him.

Stupid, naïve, horrible *children*, every one.

They were wrong. Pilot did not love them.

Chapter 13

There was only one person that Pilot loved.

And, until this morning, Max had never set foot in his father's Coliseum.

Pilot glanced back at the boy, who sat cross-legged on the bench, as far away from the window as he could get. Lila had just been called onto the arena, he'd seen her released into the playing field just seconds ago. There'd been a moment—just a passing fear, really—when he'd thought the audience would not accept her.

She was so very beautiful, and he thought that her fear was going to be too much for the crowd. But the moment passed. The mob cheered. Pilot always underestimated them.

"Don't you want to see the fight?" he asked Max.

The boy looked up, his face set in stone, frightened and disgusted. He'd been such a soft child before the war, and in those days when Pilot wasn't sure that he would survive the fire and the disease, he'd grown even softer.

Pilot turned away from the arena and gestured for Max to join him at the window. His son stuffed his hands into the pockets of his coat—the boy was always cold, even when it was a hundred degrees outside and suffocating—but got up obediently.

He didn't look at his father as he stepped up beside him.

The announcer, his voice hollow and artificially amplified, called, "Coming out of the north, Creed Tenison!"

Creed was already moving out of the gate, cutting across the field without a second's hesitation. He should have checked his blind spot on the west side, probably, but Pilot had promised him that Aiden would not kill him today. At least, not until Lila Sinclair was dead. So he didn't hesitate.

Beside him, Max stiffened. "She looks scared."

Lila looked terrified. She saw Creed and took one stumbling step backwards. It took her fatal seconds to understand that the boy was coming for her. She took a second step back, a third, retreating but not at all fast enough.

Pilot heard Max inhale sharply, echoing the hushed anticipation that rushed across the stadium. He smiled tightly.

Then, unexpectedly, Red screamed her name.

His voice echoed across the arena, a roar and a threat. Lila turned and now Pilot could see her face. She did have startling eyes. They were wide, colorless. She didn't see him.

But she did see Red. He yelled again, wordless, but she had finally understood. She ran.

Out of the corner of his eye, Pilot saw Max tug his hands out of his coat pockets and lean against the windowsill. His gaze, and that of the entire audience, followed Lila's progress.

She was not fast enough. Pilot could see that immediately. Creed had the distance on his side, and he was moving faster than she was. He let out a cry and raised the knife, moving suddenly diagonally to cut her off from Red. Smart.

Lila slowed, hesitated, then took three uncertain steps backwards. Max pressed his hand to the window.

"You said this was a fight to make a hero," he said quietly.

Pilot glanced at his son, but the boy's face was soft and unreadable as ever. "Yes."

"Who is the hero supposed to be?"

Pilot couldn't bury his smile. "You'll see."

He felt Max's eyes on him and turned expectantly. But the boy just looked at him, quietly, with that thoughtful knowing glance that his mother had been so good at. He did have his mother's temperament. Her contented smile.

But he had proved to have the better luck.

Pilot turned back to the arena.

Aiden had almost reached engaging distance with Red. He was steady on his feet as he slowed, brandishing his knife. He was keeping just enough space between them to keep Red from making quick work of him but close enough that Red could not retreat. Aiden took a step forward. Red rotated the knife in his right hand. He was at a disadvantage today.

Even from here, Pilot could see that the brace the boy had created to protect his broken left arm wasn't secure enough. It would only take a single, well-aimed hit to debilitate him completely. Any other day, it wouldn't be an issue. Red never left himself open to attack. For more than a year and a half, longer than any other resident of the Coliseum, he'd watched the boy cripple opponent after opponent, and he'd never seen anything happen on the arena that Red had not planned for, that he could not cope with.

Until today. Red retreated several steps and glanced to Lila. He saw her stumble. The crowd gasped and Creed lunged, but suddenly she found her balance and swung low, nicking Creed across the cheek.

Creed wiped away blood.

Lila used her momentum to crawl away, clambering to her feet. She whirled, lashing out, and this time Creed had to leap to get out of the way. He threw himself backwards, flailing, and still only narrowly missed the arch of her blade. He fumbled, looked up.

The surprise was written all over his face.

Pilot saw Max smile. And on the arena, Red smiled too.

Red turned back to Aiden, swinging his knife in a sudden, wide arch. It would have never made contact, but Aiden clearly didn't expect it. He leaped backwards, barely avoiding another suddenly slash from the other direction as Red pivoted to attack again. The crowd roared.

Aiden darted forward, feigning an attack on Red's damaged arm and then using his weight to ram instead directly into Red's solar plexus. The boy tumbled, crashing to the ground. Aiden raised his knife, but he should have known something was wrong.

The audience was on its feet.

Red caught his weight with his good arm and then kicked hard, forcing Aiden's shin back with such force that made the boy scream. His leg bowed. On the ground, Red grappled with his knife and climbed to his feet.

He turned to find Lila again. So did the crowd.

She was holding her own. Every step Creed took forward, Lila darted back. One. Two. Three. He swung wide, she blocked with her knife arm, using her stance to twirl and catch his open ribcage with her other hand.

Creed coughed, stumbling back.

And Lila attacked. At first, it was a flurry of practiced, deadly patterns. She forced him back, one step, and then another. Gaining ground. She ripped open the air in front of him, Creed was lucky it was not him, and he tripped. Lost his balance.

Lila swung high, forcing him to duck. She kicked as he dropped, and Creed caught the blow right under his chin. He flipped and barely caught himself, braced like a crab-walk on the arena floor. There was a moment.

Lila could have had him.

But she didn't. The moment passed. Creed was on his feet. Lila faltered. When Creed slashed forward, it was a half-second before Lila parried. She almost missed the next one. She gave, and gave, until finally she had to *give*—Pilot saw her strange, grey eyes cool—and she abruptly barreled, ducking, and slipped away.

At which point it would have started all over again.

If Creed hadn't seen it too. Her tell.

Those strange, grey eyes.

He caught her, just above the forearm, when she tried to move past him.

Lila faltered. Creed moved left, feigned right, and Lila spun, her hair cutting like a blanket across her face.

She hesitated. In her blindness, Creed lunged.

This time, she wasn't ready for him. He slashed his knife across her right arm, slamming her with the full force of his body. She stumbled, crumbled, and her knife fell, stained, to the ground. But she did not.

Creed was already moving.

"The knife!" Red screamed.

Pilot had forgotten about Red. It was clear the crowd had too, because they erupted into a flurry of noise. They echoed his direction, a wall of frantic sound. Red looked up.

Aiden sprung.

Then everything happened at once. Lila ducked, half-somersaulting but mostly tumbling. Creed missed the movement and he didn't turn in time, catching the full force of her punch at the side of his head. Then she was gone, scrambling in the dust.

Creed blinked, pressed his empty hand to his head, and then, before Lila could find the knife, before she could get to her feet, before she could do anything, Creed leapt at her.

Red caught Aiden's arm as he stepped out of the way of the attack, used it to shove them both in a sudden arch to face the east gate. Aiden's shoulder gave an awful crack and Red released him. The boy stumbled forward and Red, who had stepped with him to bury his knife into Aiden's back, hesitated.

Lila was still on the ground. She'd never be fast enough.

This was it. This was the moment. Pilot smiled grimly.

And then Red's face changed. He seemed to get bigger, taller, and something in his expression turned his rage to unbridled hatred. Senseless. Wild. Uncontrollable. Pilot watched Red snap.

But it was too soon, much too soon. And Pilot suddenly knew what was about to happen.

Because then, almost imperceptibly, Red smiled.

He threw his knife.

Creed crumbled.

Lila started and looked up, first at Creed and then at Red. Her bright eyes lit, and beside Pilot, Max swallowed hard.

Then she screamed.

Aiden turned in one, smooth motion. He buried his knife into Red's abdomen. Red choked. He bled.

The mob roared.

And it was over. Red Ferris was dead.

Pilot's Coliseum went silent. Aiden stood over Red's body, heaving against the pain of his dislocated shoulder. At his back, Creed lay, bleeding in the dust. Dying.

Two dead boys, and no heroes.

No heroes.

Nothing.

Pilot stepped back. How could his golden boy have died? He pressed his hands along the front of his shirt, ironing it with his fingers. Then he turned his back on the arena.

Max made a soft, frightened noise. "Wait. Look."

Lila was crying. She got to her feet and ran across the arena. Aiden didn't stop her. He just watched as she stumbled and crumpled and crawled to Red's body. The whole crowd watched. She pressed her hands to Red's hair, his cheek, his chest. Her fingers turned to red, covered in his blood. She leaned down and kissed him, on the lips, on his forehead. She cried.

Then Aiden took a hesitant step forward. He looked up at the audience and they looked back at him. Pilot felt the uncertainty, the anticipation.

Was Aiden going to kill this girl?

Lila heard him at her back. She froze.

The dust rushed across the arena.

Aiden decided.

Max screamed, but Lila had already moved. She put one bloody hand on the ground and sprung to her feet, spinning as she did. For an instant, they were face-to-face. Aiden lunged. Lila pivoted, just as Red had done only minutes before. She grabbed Aiden's dislocated shoulder and shoved him forward.

Aiden screamed and Lila raised one bloody arm, knife in hand, and buried it into his neck.

Silence.

Then: "Ladies and gentleman—your hero."

NEW TESTAMENT

Chapter 1

Lila was drowning. There was so much. *Too* much. Sound. Echoing. Amplified. The noise was throbbing. It shook the dusty floor. The smell of the sweat and blood hung in the air, dense and rusty. The cloudy sky was too bright, the mob was shaking. The people—everywhere, teeming, suffocating her.

They adored her. They wanted her.

Lila was going to be sick.

Red was lying at her feet, a bloody mess that transformed his perfect face into a grotesque, mocking forgery of what it had once been. She stumbled, climbing over the other boy's body, to put her hands on Red's chest.

His eyes were closed. He did not stir. He did not breathe.

Lila leaned over him, pressing her body to his. She kissed his closed eyes, his forehead, his cheeks, and finally his lips. He tasted of salt-water and blood. That was all. Red was gone.

He'd left her here alone.

Lila spoke then, in a soft, panicked spree. She cried against his mouth. She begged him for something, something he'd promised not so very long ago but couldn't give her anymore. She whispered his name, over and over, like it was a mantra that could drown out the sound of the mob.

Lila cupped Red's face in her hands. The knife in her right fist touched his cheek, the flat of the blade against his skin, but she couldn't bring herself to let it go. She whispered his name again, but there was nothing. He refused to answer her.

Then, suddenly, Lila felt a weight on her shoulder. Someone grabbed her, dragging her to her feet.

She spun wildly, pulling out of the grip and slashing frantically out with the knife. The man took several steps back. He swore. Lila watched him.

It was suddenly quiet. The audience had stopped calling her name. She was glad.

Then someone else entered the arena, sprinting from the west gate. She shifted her weight to her back foot.

If they touched Red, she would kill them.

But then the second boy slowed. He had a purpling bruise on the left side of his chin and a gangly form, and the way he looked at her—like he knew her. And he was not afraid.

She didn't understand that. He *should* be afraid. There was nothing left, nothing but Lila and this barren, bloody arena. Didn't he know that when the mob cried her name, they were secretly calling out for someone else? Didn't he know what they'd lost—what she'd lost—was irreplaceable?

It was over.

He knew. He had to know.

"Lila," he said quietly.

She stepped back.

"Lila," he said again. Then his eyes flickered passed her. She saw him see Red. She saw his face change, just for a moment.

When his eyes found her face again, she held his gaze. She thought-

"It's Alec, Lila. Do you remember me?"

She didn't. She didn't remember anything except the roar of the mob and this throbbing in her body, under her skin, that hurt so badly she couldn't breathe. She didn't remember anything except the way that Red tasted—like salt water and blood.

Alec took another step forward.

And then Lila remembered something else. She remembered the box, her chains, the key that had set her free. She remembered a promise.

"*And then we're gone. You, me, and Alec.*"

Alec. This Alec. This boy with the broken jaw, the dirty green eyes and the halting, cautious voice. This boy from another place, another time, another reality.

A reality where Red loved her so much that he was going to take her away.

Lila let the knife fall to her side. She let Alec come and take her under his arm. She let him turn her away from the broken, bloody body of the boy she loved. She let him whisper her name, carefully, and tell her that it was going to be okay.

She let him lie.

***

For all the noise the boys made, no one approached Lila. She sat on Red's bunk, his knife in her lap, running her thumb along the flat of its blade. She could hear them whispering to one another, some in louder voices than others. They asked if she was really the hero. They asked what Pilot had meant, if there would be more fights. They guessed who would be next to fight her.

In quieter voices, in corners of the room, a few dropped terrible words about what they would do if they got to fight her in the arena. She saw Alec stiffen. He looked over at her and she had the sudden urge to reach out to him. He would hide her.

But though he was only inches away, leaning against the bed frame at her side, it was an unfathomable distance. She could not reach him. She could not feel him.

She ran her thumb across the tip of the blade, drew just a bubble of blood.

Alec inhaled sharply. “Lila-”

She was disappointed. It hadn’t hurt.

There was another sudden commotion, as the boys near the door were abruptly cut short. They settled into uncomfortable silence. Lila felt the tension in the air shift.

Alec took a step closer to her. His eyes turned to steel. No one spoke.

“Where is the girl?”

She looked up. It had been months since she’d heard his voice. The last time she’d seen him, she had been something different, not a person at all.

She’d been a possession.

And now here Pilot was, just when she’d become a possession again.

Pilot’s hero.

He looked the same. His overcoat was still too large. His clothes were still too clean, his skin too smooth. He still had that barely-contented expression, the one that had driven orphan after orphan out of the ruins of the old world, under his wing, and into the arena. When he saw her, he smiled.

Lila did not smile back, but she did stand up. She held Red’s knife in her left hand, limp at her side, and waited for Pilot to tell her what to do. For *anyone* to tell her what to do.

She felt Alec touch her forearm. The shock of the contact surprised her. She pulled away. He didn’t leave.

“You don’t have to go with him.”

Lila put her fingers to her arm where he’d touched her, the knife shaking at her side. She searched his face and remembered the way Red had looked, with that same belligerence in his eyes. She remembered his soft promises in the darkness, when she’d stand so still that she would forget she was chained and could pretend that she was somewhere else, somewhere wonderful, where no one could hurt them again.

Lila pressed the flat side of the blade against her thigh. “It’s fine,” she said, because it wasn’t.

She didn't understand Alec's expression.

Pilot, at least, seemed pleased. "Let's go."

Lila followed him, without looking at the other boys. Still, she heard their whispers follow her, the questioning glances, and the weight of Alec's gaze on her back. It was heavy. Everything was heavy. Lila followed Pilot, feeling dizzy and sick.

He led her through the hallway, around to Entrance C, where the Coliseum's audience had finally filtered out of the bleachers and away. He hesitated in the archway and turned back to her.

"I'm going to take you back to the house. You'll be safer there."

Lila looked up at him.

His face was open. He leaned towards her, bending his head to catch her eyes. "You don't have to be scared. I'm going to take care of you."

She dropped her gaze to her hands, where she held Red's knife to her chest. Her fingers were steady as she ran her left palm along the blunt edge of the blade. Pilot made a sympathetic noise.

"You'll be okay. I promise."

Lila's eyes flickered to his face. "I know," she said. As if it mattered whether or not she was ever okay.

This seemed to satisfy him. Pilot turned again and led her out into the open. She hesitated for only a moment before following him, gripping Red's knife hard enough to keep her hands from shaking. To keep from throwing up.

Lila didn't know why she felt so sick. She was leaving the Coliseum, just like she'd always wanted.

When the tip of Red's blade slipped and sliced a gash open across her left palm, she didn't even feel it. She looked at the cut, already dripping a single line of blood, and wiped it away on her jeans. The wound remained, aching dully, but Lila trailed obediently after Pilot.

Last time she'd been in his car, it had surprised her. She'd wondered where the gas had come from, how he'd managed to hold on to the vehicle through the fire and the famine and the massacre. She'd asked him. Pilot had told her, in that other life, the answer to all of those questions. He'd promised her that she would see a great many new wonders where he was taking her. He had flashed his greedy smile and said that she'd see the beginning of the new world.

Now Lila just got in the backseat when he opened the door for her. She didn't look out the window. If Pilot said anything, Lila didn't notice. She watched Red's knife shake as the car sputtered to life. Minutes later, Pilot slowed to a stop to let someone in—someone who slammed the door violently closed again and spoke in a wild, bitter stream of words. Lila looked up at him. He froze at her expression. Then he slumped into his seat and didn't speak for the rest of the ride.

They left the Coliseum.

The boy in the passenger seat said something quietly about 'home'.

Lila pressed her left palm into the leather seat cushion at her side. It left a small sliver of red in its wake. She leaned her head against the window and closed her eyes.

In her dreams, Red pressed his bloody lips to hers and whispered promises that he could not keep and cried into her hair and died—over and over again. Until she couldn't take it anymore. Until, it wasn't real because it couldn't be real. It was just something that happened to someone else, in some far away nightmare.

Lila opened her eyes. The boy in the passenger seat was quiet. Pilot looked at her in the rearview mirror and Lila turned her face away.

***

Pilot pulled into the driveway of a two story, unobtrusive house at the end of a cul-de-sac in the middle of nowhere. They were outside of New Chicago, but not far.

It had once probably seen the Chicago skyline, just over the horizon, but there wasn't a skyline to see anymore. So instead there was nothing. *It* was nothing. Left behind by all but Pilot—king of the new world. Lila did not get out of the car.

Pilot did. He turned back to face the vehicle, shutting the door and pressing his palms on the roof. Seconds passed. Lila didn't move. Neither did the boy in the passenger seat.

"Come inside."

Lila started at the sound. Her eyes flickered to Pilot's face, but he wasn't looking at her. His gaze was leveled on the boy.

Something about his tone surprised her.

"Please, Max."

Was he *begging*?

"I need you to go inside." Pilot's voice was strained. Something was wrong.

And then Pilot looked sideways at Lila.

He should not have.

Her mind, all hazy and adrift, became suddenly focused. Lila's palm ached. She looked down at it, at the blood, then back up at Pilot. And still she did not understand.

Everything was wrong—misshapen and jagged where it should have fit. Panic bloomed in her stomach.

Something was missing inside her. Something important.

She said the first thing that came to her head. "Where am I?"

A shift in Pilot's expression.

The boy in the passenger seat replied first, however. "We're at the house. I don't know why he brought you, though." His baby blue eyes caught the light when he turned suddenly to glare out the open window. "Why did you bring her here? It seemed pretty clear what you thought of her earlier-"

Pilot cut him off. "Not here. My God, Max, have some sense. Not here."

Max's face was flush. His eyes went to her face, then away. The panic in Lila's stomach was rapidly becoming something else, something angry and unsatisfied that she couldn't quite put a name to.

But it was clawing its way out from under her skin.

Lila rolled Red's knife between her hands.

Red's *knife.*

"We have to go back for him," she said suddenly. Her grip on the knife tightened. "He's hurt. He needs me-"

Max made a strangled noise.

Lila's head jerked up.

Ladies and gentlemen, I give you your hero!

Red.

Red.

The boy she loved with his head held high, eyes wild. Watching her. The knife in her hand, heavier than she was used to. No more chains. Another boy's knife. A sudden attack.

Saved.

Then lost.

And the rest—gone. All of it—Red—just *gone*.

Lila exploded. "You *killed* him," she screamed. She was out the door, one hand on the door handle, the other gripped tightly around Red's knife. Pilot stepped back.

Not fast enough. If she moved now, following the curve of the car, she'd have him. She'd kill him.

But Lila hesitated. She saw Max.

He'd scrambled out of the car on the other side, trying to keep his balance on the frame of the door and accidentally catching his hip against the car hood on his way around. He inhaled sharply, stumbled, and looked up. His wide, baby blue eyes landed on Lila's face.

He was terrified.

It stopped Lila in her tracks.

How was that possible? Lila was the one that was scared. It was *always* her. She was the one who'd hesitated in the arena. She was the one who'd forced the gamble, the sacrifice. Too scared to fight. Too scared to live.

Her terror had *killed* him. The boy she'd loved.

Would it kill this boy too?

Lila's grip on the knife loosened.

And, just like that, it all came undone. Her rage, the only levy between Lila and the tide, just gave way. Guilt dropped like a stone in her stomach. Crippled her. Then the desperation came. The fear. The sorrow. A torrent of grief that broke over her head.

The anger wasn't worth this. This was too much. It would bury her.

Lila's fingers shook as she pressed the blade against her palm, frantic. She'd barely broken skin when she felt it—just a buzz in the back of her spine, erupting like a shiver at the base of her neck. A shock.

It wasn't enough. She wanted less than this. She wanted to feel *nothing*. Lila was still shaking when she dropped the knife to her side. She raised her face to Pilot's.

He spoke stiffly. "Max, go inside."

This time Pilot's son obeyed.

Long seconds passed.

"Was that-" Pilot watched her warily. "Was that all?"

Wasn't it enough?

The words must have been in her eyes, because Pilot thinned his lips. There was another beat of silence.

Then he held out his hand. "The knife," he said.

Lila hesitated, then shook her head. She stuffed it into the waist of her jeans, at the back, as Red had done before her.

Nothing changed in Pilot's expression. "I have to know you won't hurt him."

Hurt *him*?

"Why would I hurt him?"

"I need the knife."

Lila stilled. "It's mine."

But it wasn't. It wasn't hers.

Too much. Lila buried it. She had to be empty. There had to be nothing inside her. Nothing at all.

"You won't use it," Pilot said. It wasn't a question.

Lila was surprised. Then she was nothing. "I won't use it."

He considered her. "You can sleep in the guest room. You'll go up first. You won't speak to my son."

Lila did as she was told. If there was a moment, in the grey shadow of the doorway, when she almost turned back—then it was only a moment. And it passed.

She didn't want what was back there.

"It's that one," Pilot said, when Lila had reached the top of the stairs. "The first door is Max's. You won't go near him. The second room is yours."

Lila nodded. The landing looked down over the kitchen, and from where she was standing, she could see just the shadow of Max's face from behind the partially-closed door to the adjoining room downstairs. His blue eyes widened when he saw her see him. He vanished.

Lila didn't look at Pilot as she turned and fled into her room.

But even after she'd gone, Lila could hear him out there. Neither of them moved. Pilot was silent on his side, and Lila was nothing on hers. She didn't know what he wanted.

She didn't know what *she* wanted.

Lila did not hear him leave. But he must have.

"I'm so sorry," Max said suddenly, his voice was a whisper behind the door.

Lila froze.

He coughed. "Are you going to be okay?"

There was nothing—nothing inside.

Lila didn't speak. He didn't ask again.

Red's knife dug into her back. Shaking hands made it hard to free it, but she managed. It seemed lighter than before, the blade familiar in this new room. She gripped the weapon by the hilt in one hand and experimentally squeezed the blade itself with the other. A sharp pain tore through her forearm, then nothing. Lila watched the blood run down her palm.

She didn't cry, but her heartbeat slowed down.

Outside the door, there were sounds. Pilot was talking to Max in the kitchen, their voices carrying up the stairs. Max was angry and loud, but Pilot was cold, and Lila could feel the chill eating at her fingertips, biting behind her neck.

Max could feel it too. Lila could tell because the silences got louder and Max got quieter, until it was just Pilot's voice, constant and quiet and certain.

Lila pushed away from the door. She took careful, even steps to the bed and sat down. It felt the same as any other bed. The blanket was dusty. It cast sprinkles into the yellow air like snow. Lila laid Red's knife on her lap, where it left a bloody imprint on her jeans.

Her left hand was sticky and sleek with blood now. It throbbed, painfully, in the back of her conscious. She turned her hand over thoughtfully, laying first her thumb and then her forefinger over the hilt of the knife.

It had been Red's knife.

Now it was hers.

She toyed with the blade. First she rolled it between her fingers, sending sharp sparks of pain like static electricity along her skin. Then she dragged the knife lower, to the wrist. She pressed down.

A soft, gasping cry.

And Lila found she was sobbing.

Shaking, she took the blade to the other wrist. It hurt. God, how it *hurt.* And Lila laughed.

The pain gave her distance. Quiet. Warmth. She couldn't feel herself anymore, not her hands or her heart or the nothingness inside of her that was tearing her apart. The walls swam around her. She smiled at them, slipping into herself and onto the bed, head lolled back against the blanket.

Then she heard something, something loud and demanding. She felt cold fingers fumble at her hands, her wrists, her forearm. She felt the weight of another body against hers. For a second, she thought—

But that was another life, a life where she could be hurt and touched and damaged.

Nothing could touch her here.

Then there was a voice. Hot breath at her ear. "Lila," he breathed. It took her a minute to realize he was screaming, another minute to realize that it was her name.

"Lila," he said again. She looked at him, at his ashen face and wide eyes, and then suddenly it was just blackness. She lost control.

Panic. Then nausea.

She was too hot now. Her body was burning, writhing, tearing apart of its own accord. *Too much.* Everywhere.

She reached for him, grasping with her bloody hands to his skin, his shirt. He pressed his palms around her wrists. Lila could suddenly hear her pulse, pounding at her head, a hammer. Max was screaming someone else's name now.

Then, with her forehead pressed to his, baby blue eyes wide, she suddenly saw him. He smiled. "Hey, are you looking at me? Do you hear me? Stay. Stay here. With me."

For some reason, she smiled back.

Max let out a terrified, choking laugh.

But by the time Lila realized there was light—so much light and sound and pressure—it was too late. Her body revolted against her in a sudden, violent spasm.

"Damn it. You stupid, stupid girl. If you die tonight-"

He'll never forgive me, she thought suddenly.

She'd lost Red's knife.

Lila tried to open her eyes. She had to find it; she had to—to make it quiet in this loud, bright, angry room. Then she passed out.

Chapter 2

Max was still standing at the kitchen sink when his father came in. He didn't look at Pilot, just kept his head down and his hands in the water, watching the red streak along the sink and away. He heard his father hesitate, but Max just stood there. He had no idea what he was supposed to say.

"She'll be okay," Pilot said finally.

Max let the water run.

"Max, please," his father said. He turned, confused, then saw Pilot gesture to the sink. "You're wasting resources."

Oh. Of course.

Numbly, Max turned the faucet off.

Pilot stopped at the foot of the stairs. "She'll be okay."

"You can't know that," Max said without thinking.

And froze.

He would choke on his own words. His father would be furious.

But Pilot only smiled tightly. "I'm sure."

Max nodded but said nothing. Gauging.

It was a risky move. Sometimes he could take a little from Pilot, if he gave a lot. Sometimes his father would accept silence as consent and Max could get away clean. Sometimes, it would be enough. Max could keep his confusion, his anger, close to his chest and keep himself safe.

Some days were better than others.

"Look at me," Pilot said. His voice was cool.

Max turned obediently. His father hadn't moved. He had his sleeves rolled up to his elbows, hair greasy with dirt and sweat. He looked worn, stretched too thin.

And while Max understood—he'd seen the state of the girl in the bedroom upstairs—he was still wary. Pilot was on edge. And Pilot on edge wasn't good for anyone.

"Lila will be fine," his father said now. His eyes were urgent. "I will fix this."

Max's hands were shaking. He looked down, refocusing his gaze as he massaged his fingers. "Okay."

He didn't ask if Pilot was talking about Lila, or the Coliseum, or the dead kid he'd left in the arena—the one who was supposed to be his hero. Max didn't want to know.

Pilot made a sympathetic noise in the back of his throat. "Nothing has changed. You'll be alright."

There'd been more people in that stadium than Max had thought were left in the whole world. They must have turned up in the hundreds. And Max couldn't stop thinking about it. Where they'd come from. How they lived.

How they lived with themselves.

Pilot's golden boy.

That was the one who was supposed to be the hero. The savior. And when he'd died, Pilot's expression had become so strange. Void.

It was the same look that Max had found on Lila's face, hours later, when she'd taken a knife to her wrists.

"Are you listening to me?"

Instead of saying what he was supposed to say, Max replied, "You built a coliseum."

He didn't even mean to. It just came out.

"Yes."

Max dragged his eyes up to meet his father. His *father.* "You built a coliseum?"

This time Pilot said nothing. Max should have done the same. He should have seen the chaos in Pilot's eyes. He should have known this was not the time.

He was not usually so careless.

But he couldn't get the look on Lila's face out of his head.

"And the kid who died," he whispered. "She loved him."

For one, confusing second, Pilot looked sorry.

Then he was not. "I did what had to be done, Max. You knew I was rebuilding the city. What did you think that was like? Did you think it would be easy? It wasn't."

Max had never asked his father what he'd been doing on those long days when he was away. He'd never asked what Pilot meant when he'd said he would make sure that Max was safe. He'd never wondered. He'd just assumed they would be okay.

Because Pilot had said it, so it had to be true.

And now there was New Chicago and a girl dying in the bed upstairs and his father was so very angry and Max hadn't been paying enough attention to stop it. Any of it.

"But I did," Pilot continued, voice rising. "New Chicago is strong. We'll survive. It will be enough."

His father closed the distance between them, eyes like steel, and hissed. "Any other questions?"

Max shook his head.

There was a beat of silence.

And then Max's vision started to cloud. Shit. He dropped his head. His father must not see him cry.

He was not a child. He would not cry.

That was when he saw the blood on his shirt. He fingered it with his thumb, clung at the fabric to keep his hands from shaking. But he couldn't help it. The blood made him think of Lila.

Lila, who terrified him.

Lila, who was dying.

Pilot touched his shoulder. Max raised his head reluctantly. Ashamed.

But his father had changed again. He pulled Max close, engulfing him with his arms, and Max buried his head against his chest.

"She will survive," Pilot spoke softly.

And his father had said it, so it had to be true.

***

Nevertheless, two long days passed before it was clear whether or not Lila was going to make it. She wandered in and out of consciousness, each time riding the wave of some terrible nightmare or another. Max suspected he knew what she dreamt about. He was pretty sure it was the same thing that was keeping him up.

Pilot was right, though. Lila survived.

Max sat outside her door most of the time, leaning back against the wall. He kept his legs tucked up to his chest and his elbows resting on his knees. Sometimes it was simply to keep out of Pilot's way. It had been a long time since he'd seen his father like that.

He'd almost forgotten how to manage it.

The other reason for sleeping in the hall, however, was that Max didn't like the idea of being too far away from Lila. He slept occasionally, in the stuffy hallway, and each time he woke with the horrified certainty that she had done it again. He'd push open the door to her room, feeling the slick stickiness of her blood on his hands already and tasting the fear like metal on his tongue. Of course, Lila had not tried anything.

She would open her eyes, though. The first two times, he'd just frozen in the doorway like a deer caught in headlights. He'd turned tail and run, retreating back into the hall and away from her blank gaze. After that, though, he at least tried.

"Are you okay?" he asked. Every time.

And every time she looked at him with her colorless, wild eyes, and said nothing at all.

So now Max remained in the hall, head buried in his arms, staying out of everybody's way. He pretended he didn't hear Lila making that horrible, strangled sound when she woke from fitful sleep. Her sleep was always fitful. Max knew because he rarely slept.

Pilot appeared on the stairs, while Max was dozing. He straightened suddenly, turning away from his father.

"You should get some sleep," Pilot said. His voice hurt Max's head. The sound of Lila breathing in the next room had been starting to hurt his head.

Max gave his father a blank look. For a second, Pilot looked angry—*not again*—but then it was gone and he padded across the floor to put an arm around Max.

"Come on, I'll take you to bed. She'll be fine until morning."

Max didn't fight him. He didn't know how to fight Pilot.

Pilot half-carried him to bed, dragging the comforter down before letting him settle inside. Max didn't look at him, and Pilot didn't say goodnight. He never did. He just stood at the foot of the bed, considering. Then, finally, he just turned and left, abandoning his son to the dark.

Max sat up, pulling the blanket with him, to see if his father ever looked back.

He should have stopped doing that a long time ago.

***

Max woke up, abruptly, to Lila not-screaming. It sounded like she was choking, sobbing on the inhale of the breath instead of the exhale. The noise would never have stirred Max at all except that, underneath it, there was a dull, rhythmic thumping.

He crawled out of bed and into the hall. The door to her room was open, as always, and the moonlight from her window flooded the floor. Her face, cast in the light, was ashen. Her eyes were closed and she was shaking violently, hitting her head against the wall behind her.

"Lila?" he asked.

She turned to him, eyes too full. The tears reflected moonlight like sparkles on her face. He saw her part her lips, but all that came out was a gasping moan.

Max stepped towards her and Lila suddenly *saw* him. Her eyes cooled, her body stilled. She saw him—saw him seeing her—and looked away. By the time he'd reached the bed, she was blank.

Except for the tears, still clinging to her face.

Max should not have said anything. He should have just sat at the edge of her bed and waited for her to fall back asleep. He should have left her alone to her grief. He should not have come at all.

But instead, because he had no sense, he asked, "Are you okay?"

Lila's head shot up. She looked angry and shocked. Then she looked nothing. Max tried not to see her, keeping his eyes on the bedspread and his hands stuffed into his pockets. She'd always ignored him before.

She would ignore him now. And he would disappear back to his own room and his own life. He'd go to sleep, vowing to decide in the morning if he was still mad about the arena thing. He'd leave Lila alone.

She didn't need his stupid questions.

But the seconds took too long to pass. Max finally had to look at her. He had to know what she was thinking.

Lila was still watching him with her strange, ethereal eyes.

Silence. Moonlight. The smell of rust and humidity.

Then, turning away, she said, "Why do you always ask that?"

"Because I can never think of something less stupid to say," Max replied, before he could stop himself.

Lila looked at him. And laughed.

It was barely a laugh, really. It was just a sort of half-hearted sigh, but she smiled. It was fleeting, but it was there, and it pushed Max on.

"Okay, better question then. Are you hungry?"

Lila looked at her hands.

"I guess," she said.

It was the most positive reaction he'd ever gotten from her. Max wasn't sure whether to laugh or cry.

"I think my dad has some soup in the pantry. If I heated it up, would you eat?"

"Yes."

Max fled into the hall, leaving Lila alone in her room. He hesitated at the top of the stairs. It was cooler out here, he thought suddenly, and the chill made him reconsider the wide emptiness in Lila's face. 'Nothing' was the wrong word for her expression. 'Numb' was better. 'Sinking' was best.

But when he thought about the girl fingering her bandages, that hostile coolness set like stone across her features, the only word Max could think was: *burning*.

He took the stairs two at a time. The steps made no noise because Max weighed a buck twenty soaking wet and he'd perfected the art of silence a long time ago. In those first weeks after he'd gotten better, when his mother's grave was still fresh in the backyard of the home Pilot had 'inherited' for them, Max had found it was much better to make silence than noise.

Pilot responded better to silence. He respected it.

The pantry was stocked, as usual. Max found a can of soup—*just add water*!—and dumped it into a pot. The mix sloshed about when he swung the saloon door open with his shoulder, but he was careful. It was easier to heat food over the fireplace in the dining room then building up a fire to stoke the renovated-gas stove in the kitchen. Pilot let Max keep the fire in the dining room going all the time, even when Max was alone in the house.

Especially when his son was alone.

The fire was just embers now. Max set the pot on the unused dining room table and crouched down, tugging out a handful of small logs from under the wobbling chair in the corner. He'd just tossed the last one in when he heard the rustling behind him.

Max was on his feet in a moment, letting out a soft shriek at the sight of the pale, ghost of a girl standing in the shadows. She gave him a small smile.

He scrubbed his face. "You scared the shit out of me," he said, grabbing the pot off the table and turning back to the fire. Anything to get back a semblance of dignity.

"Am I allowed down here?"

She had a warm voice. Max hadn't really noticed before, but now it surprised him. Her skin was so pale, her whole body shades of grey and white, that he'd expected her voice to be marble. Cold. Unyielding.

It wasn't.

"I don't think my dad gives a rat's ass where you go," Max replied, eyes on the pot.

Lila knelt at his side, surprising him again, and Max had to resist the urge to flinch at her sudden closeness. They both looked at the fire.

"And you?" she asked.

Rolling his weight onto the balls of his feet and switching the pot carefully to his other hand, Max shrugged. "As long as you don't have a knife, I don't think it matters."

Lila stiffened.

Did he really just say that?

"Oh God, I-"

Lila dropped her eyes to the floor. "Don't. Please."

Gripping the pot handle tightly, Max nodded. He stood up shakily. Lila followed.

"It's probably warm enough. I'll get a bowl," he said to the simmering pot of soup. Out of the corner of his eye, he saw Lila nod. The strands of her red hair stood out against her ghostly face. It distracted from the careful, burning expression underneath.

Max padded back to the kitchen. He took two bowls from the cupboard and poured the contents of the pot equally between them. He met Lila's eyes only briefly, to gesture towards the kitchen table.

"Sit," he said. She did.

They ate.

"What happened? To the knife, I mean," Lila asked suddenly. Max glanced at her from beneath his eyelashes, relieved to find that she wasn't looking at him.

He shrugged. "Not sure. My dad has it, probably."

"Oh."

Max pushed the soup around with his spoon. Lila lifted another mouthful and blew on it. The silence pressed in around them, full of grief and questions and hesitancy.

Then Lila sighed. Max made a noise that sounded like concern.

"Could you-"

"No," Max interrupted, finally meeting her gaze. Lila looked surprised. Max swallowed, "You can't have it back."

Something shattered between them, something Max did not understand. But the look on Lila's face made him want to eat his words.

Then she dropped her eyes to her spoon and mumbled quietly, "It's not that. I just…I just don't want Pilot to have it."

She said his father's name like it weighed too much. She said it like the syllables alone were going to make her sick.

Max understood. Looking at Lila, looking at her bandaged wrists and the wary way she sat, thinking about the arena, the dust, and the horrible thrill of the people in the audience, all of it only made Max hate his father more. His goddamned, unholy excuse for a father. A man who'd had the audacity to take advantage of a world on its knees.

Of a girl on her knees.

"Okay," he said.

Lila's colorless eyes flashed to his face.

"Okay," he repeated. "I'll get it from him."

She blinked, dropping her gaze to her spoon and then raising it, abruptly, back to him. Her eyes were too full again. But she smiled.

"Thank you," she said. It was enough.

Chapter 3

Pilot's son was named Maximilian Archer. He was five foot nine on a good day and his baby blue eyes were the biggest thing about him. When he slept, he was quiet, but when he had nightmares, he talked. It was soft, usually, but his voice was still there, whispering, on the other side of the wall. He was almost as afraid of his father as he was of Lila, but that hadn't stopped him from fighting for her. Fighting her back to life. The strangest thing about him was the sheer blonde color of his hair. If it weren't the end of the world, Lila would have sworn it was bleached. But as it was, she was sure the color was natural. Everything about Max was natural. He was small and slight, soft-spoken and tentative, but stubborn. He was stubborn enough to look at Lila in that early afternoon light—back when he hadn't known her at all—and clasp his hands around her wrists, her blood leaking through his fingers, and tell her that she simply was not allowed to die.

"*I know it's not fair, but you can't go. Not today. Not now.*"

These were the things that Lila had learned about Pilot's son.

He sat at the end of her bed now, leaning on the baseboard and reading aloud from Homer's *Odyssey*. Lila was curled up at the headboard, arms wrapped around her legs, chin on her knees, watching him. Two feet of distance between them. Careful.

But comfortable.

Max raised his voice, tripping over the rhythm of Odysseus' experience with the Sirens. After his precarious escape, Max stopped. He laid the book down, still open, on the comforter.

"Your turn," he said.

Lila crawled forward. She took the book from where it lay, eyes on Max. He didn't move. He barely breathed. Lila was grateful. She settled back with the book in her lap.

Pilot left them alone most afternoons. He was never far away in his study, but he rarely interrupted. Max didn't talk about him. And in the daylight, when Pilot's work kept him busiest, it was as if he wasn't even there. He kept his distance from Lila, and she kept her distance from him. Days passed. It would have been like none of it had ever happened.

Except that, when Pilot chanced a glance in her direction, she could see it in his eyes. The whole world—*her* whole world—that he had destroyed.

Neither one of them would forget that.

The knowledge made Pilot cautious and hostile. It made Max gentle, consoling.

It strangled Lila. The nothingness inside of her was frightening. It hurt. It swelled. Sometimes, when it was dark and she was alone and sleep would not come, it seethed under her skin. It turned from nothing into something, and she was afraid that she would be swallowed whole. But it never happened.

So instead, she sat on her bed and watched Max read aloud. When he'd put the book down the first time, she'd been surprised.

"Do you want to read now?" he'd asked, not looking at her.

The not-looking helped. It made everything he said—everything he did, everything he was—seem distant and dulled. Less terrifying.

"Okay," she'd said.

And they'd been passing the book between them ever since.

"You know," Max interrupted her, just before she turned the page to renew Telemachus' escapades in Sparta. "There really doesn't end up being a reason for him to fight."

Lila paused. "What?"

"Telemachus," Max explained. He was looking out her window, tracing patterns in the comforter at his side absently. "He leaves to find his father and pretty much fails. It's by accident that they run into each other, and even that is way later. On his way home."

Lila ran her fingertips along the paper. "But he has to try."

"If he'd stayed, maybe the suitors wouldn't have been an issue. Maybe Odysseus wouldn't have had to slaughter them all."

"It was revenge. For all the time he'd been away. For all the things he'd had to do to get home."

Max sighed. "Yeah, but what does the revenge get him? His wife was always faithful. She'd never have said yes to any of them. He was home. It was over."

"But it wasn't over," Lila persisted. She stared at Max until he turned to her, willing something akin to determination onto her face. The talking was making her warm inside. Urgent. Insistent. "After everything the gods put him through. They owed him."

"They owed him the kill?"

Lila's felt her face flush and she glanced down at her hands. Her wrists. She thought of Red's knife.

"Well, I don't know," Lila said, voice rising. "But they owed him something."

Max raised an eyebrow. "Too bad it wasn't the gods who paid the price."

Lila looked away. Her words had all dried up.

He waited a moment, then said quietly, "I'm sorry."

"Don't," Lila said.

Max flinched. "What?"

"Don't apologize."

"I only-"

All Lila had to do was look at him. "Stop it."

Max swallowed. For a long second, he just watched her. Expression open, gentleness all over his face. Waiting for her. *Too much.* Lila shied away.

"Please."

She hated when he did that. He made her feel soft.

Didn't he know how it hurt her? To *feel*?

Then Max touched her hand. It was just the brush of his thumb against her fingers. She pulled away. His hand remained, palm down on the open book.

"I think it's my turn," he said, holding her gaze.

Everything he did was deliberate. Persistent. Certain.

He scared her.

But he also made her feel safe, so she reached her hand out and pushed the book back in his direction. Their fingers did not touch. Max did not move.

Lila smiled tentatively. "It is."

She did not say thank you, but she was pretty sure he heard it anyway.

Chapter 4

The kid's name had been Red. Red—the first time Max had heard Lila say that name, choking and wrecked, whispered into the darkness with her eyes closed, Max had nearly cried. He hadn't known she could put so much emotion in a name.

He hadn't known she could *feel* that much.

That was the first time Max had realized how angry he was.

At first, he'd been scared. There'd been so much. The Coliseum, Pilot Archer who was a man and a leader and not just a father, and of course, there was Lila. He couldn't react. He couldn't even keep up.

But he'd caught up now. It had caught up with him. All he had to do was look at Lila's strange, burning eyes to remember what it was that churned in his stomach, the feeling that settled heavily in the back of his mind.

Hatred. For the Coliseum, for New Chicago, for his father.

And yet.

His *father*.

Max had no idea what to do with that hatred. So he didn't do anything. He said nothing. He did nothing. And nothing changed.

He was a coward.

He was such a coward that at first, when he saw Pilot in the kitchen that morning, he tried to sidestep back out of the room. Quickly and quietly, and his father would be none the wiser.

Not quick enough.

Pilot turned, his narrow face pinched. "Wait."

Despite himself, despite the fury and flush of heat that burned in his chest, Max stopped. He couldn't help it.

He didn't know how *not* to be an obedient son.

"You're still angry with me," Pilot said. He sighed.

Max didn't say anything. He wasn't even sure that he was supposed to answer.

"Is it about the Coliseum?" Pilot asked. "Or Lila?" He strode to the kitchen table and took a seat, looking pointedly at Max.

"It doesn't matter."

Pilot closed his eyes and exhaled. "Of course it matters. Sit down."

Max was seething.

He sat.

"Lila survived," Pilot said. He leaned in, searching Max's face, and Max had to resist the urge to shy away. There was something devastating in his father's voice. Something tired.

Something he didn't like at all.

"But we're still here. You won't talk to me. You won't look at me. Please, Max, tell me what's wrong."

Like he didn't know.

In the sudden silence, though, Max couldn't say anything. It was always like this, with his father. He was angry when his son was scared. Brave when Max was weak. Determined when Max was lost. And finished—at the end of his rope, just trying to make it work—when Max was finally ready to fight. And Max was ready for a fight, but it wasn't just about him.

There was so much more.

There was everything that happened in the arena. There was everything that his father had done. Worse than all the rest, though, there was the fact that, even knowing what he knew, Max couldn't seem to make the ends meet: that man was *this* man, Pilot Archer was his father.

Which made this his fault.

"You know what's wrong," Max said finally.

Pilot looked exhausted.

"Don't be like that. I know what happened. I want to know what about it upsets you."

Max floundered. "*You* do. You're the part that—how could you have done it? I thought you were going to save us, but instead you...instead you built a coliseum."

The words were supposed to be a whip. They sounded like a plea.

So did Pilot's. "What would have had me do?"

Max was going to be sick.

"What's wrong with you?" he asked. He didn't yell it. He didn't even look up. He just said out loud all the true, horrible things his father had done. "You *killed* them. You did that. The fights, the Coliseum. Your New Chicago? It's just a place where people come to die."

He paused. Breathed. Then added, "Don't you see that?"

But Pilot did not see.

"They come voluntarily, Max. It's the only place on Earth with an economy, an exchange of services. And it's right here in New Chicago. Everyone has food again, and shelter. The fighters are safe-"

"Safe?" Max interrupted. "They *die*. Maybe it's one at a time and maybe it feels better than it does out here. But don't pretend that makes them safe. They don't come out of there alive."

"Lila-"

And then, abruptly, Max had had enough. He lurched to his feet, palms pressed to the tabletop. The chair toppled behind him, echoing in their huge, hollow house. "Lila? Really? Do you call that alive?"

Pilot got up. He passed his son and kneeled to right the chair Max had knocked over. Both hands on the chair's back, he closed his eyes. "I didn't mean for the boy to die."

"No. You meant for it to be Lila. Is that supposed to make it better?"

Max was breathless. And his father wouldn't look at him.

"I can't justify it to you. Not really. Max, while you were safe in here, with locks on our doors and food on our shelves, others weren't. The war killed everyone. There was no food, no plan, no future. I couldn't take care of you forever. How was I going to keep you safe? How was I going to keep you fed?"

Max didn't say anything.

Pilot scrubbed his face with his hands. "This was the only way."

Max could see his father was tired. He could see that he honestly believed that he hadn't done anything wrong. He could see that this was supposed to save their world. But Max was still angry. And he couldn't help himself. "Kids killing each other? That was the best option?"

If it was supposed to incense Pilot, it did a poor job. Max's father simply sighed. "There are kids killing each other everywhere, Max."

Even though it was true, it didn't help. It didn't make Max feel any better. He sank back into his chair. Pilot followed suit.

"I do have a question though, if we're finished with this."

Max looked at him.

"Everything else aside, do you feel safe with Lila?" Pilot asked. He watched his son carefully.

Let him. There was nothing in Max's expression that Pilot could not see.

"Yes," Max said. Simple as that.

"And you trust her?"

Max crossed his arms. "Why?"

For a second, Max thought his father wasn't going to answer. He looked so—lost. Then Pilot sort of crumpled, propping his elbows up on the table, forehead resting on his palms. He seemed smaller.

"I need to be sure that you're safe. They need me at the Coliseum, but-" His voice was quiet. Thoughtful. Full of things he never said aloud.

Not since Max's mother died.

"-but I won't go until I know you're okay."

Max rubbed his eyes. It was so like his father to remember how to love, just when Max was finally ready to give up on him.

"I'm okay," he told Pilot. Hesitantly, he reached out and squeezed his father's hand.

When Pilot finally looked up, he gave his son a gentle smile. It was weary and soft, but it was genuine. The only sincere thing about Pilot, and all the more hopelessly rare for it. It was Max's favorite kind.

And that was the last time he ever saw it.

Chapter 5

Pilot wanted something from Lila.

When he came in, she thought he was Max. She didn't turn around. "Hold on," she said quietly.

Pilot waited.

Lila was standing in the middle of her bedroom, the cuffs of the dress shirt she'd borrowed from Max hung much too far from her arms. They dangled at her fingertips, burying her hands. Her hair was clean and razor-straight down her back. It was still wet.

"You found the bath, then," Pilot said.

Lila turned.

The afternoon light swelled at her back and struck Pilot at an odd angle. He looked older, more weathered. His narrow face was calm.

"Lila," he said.

She didn't know when her name had become a greeting.

Pilot took a step forward, Lila took a step back.

"How are you feeling?" he asked. His hands were clasped behind his back.

Lila looked down. Something was stirring in her stomach. She felt nauseous. "Fine," she said.

There was a moment of silence. Lila wondered if Pilot knew she was lying.

She wondered if either of them cared.

"That's relieving," he said.

"Relieving?" she echoed. The word angered her. It was unsatisfying, fickle. It tasted like half-rations and broken promises.

Pilot weighed that. "You've been spending a lot of time with my son," he said finally.

The way he said it made her pause. She'd forgotten that he was Pilot's. The boy with blonde hair, blue eyes, and a desperately positive outlook on life. *Max.*

The boy who was trying to save her.

She hadn't meant to let him. She had meant to die of the nothingness inside her and, failing that, she'd planned only to fill her present with enough sound and touch and taste to bury the way that Red had sounded and felt and tasted. If she buried it deep enough, maybe it would die. And then she wouldn't have to.

But then there was Max. The last of his kind.

The world would only hurt him. He was a fool to hope, to dream, to care.

But Lila was glad that he did.

"He's good to me."

Pilot's voice was strangled. "Max is good to everyone."

Well yes. There was that.

Lila shifted her weight to her heels. She gathered her hair, still damp, over her left shoulder. Then, tone utterly neutral, she looked up. "What do you want?"

Pilot thinned his lips and his eyes darted towards the door. He crossed the room in three even steps. His voice was a rushed, rough whisper. "You think you know me. You hate me. Fine. But Max is my son. My *son.* And I am warning you that there is nothing that I wouldn't do for him."

Would you die for him?

She didn't ask it. She didn't even feel it.

Pilot went on. "My son seems to trust you. He likes you and he thinks that, given the chance, you wouldn't hurt him. I want to know if it's true."

He likes you. Something light and warm seeped into Lila's skin. It was comfortable and gentle and, for just a second, Lila forgot that she wasn't supposed to feel anything anymore. "He said that?"

Pilot was too quick. He searched her face before she could bury it.

"So it's true."

Too late to deny.

"Yes."

Pilot's expression was fleeting. Lila missed it.

Then he turned away. "God help him."

He left for the Coliseum the next day.

Chapter 6

Lila still wasn't sleeping. Instead, as she did most nights, she sat on the floor at the end of the bed. The floor was cooler in the darkness and, with her head buried in her arms and her hair cascading like a shield around her, Lila could close her eyes and keep the nightmares away. As long as she did not sleep, nothing bad could happen.

No one would die.

She listened to the ticking of a clock, somewhere downstairs. It marked the seconds passing, one by one. After a few minutes, Lila started counting them. She counted the seconds and breathed in for three, out for three, until she was sure that time was still moving forward and she was still breathing. Life went on.

It didn't feel like it though. It didn't feel like anything was going on. It felt like it was just *going*, round and round, burying her in this stuffy darkness and empty terror. Her hands shook. She willed them to stop. Then her whole body shook.

Lila stood up. She drew the blanket off the bed, wrapping it around her like a cape. A chill all her own ate at her fingers and her bare feet. It tickled her skin until she itched and sweat and shivered. Feeling nothing. Feeling missing.

The clock downstairs chimed.

Lila stared at the blank wall in front of her, grey and ambiguous, and imagined that it was another wall, in another place. She thought that she was standing in her box at the Coliseum. She imagined voices in the arena below. Red was coming. The sun had just set, greying her room. This was the time of day that they both loved best. He loved it because it was cool and gentle, because it reminded him of her. Lila loved it because Red was more beautiful in the setting sun, once the night had melted the arena from his skin. He always held her closer in the darkness. Lila could almost feel his cool fingers on her collarbone. She turned—

But her feet were weightless. Her ankles carried no chains.

And Red was not there.

Downstairs, the clock ticked on.

Lila cried soundlessly.

***

"Can I ask you a question?" Lila said. She and Max were sitting at the kitchen table, having just finished both *The Odyssey* and the dredges of the instant oatmeal Max had made for lunch.

He looked up expectantly.

"Do you know what Pilot meant? About me being the hero?" Lila asked.

Max got up, carrying the book with him, and shrugged. "Not really." He grimaced, "I'm sure he'll tell you when he's decided you should know."

Lila rubbed one of her wrapped wrists. It always ached when the bandage was still new, or Max had just dabbed the scabbing wounds with hydrogen peroxide. Four times already, he'd put Lila through the motions, making her hold out one hand and then the other while he went to work.

And Pilot had only been gone three days.

Her hands hurt all the time now. A whisper, a throbbing reminder of what she'd tried to do. Although Max, to his credit, had never said anything about it.

He never said anything that she didn't want to hear.

***

It was night again.

Red gave her the most beautiful smile. He kissed her on the lips, softly, and touched her cheek with his palm. Then his hand was a knife and it was hurting her. Lila made no sound, but she bled. Red cried into her palms. He whispered her name. Then he crumbled, a mess of blood and dust, and died.

Lila woke. She was crying.

Max was a shadow in the doorway, his baby blue eyes soft.

He offered an ironic smile. "Are you okay?"

Lila laughed. It sounded like choking.

Max padded across the room. He didn't say anything. He just stood at the side of her bed, not touching her, until she got her breathing under control. Lila drew her legs up and rested her forehead on her knees, shaking. She never really stopped crying, but she stopped making noise.

The silence, in the end, was enough.

She cried herself back to sleep.

***

When she woke again, it was morning. Max was still curled on the floor at the foot of her bed, legs pulled up to his chin. His eyes were closed.

But when she stirred, he blinked them open groggily. "Lila?"

"I'm okay," she said, before he could ask.

Max was surprised into a grin. Then his eyes flickered to the open door and the smile slipped from his face. "He's back," he said quietly.

Lila didn't have to ask who he meant. There was the only one person that could make Max look angry, heartbroken, and hopeful all at once.

"Did you hear him come in?" she asked.

Max scrubbed his face with his hands. He sighed. "I saw him. Last night."

Last night, when he'd ended up holding Lila's hands because she couldn't stop shaking. When he'd whispered over and over that she would be okay, it would all be okay, and that he wasn't going to leave her. Last night, when he'd stayed for as long as it took. Until she finally fell back into fitful sleep.

Last night, just like every other night.

If it wasn't the nightmares, it would be something else. Red. The Coliseum. Her parents. That scene in the box that she simply didn't want to think about anymore. All the horrible things that had happened to her—and the one good thing.

Max would deal with it, whatever it was, and Lila would be sorry. But she'd never tell him.

And he'd never ask. Max never asked Lila for anything.

He yawned and climbed to his feet, scrubbing his face with his hands. "He'll know I'm awake. I should go."

Lila thought Max didn't look particularly happy about it. Actually, it was worse than that. He looked exhausted. He looked like one more accident, one more harsh word, would be just enough to break him.

And still, Max's eyes sought hers. "Are you going to be alright up here?"

Lila could die of his gentleness.

How much more could he give?

How much more would she take?

"Let's go outside," Lila said suddenly.

Max's surprise flickered across his face, just a flash. Then it was gone.

He shrugged, blue eyes wide. "Okay." As if it was nothing. As if he would follow her anywhere.

He smiled.

And Lila realized that there was something inside her after all. She was not dead. She was not empty. She was not nothing.

Because where there should have been nothing, instead there was Max.

Chapter 7

The sun was a surprise. It looked different. Brighter.

The sky was different too. The clouds hung higher. There was not so much smog and soot. It was clear now. Clean. Limitless. And it was cold, finally.

December.

There was a time when Lila wasn't sure it would ever be cold again.

Best of all, Pilot was on the other side of a closed door. He was inside the house and she was outside of it, and there was nothing he could do about it. Because he didn't know.

He had no control over her after all.

Lila laughed.

And it made something burst in the center of her chest. She rounded on Max.

"Why do you keep trying?" she blurted out.

Max furrowed his eyebrows. "What?" he asked. He squinted at the pavement. Their shadows stretched long, mingling in front of them.

"With me. Why?" The brightness was wild in her voice. She sounded frantic.

This time Max's voice was strained. "You know what my father did."

That was not an answer. The things that had happened to Lila had nothing to do with Max. He was an angel. The fact that his father had destroyed her world—that was nothing. Sons were not responsible for their fathers.

"So? What does that have to do with you?"

Max's head shot up. He looked hurt. "What do you mean? Of course it has to do with me. Someone should have *stopped* him. Before he built a goddamned coliseum. Before he started killing people. Before-"

He turned his back on her suddenly, shaking his head. "-before everything else."

Lila wrapped her arms around herself. "But why you?"

Max scrubbed his face with his hands and grunted. He threw his head back. Lila stepped forward. She didn't move to touch him, but she drew closer. He must have felt her, because he spun around.

They stood face to face, not touching. Inches and light years apart.

Lila was an island. Max's face was red.

"My God, Lila, because I'm the only one who's here. Who else is going to do it?"

Who else would care?

Max sighed, lowered his voice. "And because I'm so sorry. For everything."

"I told you not to apologize to me. Remember?"

Max rolled his eyes. "Fine. No more apologies, from either of us." Something flashed across his expression. He smiled grimly. It wasn't a smile Lila had ever seen from him before. "But you have to promise me something too."

"What?"

He hesitated. His eyes flitted away. "You don't get to-you can't...give up. That can't be an option anymore. I-I can't…"

He bit his lip. The color flooded from his face. But his eyes found hers.

Max had asked it and she could not refuse.

"Okay," Lila said. "I'll stay."

A beat. "Good," Max said, withdrawing. He didn't believe her.

"I mean it," Lila said. His expression didn't change, so she reached out. Her fingers brushed the back of his hand, not quite holding on, not quite letting go.

Max's eyes widened.

"You don't give up on me, and I won't give up."

"Yeah?"

Do you promise? He didn't ask it.

Lila answered anyway. "Yes," she whispered.

Max's smile was almost enough to warm her freezing heart.

Lila looked away first.

"So what's out here?"

Max stuffed his hands into his pockets, his shoulder bumping against Lila's arm. She glanced at him, but he just shrugged. "Nothing, really," he paused. "But my father will know we're gone."

"God forbid we do something Pilot wouldn't like."

Max flinched at that. Lila felt him look at her, but she was watching the horizon. It was cold and dusty out there, but it was stifled and hot behind her and she wasn't going to go back inside until they dragged her. Forced her.

Max didn't leave.

"Are you scared of him?" Lila asked suddenly. She was thinking of Max's silence, of his small anger and his father's insurmountable determination. She was thinking that, if Pilot had always been so cruel, the fact of Max's gentleness was astounding.

"Isn't everyone?" Max answered.

It was no small wonder that he existed at all.

Lila didn't look at him, but she reached over and entangled their fingers, squeezed his hand.

Max didn't look at her either, but he held on tightly.

That was the first time that Lila Sinclair thought it. She didn't say it aloud, though. Not then.

Instead, she said, "Let's walk. I don't want to go in yet."

When Max flashed a guilty look at the house, Lila smirked. "You are coming, right?"

Then his big blue eyes were on her, glaring.

Lila didn't mean to smile.

But Max's expression melted at hers, and he gave her a surprised, easy grin. "Of course I am."

It was beautiful, that 'of course'.

They walked, side by side. Max started to look back, but stopped, catching Lila's eye instead. He grinned guiltily and turned his eyes back to the sidewalk.

Lila standing beside him was enough, apparently, for Max.

It made Lila think that thought she shouldn't have been thinking again.

Was she supposed to be afraid of Pilot Archer?

He was the creator of the Coliseum. He'd bought her. He'd chained her. Then he'd let her have Red. For a day, a week, a year. Just enough time to destroy her. He'd *wanted* to destroy her.

But here she was, not destroyed.

Not scared.

Not anything.

And it occurred to her that there was nothing Pilot could do to hurt her now. She was not scared of him. Pilot may have made her, but he was still just a man.

She was the hero.

Chapter 8

Max would have felt better if they were sneaking around behind his father's back. He was used to hiding from Pilot. Keeping that up, for Lila's benefit, would have been second nature. He'd have been comfortable with that.

Lila didn't hide from his father, though. She went out whenever she wanted, and always with this cool, empty glance at Pilot's office door. Sometimes he was at his desk, door propped open, and he'd look up. Max never knew what his expression meant, but it was subdued and foreign.

It would have been remorse, if Pilot was sorry. Or wrong. But Max had never known his father to be wrong—cruel, violent, absent, and calculating certainly, but never wrong. His Coliseum was the making of the new world, whether or not Max approved, and that new world named Pilot Archer as its leader.

So Max never knew what to make of the expression on his father's face when Lila looked at him. He could not imagine a world where his father doubted.

Faith was all Pilot Archer had. Faith and a Coliseum.

But Pilot never said anything when Lila left for the afternoon. He never tried to stop her. As for his son, Pilot didn't even look at Max. Not the first time he followed her, nor any time afterwards.

Max pretended that it didn't hurt him, at all, that his father never asked him to stay.

***

"Can I ask you a question?"

Max snorted. There'd been nothing but questions between them for the last few weeks. Out of his father's careful watch, the silence had given way to words. Lila didn't like Pilot, maybe even hated him, but she didn't seem to hate Max. And though he couldn't imagine what difference she saw between them, Max accepted it. He'd been answering her questions as best as he could.

She'd asked if he was living here before the war.

The short answer was no. They'd lived in downtown Chicago, where his father worked. Max went to private school. He lived in an apartment complex with a night guard and a doorman. Safe, even then, from whatever Pilot was so afraid of.

Why didn't they go back?

Max's mother died in that apartment.

The whole apartment had been leveled in the second bomb raid, while Max was at school. She'd been the only one home. Max had known the moment the first explosion rocked the boy's bathroom where everyone in his class was huddled.

There were no bomb shelters in apartment buildings, after all.

That hadn't stopped him from trying to call home. Twelve times. Until the telephone lines came crashing down and the fires started and school was closed for good. Pilot had come to get him from the school basement.

His father didn't even let him say goodbye.

They'd walked away, on foot and in mass, to an evacuation shelter outside of the city.

And they, like so many others, had almost made it.

Not that Max told Lila about that. He didn't tell her about the time he'd stolen Pilot's car either—without a license, even, just his driver's permit—to go back. Back to the home where he'd lost everything.

He'd had trouble finding it, at first. Everything was different. Streets weren't paved flat. Whole skyscrapers had crumbled at the feet of brick houses. None of the signs were right, because there was nothing left to point to. Just dust and decay.

He found it, in the end, nestled just as it always had been between the deli and the supermarket. Except that the whole third floor was gone. In its place, there was just a hole, filled with broken glass that reflected the sky.

His mother's body was gone by then. Max had never had the courage to ask Pilot if she was buried beneath the gravestone in their new backyard or if someone else had found and taken her instead. There were places, he knew, full of dead loved ones, piled together to be forgotten, already left behind.

Mass graves, they called them.

In the beginning, he'd hear crying in the streets all the time. Sometimes it was because of the lost, never to be buried, never to be found. Sometimes it was because of a new, terrible grief. It was always unbearable. It was always universal.

People didn't cry as much lately.

Lila said it was probably because people weren't as surprised by death.

Max hoped it was because fewer were dying.

Lila bumped his shoulder.

"What?"

She rolled her eyes. "I said, can I ask you a question?"

"That isn't what you've been doing?"

They were walking along the south side of the neighborhood, behind the exit ramp from the highway. Most of the asphalt was broken into uplifted segments on the other side of the street, but where they walked it was level. Both of the houses that were still standing had clearly been ransacked. There was broken glass all over the overgrown grass and doors hung open limply.

But Max and Lila had the road to themselves now.

For days they'd been walking like this, side by side, and they'd never seen anyone at all.

Lila looked up, squinting at the sun. "Well this question's different. You don't have to answer it if you don't want."

"Shoot."

"Do you still miss your mom?"

Max thinned his lips. "Every day."

He heard Lila clear her throat, but he didn't look at her. They reached the next intersection and didn't hesitate, stepping off the sidewalk in sync.

He almost didn't hear her next question.

"Does it ever get better?"

Max scrubbed his face with his hand. "I guess I don't cry when I visit her grave anymore."

"That's not what I asked."

He closed his eyes.

They walked on.

"Did you really not know about the Coliseum?" Lila asked suddenly.

Max turned his head and met her grey eyes. She didn't look angry. But then again, Max had never been good at reading her face. He shook his head, making a noise in the back of his throat that didn't even begin to do justice to the sick way his stomach turned over. "I really didn't."

"Pilot doesn't tell you much, does he?"

It didn't hurt as much as he'd thought it would, to hear it aloud.

On the afternoon his mom had died, Max and Pilot had walked one hundred and thirty two blocks to get out of the city. They were two in a thousand, a wave of refugees walking on blind faith towards the shelters that they'd heard days ago would be standing in the suburbs of the city, waiting for them.

That was before the Willis Tower crumbled.

It was not the only building to fall, but it was what Max remembered best. He remembered the smoke next—not the fire, just the smoke, everywhere, swimming like a fog at his feet. Pilot told him that the riots had started later, that people hadn't really started running until the telephone lines whipped out into the muddy streets.

But all Max remembered was that it had smelled like fire and gasoline—which was strange, because the oil shipments had stopped last year and no one drove anymore—and then suddenly there was just panic. Everywhere. He lost Pilot in the crowd.

That was when the billboard dropped unceremoniously from twenty-seven stories to crash in the middle of the street, crushing several people to Max's left. He saw them—standing there and then suddenly *not* standing there—and he didn't even have time to scream before the wires that it had ripped down with it lashed out, a flurry of electrical tendons.

It was the wire slicing him open, a clean cut that had left a scar from his left shoulder and down his back, that made Max lose consciousness. It was the trampling by terrified refugees that broke his leg, two of his ribs, and left a vicious, blue-and-purple bruise along his jaw.

Pilot must have thought he was dead, when he finally found him.

"I don't think he wanted me to know. It was always about keeping me separate from everything else. If I was here and no one knew that I existed, I couldn't be hurt."

Lila glanced at him, eyes narrowed. "You think he wants to protect you?"

The way she said it, like Pilot was incapable of love, made Max ashamed. Of course she would think that.

Look at what his father had done to her.

But Lila didn't understand. Pilot had come back for his son. He'd found him, broken and bleeding, and carried him out of the city. He must have known that Max would probably die. He must have known that he was about to lose his wife and child in the same day. It was over. He must have been ready to give up.

Like everyone else had.

Like Lila had.

But Pilot didn't. He carried Max almost three more miles, to the emergency hospital tent that the Red Cross had set up. He'd carried him to safety. And he'd gone on carrying him when the evacuation began. When they told him that he couldn't bring the boy. No one in Max's state was allowed to leave the city.

Survivors only.

And it was clear that Pilot's son was going to die.

So Pilot Archer had stayed. He stayed and he fought and he did the impossible.

He brought Max back to life.

Of course Max couldn't say something like that to the girl that his father had tried to kill. The girl he'd tried to destroy. Instead, he said, "Keeping me safe was pretty much the only thing that ever mattered to him."

"But he brought you to the Coliseum eventually," Lila said. Her voice was neutral.

Because, for some reason that neither of them knew, the creation of the Coliseum's hero was important to Pilot. The only thing that had ever been as important as his son.

"After we got to the new house," Max began. He felt Lila look at him, surprised by the change of subject. "He never told me that my mom was dead. He just carved her name on this big slab of concrete and put it in the backyard. For days, I stood outside and just looked at her name."

Max laughed dryly, feeling like he was going to throw up. "It took me a ridiculous amount of time to understand what it meant. That it was supposed to be her grave."

He felt Lila's hand take his. Their fingers intertwined and she squeezed.

Max looked at the sidewalk. "When he found me crying, he said that I shouldn't worry, because he wasn't going to let anything happen to me."

I'll keep you safe.

He'd said it that first night, when Max was sitting cross-legged in front of the engraving, tears rolling down his face, whole body shaking. And he'd said it a thousand times since. It was the only thing that Pilot could ever promise, and it was the only comfort he could ever offer.

I will keep you safe.

Until one day, he'd come home and said something new. He'd smiled his frightening smile and told Max that everything was going to be okay.

I've done it. I've made a hero.

Max hadn't asked him who the hero was supposed to save. Max never asked his father anything.

Not until Lila had crashed into him, bleeding her heart and her fire all over his safe little life and making him wonder, suddenly, if he should have been asking questions all along.

"What is he going to do with me, Max?"

For a second he thought she was asking him what it meant that she was Pilot's hero. But her voice was wrong. It sounded like a threat. Like she was daring him to tell her that his father could do *anything* to her.

Max didn't rise to the bait. "I don't know. You know I don't."

There was a beat of silence. They had almost walked the whole block. Max could see the top of his house, just around the next corner.

Lila's next question caught him by surprise.

"What if I refuse?"

Max stumbled. "Refuse?" he repeated dumbly.

His first thought was that Lila was fearless. She was invincible.

Then he remembered that you couldn't refuse Pilot. He was the leader of the new world. He was Chicago's savior. He was the future. And so, even when he wasn't right, he had to be *right*. If he wasn't, then everything else was lost.

And truly, there wasn't much everything else. The future wasn't beautiful. It was full of Coliseums and death. It was hundreds of people destined to be crushed under the power of a select few. It was autocracy. It was starvation and dehydration and not enough to trade for tomorrow's dinner.

But at least there would be a tomorrow.

No one else had been able to promise that.

Chapter 9

Whatever Max had been about to say was interrupted.

Lila heard it first and squeezed his hand suddenly, cutting him off before the words escaped his lips. He looked at her and slowed down, something about her expression making him glance around.

But apparently he didn't hear it. She pushed him off the sidewalk, into the iron gate that encircled the last house on their side of the intersection.

He hit the metal harder than she intended and when he winced, she cupped her hand over his mouth to keep him from speaking.

Max looked even more concerned.

"Sorry," Lila mouthed, then gestured towards the intersecting street, where she could hear the noise rising again.

It was two voices, she realized now. One girl and one boy.

The girl made a startled scream. "My god, back *off*!"

This time Max must have heard them, because his eyes got big and he stiffened. When she was sure he wasn't going to do something stupid, Lila stepped away.

"Who is that?" Max whispered. All at once, he sounded young. Breakable.

Lila closed her eyes. She could hear them both now. Their voices carried like a funnel along the street.

"Don't give me this *shit,*" the guy said. He had a lisp. "I know you've got more than this. You've got the shoes. I want 'em. And whatever's in your pockets."

The girl made a gasping noise.

Then there was a snap and the girl screamed. The guy said, "Well, if you didn't give me so much trouble it wouldn't hurt so much."

Lila felt something fall away inside her. Something that had been warm and steadying, that had everything to do with Max. It had been keeping thoughts of death and blood as far away as possible, and lately there had been a fullness in her body, a gentleness that she'd been craving like a drug.

But, just like that, it was gone.

Her eyes flickered to the street's intersection, measuring. She could make it to them in a matter of seconds.

If she wanted.

Max touched her shoulder but she didn't feel it. She didn't hear what he said.

The girl screamed again, this time in anger, and though she was still out of sight, her voice was panicked. "*Please.*"

A clatter.

Then, low: "Bitch."

Lila hesitated. The coldness inside her was almost foreign now. It fit her like an old coat—not quite her size and tight in all the wrong places—but it felt good. Brutal. Certain.

It felt like the arena. It felt like Red after a fight, all fire and burning.

But it also hurt. Because it felt like Red.

Then the girl screamed again, and this time it was a scream that Lila recognized. It was pain. It was a broken bone and a scatter of applause from the Coliseum crowd. It was hurt, all-consuming, unbearable.

And in the end, it was the scream that drove Lila into action. She moved suddenly, off the sidewalk and across the street. All at once, Lila was alive.

The guy froze mid-swing when Lila appeared.

The way she must have looked to him—red hair in strands across her face, eyes hot and raging, straight-backed and proud. Wild. She was not surprised that he paused. He would be a fool to not be afraid.

But his fear would not save him.

The girl was on all-fours on the ground, the back of one hand raised to her cheek. Lila could see the blood, but little else. At least she was conscious.

Then the guy swiveled to face her. “What do you want?”

It was wonderful, to be the target of his disgust. It made it easy to hate him. He was all the horrible things she was feeling—the dirtiness, the sickness, the nausea, the throbbing anger that ached inside her all the time.

Maybe this wasn’t the boy that had killed Red.

Maybe he hadn’t raped her, or sold her, or abandoned her.

Maybe he wasn’t the one who had single-handedly destroyed her world.

He wasn’t the reason that she felt the way she did—so empty and so full, so cold and so hot—but it was okay, because she could blame him for it.

And she could *hurt* him for it.

Lila smiled.

The guy hesitated again.

And then she was in front of him.

He had a weapon. It was a little switchblade, and he didn’t even get a chance to properly swing it before Lila had his wrist. She twisted with both hands, forcing him around until his back was to her.

He writhed. He tried to use his weight against her, pulling suddenly forward. It was a mistake. Lila moved with him, shifting her stance, and caught his groin with her knee. He doubled over, half-crumbling against her, but she didn’t release him.

She wasn’t done with him yet.

Lila used her grip on his wrist to force him to make a quarter turn. Then she braced her arm between his shoulder blades and wrenched one last time against his wrist. Snap. He screamed, short, and then whimpered softly.

This time she let him crumble to the ground.

He was still making gasping, moaning noises, but it wasn't enough. He struggled, trying to get to his feet. On his knees, he looked up at her. Bloodless. Unrepentant.

Lila kicked him. The motion must have surprised him—or his broken arm was enough to upset his center of gravity—because he toppled over.

When she kicked him again, he grasped out wildly. "Stop! Fucking *bitch*, I'm going to-"

The last kick silenced him and rolled him onto his back. Lila dropped, hard, onto his stomach. He gasped, but didn't start crying until she punched him, breaking his nose.

It took only one more punch before he was sobbing, and his messy, bloody words turned from threats to pleas.

He was still begging when Max came.

She knew him immediately, because his grip was gentle and he touched her like she could not scare him, like she could not let him down. He wrapped his arms around her and dragged her backwards off of the bleeding, begging boy.

"That's enough," Max whispered. "That's enough, Lila. It's over. It's over now."

Lila fought him. He was wrong. It wasn't over. It would never be over.

The thought made Lila feel sick. Unstable.

Was she crying?

The emptiness inside her started to fill with something else—something sad and hurting and unfulfilled.

She didn't want this.

She didn't want to *feel*.

Lila wrenched herself from Max. He tried to stop her, but she shoved away from him blindly. Her hands were covered in blood, her hair was sweaty and sticking to her skin. She was desperate, feral. She had to get away.

She didn't mean to look at the boy again.

But there he was. Only it wasn't just him, it was blood and gore and the way his arm lay at an awkward angle, the mess she'd made of his face, his body. The mess *she'd* made.

She was a monster.

Lila ran. It was the only thing she could think of to do.

Chapter 10

Max was pulled in all directions. As soon as Lila was gone, the guy scrambled to his feet and, with a last bloody glance at Max, he bolted the other way. Max started after him, stopped, changed directions to go after Lila, then stopped again.

His hands were shaking. There was a cotton taste in his mouth that wouldn't go away. He kept reaching out, brushing the brick of the alleyway with his fingers like he wanted to be sure it was still there.

Max had never seen Lila like that. Not up close. Before, in the arena, there was a sort of distance to the kill. They were in another world. This time, he hadn't had that luxury. There was blood on his hands, his shirt, from where he'd grabbed Lila. And the way she'd looked at him—like for one, terrible moment she didn't even recognize him.

But she had. She'd recognized him. For now, that would have to be enough.

Max turned around.

The girl Lila had saved was sitting on her knees now, one hand paused halfway through her hair, the other pressed over her mouth. Her eyes on the ground, where blood mixed with pavement. She was pale, shaking.

"You alright?" Max asked.

She looked up at him, unseeing.

Max waited. For several seconds, she just stared at him, but finally realization settled on her features. She slouched onto her heels and let her hand fall to her side. The fingers she was holding to her lips stayed where they were.

"What?" she asked. Her expression was open and perplexed. Like she was doing basic math in her head and two plus two kept coming up with six.

Max took a step forward. "Did he hurt you? Are you okay?"

The girl looked blankly at the ground. One hand was still cradled against her face. She swallowed. "Oh my God."

Max started to say something comforting, but at the same time, the girl tried to get up. She rested her weight against one arm and started to stand, but lost her balance and had to brace herself with the palm of her other hand.

The movement left her face exposed for the first time.

A fresh cut, shallow but long, was etched across her cheek. It ran from the corner of her right eye to the corner of her mouth, purple around the edges and still bleeding.

"Shit," Max said.

"Is it that bad?" the girl replied.

Max nodded, realized what he was doing, and quickly shook his head.

The girl barked a laugh. "Awesome."

"Do you need help?" Max asked, crossing the space between them. He held out his hand.

The girl's eyes darted back to the ground, but then she turned resignedly towards Max. She grimaced and grabbed his hand, hoisting herself onto unsteady legs. "Thanks."

"Yeah. I'm glad you're okay."

The girl wasn't really looking at him. She ran her thumb across her wound, trying to clear away the blood. It ended up smearing like war paint across her cheek instead. “I can’t believe he tried to jump me. This place has been a ghost town for weeks.”

Max stuffed his hands into his pockets. “I know.”

She gave him an irritated look. “And then you show up. Nothing for ages, and then all of the sudden we’re having a frickin’ party out here.”

Max watched her tie her hair back up into a ponytail. She flinched when she raised her left arm too high, but when she caught Max staring, she rolled her eyes.

“Oh, please. I’m fine.”

Max eyed her disbelievingly.

“Okay, so I wouldn’t have been fine if you hadn’t happened to be walking by, but you were and I am. Plus I’ve got to get home. My uncle will be pissed enough when he sees my face, it won’t help if I worry him sick by taking my time getting home.”

Max nodded.

The girl smiled half-heartedly. She touched her cheek carefully and then straightened out her clothes. Max didn’t notice the blush creeping across her cheeks until she looked up again, face flush against her hair.

“You’re staring,” she said.

It was Max’s turn to blush. “I’m just trying to make sure you’re alright. You just got attacked, and then Lila…well, you saw. Not to mention what happened to your cheek.”

The girl’s expression softened. A flicker of something caught Max’s attention, but it wasn’t until she looked at him neutrally again that he realized what it had meant—she was measuring him, keeping her distance.

They were, after all, two strangers alone in an alleyway at the end of the world.

Max shuffled back gingerly. “You should get home. You said your uncle can take care of you? I don’t want that cut to get infected.”

The girl nodded. “Yeah, he’ll deal with it.”

There was an awkward moment of silence, then the girl reached down to pick up her backpack from where it lay abandoned at her feet. She winced when she rose again.

"Okay, well thanks." She started to move past him. Then she stopped. After a minute's hesitation, she turned. They were standing side by side.

Her eyes were green. Vivid.

"I mean it," she said quietly. "Thank you."

Max smiled wanly. "Any time."

She stayed for a moment longer. Then she walked on.

Max spun around. "Wait!" he called. "I don't even know your name."

The girl flashed him a smirk, but he could tell she was relieved. She ran her hand through her hair again, curling an already curly strand around her finger when she reached the ends. "It's Zoe."

"I'm Max."

Zoe grinned. "Thank you, Max."

Again, there was that moment. They just looked at each other. Max felt like he should say something, but he wasn't sure what it was. And Zoe just kept looking at him, her expression a cross between expectant and amused. Then, abruptly, she shook her head.

"I have to go."

Max made a noncommittal noise. "It's not far, is it? Wherever you're going?"

"No," Zoe said. "My uncle lives like a block away." She seemed to weigh her words, then asked, "Why haven't I seen you here before?"

"I don't get out much."

Zoe laughed. Again. Zoe laughed a lot.

Max liked it.

"No kidding?" she said. "Can't say I know a lot of people who *do* get out a lot. Especially around here. That's why my uncle is taking us east. Supposedly there are actual cities out there. Real people."

Max didn't say anything about his father's Coliseum. He didn't figure the kids there counted as real people, and he was pretty sure a football stadium didn't count as an actual city anyway.

And he didn't want Zoe to know that he was Pilot's son.

"East?" he asked instead.

She nodded, then gestured behind her. “Would you mind walking me?”

Max smiled. “Of course not.”

“We’re going to try for the coast. My uncle knows some guys who know somebody that made it. They say that Boston is still standing. Maybe even Philadelphia.”

It had been a year since the last bombs fell. His father was rebuilding Chicago. It shouldn’t have surprised Max, then, that other cities were rebuilding. But it did. Pilot had always told him that life went on.

Max had just thought that Pilot was the only one making it go.

“That’s a long way.”

“I know. But my uncle thinks we can make it,” Zoe continued. She kicked a pebble. It skipped into the street. “And honestly, anywhere is better than here. The suburbs are so depressing now. At first, it was great because the bombs weren’t falling and there was food. Plus, you know, there’s the whole lack-of-people thing. That can be really nice. But it’s time now. It’s been like two years. It’s time to get some shit done, you know?”

Max did not know. But he thought it sounded absurdly brave.

They made it to Zoe’s house without incident. It was a small, two story townhouse. The front porch had been hollowed out, so Zoe had to pick her way carefully around the debris to get to the door. She balanced against the doorframe, bracing herself on the knob, and smiled at Max. Her face lit up. “Thanks again. For everything.”

“Yeah, well, if you need anything before you leave, I’ll be around.”

Zoe’s face flushed. “I hope I see you.”

Max grinned. “Me too. But I’ve got to go. I have to find Lila.”

This time he was sure he saw her expression darken. She turned thoughtful. “Could you tell her thank you for me?”

All fire and burning.

At least she’d kept her promise. She hadn’t given up. This was something very different, something wild.

Maybe something worse.

Max sighed. “Yeah. Look, I’m sorry if she-”

Zoe interrupted him. “I’m not. She saved my life, Max.”

He gave a halfhearted smile. “That’s all she was trying to do.”

That, at least, was true. It was the secret that Max had never told anyone. He was pretty sure that he was the only one who knew. Pilot certainly didn’t. And Max didn’t think that Lila had realized yet either.

The secret was that Lila cared. She loved. She loved fiercely. Still.

It had very nearly gotten her killed.

“Look after her,” Zoe said, as if she were reading his mind. He looked up sharply, surprised, and she laughed. “Even I can see she needs someone to take care of her. You will, won’t you?”

“She’ll be fine.” Max grimaced at the sidewalk.

Zoe sighed. “Max,” she said gently. He raised his eyes to her face. “She *will* be fine.”

This, for some reason, seemed like a promise.

Then she smiled, raising her eyebrow. “Now go.”

“Thanks,” Max said.

Zoe flashed him a grin, but her voice was serious. “No. Thank *you*.” Then, with a last inscrutable glance, she disappeared into her house and closed the door.

It would be almost a year before Max saw Zoe again.

But he would remember her.

***

Max found Lila sitting on the steps in front of his father’s house. She had her fingers splayed in front of her, arms resting on her knees. The blood on her hands could have been dried paint.

She looked up. The tears were still wet, clinging to her eyelashes and hair. Her body shook. She didn’t say anything.

Max didn’t either. He just reached out and took her hands, squeezing them between his.

She was so cold.

It wasn't until he sat down next to her, shoulder to shoulder but not touching, that she said it. The thing they were both thinking.

"Is this it? Is this what Pilot wants?"

Chapter 11

The worst part about getting blood on her hands was how easily it washed off. It would stain, irrevocably, to the T-shirt Lila had been wearing. The smears she'd gotten on the thighs of her jeans would never go away. Water was a commodity, even for Pilot. It wasn't something to be wasted on blood-stained clothes.

It wasn't like there hadn't been blood on her jeans before.

But Lila was glad when Max gave her a pair of his slacks and a long-sleeve, cotton shirt. He was taller than she was but not much bigger, so she'd changed gratefully, shedding her jeans and retreating to the kitchen sink.

It was much easier to get the blood off her hands. All it took was a little soap and thirteen seconds under the running water. Good as new.

Max stayed at the top of the stairs while she worked, sitting on the landing and watching her. "Do you need help?" he asked.

She shook her head.

Max weighed the silence. Lila could tell because she felt his eyes on her. She dried her hands on the kitchen towel and then turned, rag still in hand, to meet his gaze expectantly.

Max had his arms wrapped around his knees and his body leaning back, braced against the wall. He wetted his lips. "Do you want to talk about what happened?"

No. "I almost killed him."

"But you didn't."

But what did that mean?

"Was I wrong?" Lila asked instead. "To do what I did?"

Max sighed. "I don't know. Do you think it would have been better if he were dead?"

Something about this conversation felt wrong. Lila looked away.

"Would I feel better?" she whispered.

This time, Lila felt the shift in Max's attention. She'd said something to upset him. He sat up.

"Would you feel better if you'd *killed* him?" he repeated.

Is that what she'd asked?

"He was hurting that girl. He was dangerous. We would be safer now, if he were dead."

"Lila-" Max stuttered. Changed tactics. "It isn't about whether or not he deserved it. It's about whether or not you should have done it."

And then Lila couldn't look at him anymore. Because that's not what it had been about at all.

It had been about Red.

"You're right," Lila said, dropping the towel onto the counter. She smiled wanly at Max and he stiffened. "But I'm not sorry I did it."

He watched her, quietly, as she climbed up the steps and passed him in the hallway. He didn't say anything. She just felt him, watching her with his big, gentle eyes until she went away.

Lila hadn't realized that letting him down would hurt so much.

Chapter 12

Max heard Pilot come in from the study, felt his father's eyes pressed on his scalp, but could not look up. He stayed where he was on the stairs, staring at his folded hands in his lap. Pilot came to stand before him.

His father cleared his throat and reached out, engulfing Max's hands with one of his. “It’s a disappointment.”

Max’s heart was sore. He was tired.

And he couldn’t even begin to fathom how to manage his father.

Pilot pressed his palm over Max’s. “I’m sorry you had to see her like that. But I need your help.”

Max stared at his father's hand. How could it be that this man was so much taller, so much stronger, so much bigger than Max was, in every way? How could one man be so much more than another?

He said, "How?"

Pilot squeezed his hand. Max felt stifled.

"The Coliseum.”

Max flinched.

Pilot went on. “I know you don’t like it. And I know that you don’t understand it. But the Coliseum is who Lila is. She’s made of this new world grit, and she will thrive there. Just like the others. Max, this is the birthing place of New Chicago, the last city on Earth. Maybe the greatest city on Earth."

Max did not want to remember. But the Coliseum was Red, and Max could not stop himself. He saw Red's graceless, bloody fall. He saw those dark, fearful eyes turn to him, impossibly, staring and clinging to a life that was already gone. And even when it was over, he could still feel Red watching him, just over his shoulder. Haunting him. Haunting New Chicago.

The greatest city on Earth.

Pilot leaned forward. "And we will be the ones who did it. You and I."

Max jerked his head up.

Pilot laughed, his voice low and in earnest. "That's right. Who else could I entrust this to? It has to be you, Max. Don't you remember, I promised I'd take care of you? But you have to help me too."

Something had gone horribly wrong. Max was caught, choking on the 'we'. He felt his father's hand steady on his, holding him together, holding him still.

Holding him *down.*

He felt his father's hand and knew that Pilot was drowning him.

"Help you?" Max asked.

Then his father threw him a line. "With Lila, Max. She’s hurting. You must see that. You know what she did.”

Pilot had no idea.

Max wanted those words to make him angry. It had been his father’s plan, his mistake, his terrible, heartbreaking disaster. Max knew that. He knew who to blame this on.

But Red's eyes still wouldn't leave him alone, and the nightmare would not let him go.

"I know she is," Max said.

His father thinned his lips but did not smile.

"She's got to go back into the arena, Max," Pilot said.

"*What?*"

Max started to shake his head, to separate himself from the sudden, overpowering feeling that he was going to be sick. Pilot pressed on his hands and Max went still.

"I'm thinking of what's best for her," Pilot persisted. His face was expectant. "She's so angry, and she has no way to get that anger out. The arena could do that for her."

"She doesn't want to go back," Max said.

Pilot looked at him sympathetically. "She doesn't know what she wants."

"So you think I should tell her?" Max retorted bitterly. He tried to tug away again, but his father only gripped his hand tighter.

"Why not you?" Pilot said softly.

Max raised his head, disbelieving. He was almost in tears. The helplessness was familiar. It was the panic that was new, and it was the panic that overwhelmed him.

It was the panic that made him speak. "I'll try," he lied.

Pilot nodded shortly, patted his hand, and stood up. "Good. You're doing the right thing."

"I know," Max lied again.

“We'll leave for the Coliseum in the morning.”

The mask slipped. “That soon?” Max asked, startled.

Pilot paused, searching his face. “The sooner the better.” He shook his head. “I've heard it's like a calling, the fight. Never goes away. A girl like that—I can't imagine that it won't call to her.”

After Pilot had gone, Max stayed at the kitchen table, examining his hands. He couldn't remember ever lying to his father before. It had never occurred to him to try.

There'd never been a reason.

Max looked at Lila's closed door.

Chapter 13

Lila was lying on the floor, stretched out with her eyes closed. It was warm in the bedroom. She kept the windows closed. Frost collected on the panes, casting the room a strange shade of blue. Winter was coming.

Lila tugged her hair up, in a red pile on top of her head. That was when she heard the knock on her door.

"Yeah?"

There was a rustle of uncomfortable movement in the hall. So it was Max.

"I wanted to…" Max cleared his throat. "Pilot said something to me. I just wanted…I guess I wanted to talk to you."

Lila didn't move. "Okay."

Max didn't move either.

"Are you going to come in?" Lila asked.

She heard him chuckle on the other side of the door. "No."

Lila lay back down. She wrapped her arms around her chest.

Waiting.

"Max?"

A muffled groan. "I don't—look. There's something I have to tell you. Something bad."

"What is it now?" she hissed. And flinched. She hadn't meant for her voice to be that sharp.

Lila wasn't angry at *him*.

Max made a noise. "That's not fair."

She could almost hear him breathing. And she was sorry.

But she didn't say anything.

"Lila. Didn't…didn't we promise to look after each other?"

Because no one else would. She found her voice. "Yes."

Max hesitated.

"I took the knife," he said softly, deviating. Thinking. "I've been keeping it safe for you."

A gasp. "You took it from him?"

She couldn't say Pilot's name. Not with Red's.

"Yes."

Lila leaned her head back, looking at the ceiling, listening for Max.

A sigh.

"I don't like fighting with you." His voice was strained.

Lila almost cried, but laughed instead. "Me either."

"Then let's not."

Oh, God, how could she ever learn to be like him?

"Okay."

"Thank you," Max said. She could hear the smile in his voice.

He let her have that, the forgiveness, for just a moment. He let her have the peace. Then he whispered his next words, in his gentle way, like he knew what they would do to her.

"Pilot is taking us back to the Coliseum. He says you have to come."

Chapter 14

It was a horrible idea. But it was Pilot's idea, so there was nothing Max could do to stop it.

Lila was sitting in the back seat, looking out the window. She didn't say anything, but then again she didn't usually say anything when his father was around. She didn't have to. The way she felt, the things she thought, were always so loud when Pilot was near. It was like he amplified her.

Because God knew that Lila was impossible to read otherwise.

Max wasn't putting up much of a fight for himself either, though. He just couldn't figure out why, after all this time, Pilot wanted him to be a part of the Coliseum *now*. And he was afraid to ask, because he was afraid that his father was going to say something that Max did not want to hear.

Lately it seemed like those were the only things his father ever said.

"Both of you have been gone for too long," Pilot explained. It was quiet in the car, be he seemed calm. His hands were relaxed, resting against the steering wheel.

His eyes were on the road, face impassive. "The most important part of advertising is exposure. We need to get your names out. Max, that means meeting the governors. I know you've heard of them, but it's time to meet each one, get your face in their memories. That way, when the time comes for new governors to be appointed, you'll be the one they remember. It'll be easier to manage the Coliseum when I have direct control over the incoming supplies."

Max pretended he didn't notice the switch from *you* to *I*. He spent his whole life in the space between those two words. Not quite strong enough to be his own, not quite weak enough to be his father's.

And still the son always seemed to imply the father.

But Lila noticed it too. "So Max can win support and you can be puppet master?"

Pilot ignored her sarcasm. "So Max can help keep the peace. It's obviously easier to get the supplies that the boys need if we have direct access to them."

This time it was Max to *we*. Max flinched.

"And by the way," Pilot continued, still looking at Lila in the rearview mirror. He was cool and smooth, a tightly woven piece of silk to smother the opposition. It didn't matter if that opposition was his governors, his son, or—god forbid—his hero. "Now that I think about it, you should be aware of the image you're presenting."

Max felt Lila look at him. He didn't turn around. He couldn't help her.

Pilot rolled on. "No matter what you're doing, people will be watching you. The other fighters, the attendees, everyone. They know what you're capable of. They know what you could be for them. They'll expect you to act like it."

Max glanced at his father. What, exactly, was Lila supposed to be acting like?

But Lila looked like she'd taken a punch in the gut.

It took Max a minute to realize that it was the Coliseum, and not his father, that had done it. Lila stared out the window as the stadium rose into view, a great acropolis in the horizon. She didn't even notice Max looking at her.

He couldn't look away. The blood rushed from her face, turning her pale skin to ash and her hair to fire, as the Coliseum erupted in front of them.

It wasn't until they'd passed through the open iron gates that wrapped around to the empty parking lot behind Entrance C that Max realized that this was Pilot's victory. The Coliseum had Lila ensnared, and it was Pilot's. New Chicago was Pilot's. He owned them.

And he owned her too.

Lila's eyes were burning, but her expression was hollow.

"You are the hero," Pilot said. "Whether you like it or not. And what you do today will decide the fate of the world."

Whatever that meant.

Chapter 15

Pilot split them up. He turned to Lila first, a hollow smile on his lips that didn't reach his eyes.

"Wait here," he said.

He didn't say the other things. The *or else*. He didn't have to. It was in his eyes, where it always was. A warning, a threat.

And a prayer.

Because what could he do if she didn't?

Lila matched his gruesome smile. "Why not?"

For a second, Pilot wavered. Then he shook his head, motioning for Max to follow him into his office. They left the door open, and Lila in the shadows.

Max was introduced to a Lieutenant Davis, who was apparently visiting New Chicago from a settlement in the south. He was young, a military man with rigid posture and a booming voice.

"It's good to meet you," Max said.

Davis nodded stiffly. "Quite a place your father's got here."

"It's not quite as scary as it looks." Max flashed a haphazard smile.

And if his tone didn't quite match his words, well, at least the lieutenant didn't notice.

He laughed. It warmed his face.

"You think?"

Max shrugged. His mannerisms were easy. He wore politician's son like a second skin. Uncomfortable, but not foreign. Difficult at first, but coming back to him.

It made Lila wonder what Pilot had been before the war. What Max's future had once looked like.

"Well there's a meeting about to start now, but if you want to come, I can try to give you a tour after." His eyes flashed to Pilot's face for confirmation. Pilot nodded briefly.

Max turned back to the lieutenant expectantly. "I know I'd be happy for the company."

And Lila was not at all surprised when Lieutenant Davis agreed.

She couldn't imagine anyone saying no to Max.

Lieutenant Davis and Max rounded a corner, disappearing from view. Their footsteps echoed in the corridor, adding weight to the silence between Lila and Pilot.

"Let's walk."

It wasn't a question. He didn't even look at her as he strode away.

But she was not his yet and two could play that game.

Lila did not walk. She stayed where she was and waited, crucial seconds, until Pilot noticed she wasn't following. He turned, expectant and demanding. Cold.

Not cold enough.

He shouldn't have brought her here. It was a mistake. The Coliseum made her brave. This was the place where she'd known Red. This was where she'd loved him. This was where he'd *died.*

This was where Pilot had killed him.

And if he thought that she was so afraid to be buried by that grief that she would not drag him down with her, than Pilot was a fool.

She would *burn* him for what he'd done.

Lila met his eyes with a savage smile. Raised an eyebrow.

I dare you.

She saw him recoil.

And, as if on cue, she dropped her eyes. "Lead the way."

She would let him make what he could of that.

If she was lucky, it would be enough to protect her from the thing that was writhing and choking in her throat, strangling her from the inside out. If she kept the mask on tight, he might never know the truth.

The Coliseum did not make her braver. It made her smaller.

Too much.

***

Unsurprisingly, Pilot's tour led them to the arena.

He took her through Entrance E, not anywhere she'd been before, and so she didn't realize they were headed towards the 50-yardline bleachers until they climbed out of the steel lobby and into the overcast afternoon.

There wasn't a fight today, so the bleachers were mostly empty. A handful of boys were lying out, sitting apart, pretending not to watch the boys that were training on the arena. Lila pretended not to watch them either.

Pilot strode up a few steps then turned to lean against the rail. He examined the fighters shamelessly, shrewd eyes narrowed. "They all expect you to go back into the arena."

Lila gripped the rail with both hands.. She didn't look at the arena. She didn't look at the press boxes, especially not the one with the iron bars that had been installed specially. She didn't look at anything at all.

"I won't do it."

Pilot shrugged, his eyes flickering to Lila's face. She shrank under his gaze.

"Why not? Is it because I'm the one telling you that you should?"

In the arena, one of the boys lost his grip on his sword and it crashed to the ground, dragging his spear with it. The two clattered against each other, echoing across the stadium.

Lila inhaled sharply. The sound should not have surprised her.

"Because the thing is," Pilot continued. He was still watching her. He must have seen. He must have known now, that she was terrified. That he could hurt her still. "It's not about me, not really. There's nothing wrong with the Coliseum, Lila. There's nothing wrong with being a good fighter. Skills like that will save your life. Coliseum fighters will survive in the new world."

It had never felt like they were surviving, when Lila watched them from her box.

But she hadn't meant to think about that.

Pilot sighed. "You aren't the only one who likes the fights, Lila. You aren't the only one who feels better when you're in the arena."

Red had.

Red had thrived in the arena.

That was what Pilot was saying. He was saying that she had loved a boy that had loved this place. And so she could not hate it just because Pilot had made it.

"If you went back into the arena, you'd be setting an example. You could show people a new way to deal with the tragedy in their lives. A new way to be strong."

No matter that Pilot was the one who'd made it so she had to be strong.

"I-I can't do this," Lila said. She pushed off the rail, stumbling past Pilot and back into the shelter of the corridor. But in the shade, she hesitated.

She had no idea where to go.

Lila was still standing there, eyes adjusting to the grey, shadowed hall, when Pilot came up behind her.

"Let's keep walking," he said gently.

She followed him.

For all the time she'd spent in Pilot's Coliseum, she'd never really seen it. The halls were darker than she expected. Most of the walls were sticky with tar and grease that had never been cleaned away. It wasn't thriving, like Pilot made it sound. It was barely getting by.

The boys always stopped when they walked by. She could hear them whispering, but it was the staring that made her uncomfortable. They looked at her like they were frightened of her—and angry. Every glance was a challenge, and the Coliseum was full of them.

These boys were proud of who they were.

Who was she to be their hero?

Lila ducked her head and pretended she didn't know they were there. She pretended she couldn't feel their hostile glares, their disappointed glances. It made her sorry, for the first time, that she couldn't be more like Pilot wanted.

Because these boys wanted her to be that way too.

They wanted a hero.

Pilot gestured around a corner. "If you don't mind, I'm going to use the portable bathroom back there. I'll be right back."

Lila nodded. "Do I have to wait?"

Pilot followed her gaze to the boys just passing on the other side of the hall. He grimaced. "One of the locker rooms is just through the next arch. I can find you there."

It didn't occur to her until after she got there that the locker room was one of the few places she'd been to before.

***

Lila didn't mean to walk in on anything.

Pilot had made it sound like no one would be in the locker room. Or, at the very least, that it wouldn't be a problem if she walked in unannounced.

But there he was, sitting on the floor with his left leg outstretched, wrapping it once, twice, three times with what appeared to be a T-shirt that he'd torn into long strips of cloth.

Alec.

He looked exactly the same as he had that day in the arena. Cautious with his height, awkward with his slight build. He was extremely gentle with his knee, taking care so that each action was mild. Deliberate.

Exactly as he'd been with her.

Lila paled when he looked over his shoulder at her.

"I'm sorry," she said, taking a step back. "I didn't know anyone was in here."

"My God. *Lila*," Alec said at the same time. As if nothing had changed. As if it was still Red and Lila and Alec.

They both paused.

And Lila thought, for a second, that she would choke on her own name.

Then Alec's face hardened. He looked away. "Didn't think you'd be back here."

Whatever she'd surprised out of him was gone.

"Yeah, me either."

She watched as he turned back to his leg, lifting his knee gingerly to wrap the cloth strip around one more time.

"What happened?"

Alec's hands stilled. He glanced at her, an expression on his face that made Lila take another step back, and then turned away. "What do you think? A fight."

"You broke your leg?"

Nothing changed in his expression. "I shattered my kneecap."

"*Shit*."

Alec just ran his thumb across the bandage. He winced as he got to his feet, leaning on his good leg. "So what are you doing back?"

The blood was already rushing from his face.

"Pilot brought me," she said.

Alec raised an eyebrow. "Oh."

She knew what he meant. She could hear it in his voice.

This time it was Lila who looked away. She focused on her hands, playing with her fingers, intertwining and untangling them over and over. "It's not as bad as it sounds. He mostly lets me do what I want."

Lila wasn't sure why she was defending Pilot. She didn't care about Pilot.

"You don't understand-"

"What the hell is this?" Alec interrupted, grabbing Lila's left hand violently. He turned it palm-up and dug his thumb into the edge of the gauze.

Not her hand, then.

Her wrist.

Lila had almost forgotten.

Alec peeled the cloth back with his fingers. It was already loose, so it slid another inch without much trouble. Her skin was mostly clean underneath. The scar of her wound was etched in blue and purple still, though. It ran straight and true, a clean cut across her wrist.

It was obvious, what she'd tried to do.

Alec lifted her chin with his other hand, eyes narrowed. "I asked what the hell this was."

His voice razor sharp.

Lila wet her lips. "It's what it looks like."

Alec didn't react immediately. He just looked at her, green eyes warm and unresponsive.

And then, abruptly, he shoved her. Hard. Both hands. Lila hit the door, the force of the blow shooting up her back. She gasped.

"You tried to commit suicide?" Alec shouted. He was in front of her again, his face inches from hers. She felt his hand yank her up again, met his eyes. "What the fuck were you thinking? *How could you*?"

And that was about as much as Lila was willing to take.

She kicked up, suddenly, and kneed him in the stomach. He choked, stumbled, and she slipped past him. When he started to stand upright again, she slapped him. It was surprising enough to stop him dead in the middle of the room. They stared at each other.

"How *could* I?" Lila repeated. It was hard to breathe. The room was too small. Her heart was too big. She was going to burst. Something had been made wrong inside her. No matter what she did, the ache wouldn't leave her chest.

"He *died.* Right in front of me. And when he was killed, they cheered. My God, didn't you hear them? Didn't you see? They killed him because it was fun to watch him die."

"So you just decided to throw in the towel? Thought you'd given it the old college try, and it just wasn't working out for you?"

Lila wrapped her arms around herself. Trying to hold it inside. Trying to stay in control. "Yes," she breathed. "That's exactly what I did."

Alec's eyes widened.

Lila swallowed her tears. She didn't want to *hurt.* She *wanted* to be angry.

But the two emotions were all mixed up inside her.

"It was over," she whispered. Her voice broke. "And I'd lost *everything.*"

Alec searched her face.

Then, his voice wrecked, "Do you really think you're the only one he left behind?"

"What's *that* supposed to mean?"

Alec squeezed his eyes closed. His breath hitched. "You left, Lila. You left, and I had to bury him."

All at once, the fight when out of her.

Lila gave a soft cry. "What?"

But Alec raised his eyes to her, expression steeled. "I *buried* him. Where were you?"

Lila didn't even have time to react. In the next second, Alec was gone, a ghost that was standing next to her, then behind her, then out the door.

Chapter 16

The governors of New Chicago were all very impressed with Max.

They liked the way he dressed. They liked his long-sleeve dress shirt, his blue slacks. They liked his language. He was precise with his use of words and free with smiles. He shook everyone's hands. His face was open and easy to read. They knew what he was thinking even as he thought it, and he was always thinking the same things that they were, in such a way as to guarantee that things would get done quickly and efficiently. He had ideas. They liked that. They liked that his ideas were vague and goal-orientated, to ensure that anyone could incorporate their own agendas into them.

But most of all, the governors liked Max's personality. None of them would know exactly what about his personality was so magnetic, but they would all agree. Max was a good kid. Pilot had raised him well.

Max knew these things because he was standing on the other side of the door, leaning against the wall, pretending to be gone, as the governors of New Chicago preened over him.

He'd had just about as much as he could take.

It had started easy. Lieutenant Davis had done the introductions for him.

"Afternoon everyone, this is Pilot's son. He's come by for a visit."

It had started easy, but it didn't stay that way.

Every one of New Chicago's governors was at the Coliseum that afternoon. Everyone except for the governor of The Yard, Jonathan Haze, anyway. But no one seemed to be expecting him. He was the oldest of the governors, but he was also the most independent. Even at his best, apparently, he hadn't always bothered with the Chicago Council's daily affairs.

And Jonathan Haze was not at his best. According to the other governors—God forbid Max learn anything from his own *father*—Haze was sick. A chest cough that he simply couldn't shake.

The dangerous kind of sick.

But, even without Haze, the Chicago Council was full. Both the Lincoln Park and the New Garfield governors had brought several representatives with them. The governor from Hyde Park looked like he'd brought at least three people for the strict purpose of taking notes. Everyone was dressed up in way too many layers for the season, all talking too fast, and all on their best behavior.

Why they were doing this, Max wasn't sure.

Because, as far as he could tell, Max was the only one here that *didn't* already know everything that was going on in New Chicago. The only thing that Max had on the governors was that he was Pilot's son.

And apparently that meant something.

The governors had more than a handful of questions for Max. They wanted to know what he knew about the Coliseum, his ideas on leadership for the future, his thoughts on how the city was functioning and how it could function better.

They'd known he was coming. They knew who he was.

And they thought, foolishly, that his opinion mattered at all to Pilot.

But Max was a good son. He did what his father had asked. He smiled in all the right places and listened attentively to every governor he spoke to. He made a good impression, one that would reflect dutifully back to his father.

When one of the governors asked him if he knew anything about Pilot's plans for the future expansion of the Coliseum, though, Max faltered.

"What expansion?" he asked, before he could stop himself. Before he thought better of it.

The governor cleared his throat. "I guess you don't know much, then?" He laughed uncomfortably.

Lieutenant Davis intervened. "That might be a better question for the boy's father," he said sharply. Then his expression softened. "Can't expect a kid to have all the answers, can we?"

The governor from Lincoln Park laughed.

Max lowered his voice, relieved that the attention had shifted—at least momentarily—away from him. "I didn't even know he was thinking of expanding at all."

If his tone sounded bitter, the lieutenant ignored it.

"I've only heard rumors. Some of the boys are saying that it's planned for the spring. Your father wants to build out enough to accommodate for a whole second slew of fighters."

"You've been in the arena?" Max asked.

Lieutenant Davis shook his head, something grim flashing across his features. "I haven't been near it. I stopped in one of the dorms to talk to some of the boys, that's all."

Max scrubbed his face with his hand. "To be honest, if we ever get to that tour I promised you, I'd just as soon avoid the arena altogether."

That earned him a puzzled glance.

Unsurprisingly, since he hadn't meant to say it aloud.

"All I meant was-"

"That the whole thing is a little disturbing?" Lieutenant Davis supplied.

Max jerked his head up.

The lieutenant chuckled darkly. He glanced around the room and leaned in to say even more quietly. "I'm only surprised that the architect's son feels the same way."

Max wasn't sure what to say to that.

Which turned out to be fine, because the conversation in the rest of the room had gotten heated.

"Well it's not *official*," one of the governors interrupted. Several heads turned his way. "No one's even proposed the expansion to Haze, let alone gotten it approved."

Max rolled over the phrase architect's son in his head, distracted. "You mean Jonathan Haze? The governor of The Yard?"

"He's still the chair of the Council," the governor who'd been speaking supplied. Max couldn't think what his name was. He thought it was something biblical. Maybe Mathew, or Gabriel. Either way, he was the governor of Hyde Park. Or what was left of the eastern half of the South Side.

"So he has to approve any major changes to the city." Max was guessing now. He'd never heard of the Council's chair. He thought Pilot did whatever he wanted.

It made him suddenly wondered what would happen if Pilot *did* do whatever he wanted.

The architect's son.

Someone else was talking. "Sure, John is the chair, but he rarely actually opposes anything. We've been at this for almost two years, and the most he's ever done is call a Council meeting to vote on an issue. He won't overturn Pilot's plan."

The governor from Hyde Park's voice was low when he responded. Max glanced over. "I wouldn't be so sure. Everyone knows that John and Pilot never saw eye to eye about the future of this city. And Pilot has never tried a stunt like this before."

There was a beat of silence. A flicker of tension and several veiled glances at Max.

The governor seemed to remember himself. "But I could be wrong," he added hastily.

"Besides," the New Garfield governor piped up. Several turned in his direction. "we've all been hearing the news from Cleveland. We've seen more immigrants to the city than ever before, and they are all saying the same thing. It's this guy Antipas. His gang, from what I hear, is nearly unstoppable. And the influence of their Coliseum is spreading like wildfire-"

Again, Max stuttered, stumbled, and intervened before he could really stop to consider. "There's another Coliseum?"

The governor from New Garfield looked irritated, but the others looked amused. The one who was named Gabriel-Mathew-Mark smiled obligingly. "For several months now."

Lieutenant Davis looked just as surprised as Max felt. But the governors were already filling them in.

"I'd say it was back in July we started hearing the rumors. They've had some trouble with gangs in Cleveland ever since the war ended, but all of the sudden this guy—Antipas—comes out of nowhere. He's got all these warring groups working with each other, a secret identity, and a brand new Coliseum-"

"Inspired by your father," someone else added.

The governor of Hyde Park nodded. "Exactly. So he's got an economy to lend him credibility and enough power to crush anyone who tries anything."

"Do people…try things?"

Davis flashed Max a guarded expression.

But it was New Garfield's governor who answered. "From what I hear, he's had some trouble. He didn't have the sense your father did to make sure his fighters were volunteers."

Oh.

Max stuffed his hands into his pockets, stepping back. He was feeling a little small-minded now, thinking that his father was the worst kind of villain.

At least he'd had the decency to ask before he'd taken control of the world.

On the other hand, Max wasn't at all sure that any of these people would have dared to tell Pilot no, even if they'd wanted to.

Did they want to?

This time it was the governors of Hyde Park and New Garfield who shared a look. The governor of Hyde Park glanced at Max then and added, cautiously, "Which brings us back to the problem at hand. Your father thinks that the only way to compete with Antipas' growing—well, let's call it "popularity"—is to expand our own Coliseum."

"And Haze doesn't agree." That was the New Garfield governor.

One of the others looked around, his face pale. "But even Haze wouldn't actually veto the expansion, would he?"

Should he?

Max was pretty sure he wasn't the only one wondering it.

But no one else voiced an opinion. Better to ask questions than give answers.

One had much less risk of being wrong.

They were all looking at Max now, like he should know. Like he could guide them best. Max didn't know what to say. He wasn't even sure what to think. He'd forgotten that there was a world to contend with.

For so long, it had just been Pilot, his Council, his New Chicago, and an empty, hopeless world.

And Zoe, Max suddenly remembered. Zoe, who was heading east. Towards somewhere else. Something new.

Something *more*?

The governors shuffled uncomfortably. The look on Max's face must have spoken volumes. He ducked his head.

They were all saved, finally, by Lincoln Park's governor. She put a companionable arm around Max's shoulders. "So tell us what you think is the most pressing thing that needs to be fixed around here?"

Max smiled hollowly. "Well, we could definitely use a janitor."

Everyone laughed.

It only took Max another twenty minutes to extricate himself. He had to guide the conversation safely back to shore first, where the governors could talk about theme ideas and ration coordination. Where they could smile and joke. Where they could forget that there had ever been a moment of dissention.

A matter of minutes, in the grand scheme of things, to convince a group of grown men and women not to worry about the checks and balances of their new government.

Except maybe Lieutenant Davis, who flashed him a thoughtful look as he left and said, “Rain check on that tour, then?”

Max had nodded mutely, and the lieutenant was gone before Max could be sure what he’d promised.

As far as the governors went, however, the fire had been effectively quenched. No one remembered Antipas or Haze or the expansion. The governors just smiled and whispered to each other about what a good kid Max was, how well he’d adjusted after his mother’s death, and how well it bode for New Chicago as a whole that the children could turn into such competent adults.

Max wished he shared their faith.

Chapter 17

Pilot was not happy to see his son.

“Where is she?”

Max looked up. He’d made his way down to Pilot’s office, hoping his father would think to find him there. Apparently he had.

“Where is who?”

Pilot pulled a set of keys out his pocket, then seemed to remember himself and shoved the door open with his shoulder. He shot Max a dark look. “What do you mean ‘who’? Where is Lila? You must know where she went.”

Max froze. “What? What are you talking about?”

Pilot ground his teeth. “I thought she would have told you. She was supposed to wait in the dormitory for me, but when I got there, she was gone.”

“She left?”

Max’s stomach turned over.

Either Pilot didn't hear the concern in Max's voice, or he didn't care. He didn't look at his son as he stormed into his office. Max followed.

"Of course not," his father said. "Where would she go?"

Oh. Max hadn't thought of that.

"But then-"

"She's here somewhere," Pilot interrupted. He shuffled through his papers, reorganizing simply for the sake of touching something. "Obviously. I just don't know where she would go."

Max watched Pilot. He watched his father rearrange his desk. He watched him slowly reassert control. Balance. Even in panic, Pilot was cool and collected. The key to being in control was to be detached.

It was just like any other problem. Pilot would find her. He would manage the things he had control over, until he could find a way to manage Lila, and then he would deal with her too. All in good time.

Max watched his father and wondered if he should tell him where Lila was. Because he knew. But Pilot didn't ask Max again. He'd asked when he thought Max might have been told.

It never occurred to him that Max might just know Lila.

***

He found her where he expected to find her.

The box was dark. He'd only seen it once before, on the day that his father had brought Lila down, frightened and stumbling, to go into the arena. Pilot hadn't known he was there. He was supposed to be waiting in the office so they could walk into the arena together.

But Max had been afraid, alone in a crowded building with more people than he'd seen in an entire year. He hadn't known then that it was a Coliseum and that the girl with the hair like fire was supposed to die. Pilot hadn't told him about the master plan yet.

Actually, Pilot never really told him about the master plan at all. He'd just figured, by the look on his father's face that horrible afternoon, that Lila was never supposed to be the one to live.

But the box had stuck with him, and Max found his way back there without much trouble.

He passed under the doorway, hesitating as he waited for his eyes to adjust to the shadows. The room was empty. There was a table, one of the feet busted, that appeared to be nailed to the floor in the corner of the room. There was a dirty sprawl of fingerprints along the wall. There was another door, leaning at a strange angle and off one of its hinges, across from him.

The floor of the room beyond was washed red from the setting sun. It meant there was a window there. Max was pretty sure, from what Lila had told him one afternoon as they traded *The Odyssey* back and forth, that this particular window had iron bars installed across it.

He padded quietly across the room and stepped inside.

Lila was standing with her back to him. She was in the center of the room, hands at her sides, hair a sheet of red that stuck in strands to her face. It was hot, unseasonably, but she was pale. Ashen. And though she didn't move, didn't make a sound, she was shaking. Her whole body trembled.

She must have heard him come in, but she didn't acknowledge it. She just stood there. And even though her too-bright eyes stayed firmly on the window and her fists clenched when Max took a step forward, she looked as though the next breath she took might just kill her.

Max said her name.

She turned, all sharp edges and glass.

"It's okay," he said. A stupid thing to say. A lie.

But enough.

All at once, she fell apart. Lila was crying. She was wrapping her arms around herself and sobbing, shaking and gasping for air like she couldn't breathe—like she hadn't really been breathing all along.

Then she was crumbling and Max grabbed her. He pulled her into his arms, holding her back, holding her up. She raged, trying to pull away from him, but also trying to get closer, clinging, until finally she gave in and collapsed, head against his chest, burying herself inside him.

And Max went on holding her even after it was only tears, and the silence in the box started to press in around them. He held on until it was just Lila shivering in his arms, and the sound of her heartbeat became the loudest thing in his world.

Chapter 18

They whispered secrets in the darkness. Pilot was asleep down the hall, so they kept their voices low. They did not want him to hear them.

Max was lying on his bed, eyes on the ceiling. Lila was curled up with her back against the wall. She was wrapped in Max's comforter, his pillow clutched at her chest. She was watching the door.

"What do you think the lieutenant wants with the Coliseum?" Max asked.

"Maybe nothing. Maybe he's just visiting."

"But how many visitors have you seen?"

"Ever?"

"Since the war ended."

Lila hesitated.

Max, still memorizing patterns on the ceiling, chuckled. "Exactly."

"So he's here for a reason."

"I know my father would be."

"Why didn't you just ask him?"

Max wetted his lips. "I don't think the lieutenant likes me very much."

Lila looked at him.

"It's just-" Max sighed. "You should have heard him. He hates Pilot."

"So?"

"So. He hates the Coliseum. *Disturbing*. That's the word he used."

Lila's colorless eyes glowed in the dark. "You hate the Coliseum too."

Max flinched.

"Don't you?" she asked, quieter.

They whispered their secrets in the darkness.

"Yes."

"So maybe he doesn't hate you. Maybe you should ask him what he's doing here, spying on your father's Coliseum."

Max sat up, bracing himself on one arm. "You think that's what he doing?"

"I don't know, Max. I don't know anything about him. But that's what I'd be doing. Especially now that there's apparently another one."

Ah, yes.

Antipas.

"How did this happen?" Max said, voice quiet.

"To us, or to the world?" Lila said dryly.

Max ignored her. "How could there be enough *people* to have another coliseum?"

"Did you really think Chicago was the only city left?"

Had he?

Had he been that stupid?

"No. I guess not. I don't…I don't know," Max fumbled.

There was a beat of silence. Then he added, "Did you?"

"I always thought there had to be something. East, at least." There was a rustling in the dark. Max looked over, but he couldn't see Lila's face. Her voice was strained. "I—I was told that the west is uninhabitable. Dust storms. There's nothing left passed the Mississippi. When—*if* you walked north from Louisville, all you see over your shoulder is desert. Miles of it."

Max knew what had been in Louisville. *Who* had been there.

He lay back down.

"So there's a grave," he said.

Lila gave a soft cry.

"Will you go to it?"

A minute went by. It was followed by another. The silence settled in.

When it was clear that Lila wasn't going to answer, Max closed his eyes.

She waited until she must have thought he was asleep. In fact, Lila must have been mulling over the question for so long that she'd forgotten he was there. She must have seen it, like a story playing in her head. She must have imagined the grave where they'd buried Red.

It must have hurt her, to know that she hadn't been there.

But sleep didn't come easily, so Max was still awake when she said it—so quietly that he knew it hadn't been meant for him.

"I have to."

Chapter 19

Lila had done it. She'd scared Pilot.

Finally. All those weeks, those months, those broken promises and weighted silences, and Pilot never flinched. The things that Lila would be able to do in an arena did not frighten him. The things she'd done, once, for Red, did not move him. She had thought that nothing could.

But then Lila had run. And that had terrified him.

Max was different too. He didn't talk about the governors, but Lila knew that they'd upset him. And, apart from that first night after the Coliseum, he'd never so much as said Lieutenant Davis' name. It was like he hoped that if he never brought it up again, it would just go away.

It didn't.

Lila was sitting at the kitchen table, legs propped up on an empty chair beside her, when Max came down. He looked tired. He also looked surprised to see Lila.

He shouldn't have been. Pilot never let her leave the house anymore.

Of course, he never said as much. He invented excuses, pleaded, harped, and pushed down on Lila until she bent under the weight of his concern. She stayed inside, as far out of Pilot's way as she dared. At first, having the power to scare him had thrilled her. She'd thought she was so strong.

She wasn't. Nothing had changed.

Max bit the inside of his cheek. "Is my dad here?"

Lila jerked her head towards the study, where the door was propped slightly open. She saw indecision on Max's face—he was always open like a book—and then he turned his back on the door, pulling out a chair and sitting across from Lila.

If Pilot heard them, if he knew, there was no sign.

He apparently didn't care.

"What are you reading now?" Max asked. He reached over to tug the book out of Lila's hands.

She rolled her eyes. "Nothing interesting."

"*The Iliad?*" Lila almost laughed out loud at the disbelief in Max's voice. "Why are you still trying?"

"I haven't exactly had anything else to do."

It was meant to be catty. But Max glanced over his shoulder, and Lila followed his gaze to the half-open study door, and she was sorry she'd said it. Max was so young, and seeing him hurt made her want to scream. Made her want to fight.

Couldn't Pilot see Max was scared? Couldn't he see the doubts growing where there hadn't been any before? Didn't he know that he might lose his son to his city?

Didn't he care?

A man like Pilot did not deserve a son like Max.

"It actually isn't that bad," Lila said suddenly. Her words drew back Max's eyes. He looked unconvinced.

She laughed out loud. Only a little forced.

"Okay. So it is that bad."

Something in her expression made Max smile. Or maybe it was just Lila.

She was glad that she could make him smile.

When Pilot finally emerged from the study, it was dark outside. He was halfway up the stairs before he remembered to say goodnight.

And that was only because Max said it first. Bitter. Resentful.

Pilot stopped. His eyes flashed to his son's face. Max was not looking at him, and so Max did not see. Pilot hesitated, pale and uncertain, and then he replied quietly, "Sleep well."

Max pressed his palms into the kitchen table.

Lila could have sworn that Pilot looked devastated. But he didn't say anything else, and he didn't stay. So she must have been wrong.

***

Three nights and four long afternoons later, Pilot finally suggested that Lila might benefit from another tour of the Coliseum. "We were unfortunately derailed in the middle of it last time," he said, not a hint of irony in his voice.

Max didn't even react. He didn't look at her.

And that was just about as much as Lila could take. She couldn't spend one more minute in this house, climbing the walls, watching Max tear himself apart inside. She couldn't do it.

So she said yes.

Max went to his room and shut the door.

Pilot scrubbed his face with his hands. "Now, then?"

The drive to the Coliseum was much quieter without Max. Lila sat in the passenger seat and Pilot drove, hands gripping the steer wheel tightly. She expected him to say something about New Chicago, about the hero, but he didn't. He didn't say anything at all.

There was only one moment between them, the whole drive. It was at the intersection just coming out of the tunnel outside the Coliseum. The last faded stop sign before the arena came into view. The part that Lila could not watch.

So she turned to Pilot instead.

And she caught him with his guard down, eyes wide and distant, grief like a familiar scar on his face. He was thinking of his wife, Lila suddenly realized. His wife and his son.

And he was thinking of loss.

But Lila did not feel sorry for him, because Lila did not feel.

The silence between them wasn't broken until they walked under the archway to Entrance C. As soon as the stuffy coolness of the stadium settled in around them, Lila heard the commotion. There was a scuffle, two sets of boots echoing along the corridor.

Around the corner, someone shouted. "What the hell is that supposed to mean?"

Another boy. "What's it sound like? I saw the list myself."

A low oath.

"Look, I'm just the messenger. You got a problem, take it up with Pilot."

At his name, Pilot sped up. Lila hurried to keep pace. They rounded the corner, but she'd already figured out who the other voice was.

"You know as well as I do what Pilot would say," Alec retorted hotly. His back was to them. He was leaning heavily on a makeshift crutch, created from two chair legs taped together.

The boy he was talking to, manning the ticket booth, didn't see Lila and Pilot either. "Yeah, I do. He'd say fuck off," the boy said.

Alec hissed. "I *won* the fight-"

"Is there a problem, boys?"

Lila had forgotten that Pilot could do this. Alec's words died in his mouth. The boy in the booth flinched, lifting his head to look at Pilot.

"No, sir," he said. Full of admiration.

And fear.

Alec, however, didn't turn. His body sort of slumped in on itself, making him look smaller. Taking his crutch more firmly under his arm, he glanced over his shoulder to meet Pilot's eye, but caught Lila's instead.

He lingered there, staring at her. Then, expression hostile, he turned and limped away. He didn't look back again.

Pilot sighed. "Has he given you trouble before?"

The boy at the booth shook his head. "No sir. Alec's usually a good guy. You saw what happened to his leg. I think it's been bothering him, is all. And he doesn't really have anybody to take it out on."

Lila watched Alec move carefully down the hall. He hesitated at the corner, resting his hand against the wall, head hung.

"But you will let me know if that changes. You know my policy on fighting outside of the arena."

The boy looked uncomfortable, but he said, "Of course."

At the same time, Lila said quietly, "Let me go after him. I don't think he means to make trouble."

She felt both pairs of eyes on her, but she was still watching Alec. He hadn't moved.

He looked like just standing there was almost more than he could take.

"Please."

Pilot hesitated. He touched her forearm and Lila looked up sharply.

"I know what this is about," he said quietly. "I remember who it was that got you off the arena that day."

It was almost as if he'd said it aloud. *Red.* Lila could hear his name roaring in her ears. It turned her to ice. She didn't want to have this conversation. Not with Pilot. Not now. Not ever.

He knew it too. He knew what Red did to her.

"What does it matter to you?"

Pilot thinned his lips. "It all matters to me. You know how important you are."

"What does that even mean?"

She'd meant it as an accusation, but it didn't come out that way. She sounded desperate. Pilot leaned back and the flicker of smile touched his lips.

"So now you want to know?" he countered. His voice was light, but his eyes were narrowed. Hawk's eyes.

Pilot was playing her, just like he did everyone else.

It should have made her angry. It should have made her fight.

Instead it made her tired.

Lila was sick with wanting—wanting to be where Red was, to see the grave that Alec had made, to satisfy this horrible, secret hope that she would finally bury all of the fear inside her—and so she relented. Whatever Pilot wanted, he could have.

"Just let me talk to Alec."

Pilot searched her face.

"You'll be the hero."

Something twisted in Lila's stomach. She ignored it. "That depends on what being your hero means."

"You have one hour. Then we'll talk about what I need from you."

Lila went after Alec.

***

"Come to tell me off?" Alec asked. He'd tried to put some venom in his voice, but his face was ashen and Lila could see he'd gotten worse. His voice was hoarse.

"No," she said.

He looked up at her.

"What's going on with you?" she asked him.

Alec glared. "You sure you want to know? Being Pilot's hero and all?"

If he thought he was going to hurt her with his words and his sad green eyes, he was sorely mistaken.

Lila waited.

"It's about the grave," he said finally, moving to grip his crutch more securely. He glanced behind him, but they were alone in the corridor now. Pilot had evidently taken Lila at her word. He didn't wait.

Alec winced as he stepped forward. Lila reached forward to lend her strength, but he flinched away. "Don't."

"I want to help."

Alec hissed, taking another step. "I don't want your help."

He *hated* her.

Lila stopped. Alec ignored her, making his way gingerly down the hall. He'd only gone a few feet, the distance between them barely more than a yard, when Lila called softly, "I'm sorry, Alec."

Alec faltered. He looked over his shoulder at her. "You don't even know the half of it."

"Then tell me."

He shook his head. "What difference does it make?"

But still he didn't go. They stood looking at each other.

Until Lila realized.

"How will we know until we try?"

Finally.

Something changed.

Alec's face softened. "Do you want to see the grave?"

***

Alec had buried Red just outside of the Coliseum. The fighters weren't supposed to travel in the outer rings of the stadium where the audience might be, but Alec had done it anyway. He'd snuck out there, under the cover of darkness, and he'd dug a grave.

It had taken two days. There were no fights. Pilot remained away, licking his wounds, grieving his losses. The boys didn't talk about Red's death. They just went about their lives as if none of it had ever happened. Lila's rations remained at the ticket booth, un-collected, and the days ticked by. No one said anything to Pilot about the grave. No one said anything to anyone about the grave.

And then, eventually, Alec had dug a hole large enough. He took Red's body, tucked carefully away in a box as it had been since the day he'd died, and he'd buried it at the top of a hill overlooking the Coliseum.

"It's beautiful," Lila said, as soon as she saw it.

And it was. The hill wasn't green, of course. Nothing was, since most of the plant life—including most weeds—in the city were all but extinct. But there was something tragic and outstanding about the hill nonetheless.

Lila and Alec stood side by side, not exactly a united front, but not dissident either.

Alec shied away first.

"It's barely enough," he said.

That was true too.

Because, although the grave was beautiful, it was also horrible. No matter the hill and graveyard, there was still the wooden cross and the inscription—"*forever and always*." It was still a grave.

Red Ferris was still never coming back.

And no matter how Lila looked at it, she couldn't seem to get that through her head. The more she looked at his name, the less it looked like his. Until finally, the grave had nothing at all to do with Red except that it happened to remind her of him. It hurt. That was all.

Just like everything else.

"Do you miss him?" Lila asked.

"How couldn't I?"

They didn't look at each other. Instead they stood side by side in front of the grave and kept their own thoughts. Neither said anything about the stray weeds, or the dirty cross. They didn't mentioned the frost settling over the bareness of the hillside. They just stood and grieved.

Finally, Alec closed his eyes. He turned his back on it.

Lila's eyes flickered to his face. "Thank you."

For his patience. For his forgiveness. For the burial. For the grave.

Alec let out a sigh. "Do you know what Pilot did?"

She was still watching him. Something in her chest hummed. "What?"

"After I won my first fight—I was in the first round after he…died. Pilot withheld my rations. Said the fight wasn't good enough. He put me in the next week. I fought twice before I broke my leg-"

Shattered his kneecap.

"-and he still won't give them to me. There's nothing to eat. And he's got me in the next fight."

Pilot was trying to kill Alec.

There was a beat of silence, then Alec added quietly, "If the starvation doesn't do me in, then he's got me registered to fight again in three days. And the arena definitely will."

He wasn't looking at her. He *couldn't* look at her. After all, what could Pilot's hero do against the injustices of Pilot himself?

And because Alec was right, because there was nothing Lila could do, she pretended she didn't understand. She didn't meet his gaze, and she let him withdraw back into the stadium.

"Happy New Year, by the way," Alec said.

Lila started, but he was already gone.

Happy New Year.

She hadn't realized it was already here. Her fresh start. Her first new year.

How many more would there have to be?

Pilot had taken *everything*, the night that Red died.

And for some reason, this time that thought made Lila angry.

***

Lila was still standing there when Pilot appeared.

As soon as she heard him at her back, all jagged edges and pressure, she stiffened. How could he come to *this* place, stand in front of *this* grave, and tell her anything at all?

"You shouldn't be here."

Her voice sounded empty.

Pilot moved into her shadow, just over her shoulder. "It's time we talk about the future."

"I don't think that's a good idea."

This time at least there was a little anger in her tone. *Something.*

The next thing would be to feel it.

Pilot sighed. "We're running out of time to go in circles, Lila."

He must have been surprised when she laughed.

"I've got all the time in the world."

Pilot moved. He touched her arm.

Lila jerked away from him. "Don't."

"Lila."

This time she looked at him. Her body was on fire. "I said don't touch me."

Pilot withdrew. His eyes flickered to Red's grave and Lila followed his gaze. She hadn't realized she was shaking.

"Can we not do this here?" she asked.

She'd meant to be volatile. Indestructible.

But she was pleading. Lila was still looking at the grave. And every word was a choked back sob.

Pilot didn't touch her again, but he stepped out of her shadow and into the fading light. He scrubbed his face with his hands. His voice was so soft that she almost didn't hear him.

"I'm sorry this happened to you."

At first, she didn't understand.

Then something dead rolled over in her stomach.

"Sorry? You're *sorry*?"

Lila's voice was all wrong. It was stirred, deliberate, charged. It was a challenge.

Which made no sense, because she was all shredded and broken inside.

"You're not *allowed* to be sorry," she said. There was a drumming starting up in the back of her head, a rhythm that drowned out everything else, pounding in her ears. "You can't stand here, where—where *he* is—and say that you're sorry. *This* is what you did. You killed him, and now he's there, and you're here, and—and so I—I…I don't want anything from you."

Pilot thinned his lips. "You won't be the hero."

"I won't be anything of yours."

It sounded so good, saying it aloud. He didn't own her, because she could not be owned. She was nothing inside. There was nothing for him to own.

Except that there was.

"What do you want, Lila?"

Pilot was looking at her now. His hot eyes were too much for her rage, and all at once the fire went out. She didn't burn. She *couldn't* burn. It was getting all mixed up with something else, something she didn't want to remember.

Red.

Because of course the thing that Lila wanted most was something that Pilot could never give her.

She raised her eyes to his face. "You don't deserve me."

But Pilot just looked at her. His face was open and his resigned smile was gentle. "And everyone else? The orphans? The single parents? All those who lost the people they loved, just like you did, and don't know what to do next? Do *they* deserve you, Lila? Do they deserve to live?"

Gentleness did not suit Pilot. In his hands, everything became a weapon.

Lila turned away.

But she could still hear him.

"What about Max?"

Lila closed her eyes. She was not crying. She was *nothing* and Pilot could not hurt her. "What *about* Max?" she hissed.

"He deserves to live," Pilot said. "We all do."

It wasn't Lila who asked it. Lila was not that weak. "And me?"

"The Coliseum needs a hero."

She could feel the tears on her face, hot trails leaving stains on her cheeks. She could feel the pins and needles in her fingertips, a numbness that spread all the way up her arms. She could feel the loss, heavy and overwhelming, where it rested on her shoulders.

Red was all around her, and Lila was drowning.

"Please don't make me do this," she whispered.

"Then what do you want, Lila?" he asked again.

Too much.

Her eyes snapped open. She turned on him. Her blood was burning and she was rising from the ashes, something clawing its way out from inside her.

"Why couldn't you just let me die?"

She screamed it at him.

Pity flashed across Pilot's face. Then he smiled grimly. "You told him you wouldn't give up."

Max.

Red.

Oh, God. Lila was going to be sick.

She was wrong. She wasn't just drowning.

Pilot was dragging her under.

"I promised him I'd be strong."

Was she talking about Max now, or Red?

Pilot put a hand on her arm and she didn't pull away. "This is the only way."

Lila was so tired. She was tired of caring, and trying, and hurting—all the time. She wanted it to be quiet, just for one heartbeat, so that she could breathe. Just an inhale, that was all she needed.

Just something to prove that she was still alive.

He told her that she would go back into the Coliseum. They would know her as the hero, and she would fight just like any of the other boys. Except that she would win. And Pilot would make her beautiful, perfect, untouchable.

A hero.

And, as far as she was concerned, that was fine. Because if she was the hero, than she wouldn't have to be Lila anymore.

The only thing she asked in return was that she be the one to tell Max.

At least Pilot understood that.

It was time, now, to count the small blessings.

Chapter 20

Max washed his face in the dark, because he couldn't find the matches and he was afraid to ask his father. They hadn't really spoken since the Coliseum and even though it had been days, Max still couldn't quite figure out how to bring it up. New Chicago. The Coliseum. The Council. Antipas.

Any of it.

And now Pilot was in a mood. The cold, thoughtful, terrifying kind of mood. Silences that Max couldn't remember being so full since they'd first moved out of the city.

The last time Pilot had smiled this way, he'd been building a Coliseum behind Max's back.

His father woke him before dawn.

"You're coming with us today."

When had the *us* become Lila and Pilot against Max?

"Okay."

Max was already dressed, so he came downstairs only minutes later. Pilot was in the office, door leaning slightly closed. Lila was at the kitchen table. Her red hair was brushed and straight as a razor down her back. She was dressed in sweatpants, cut with a ragged edge at the bottom to make up for the several inches of height difference between her and their previous owner. Her sweatshirt had been massacred at the collar by a pair of scissors.

But against her careless, haphazard outfit, she sat up straight. Her hands were clasped neatly in her lap. Every muscle was tense and still. *Deliberate.*

The effect was unnerving.

She was surreal. Impossible. *Alien.*

Then, as if she could hear him, she looked up. And all at once, she was just Lila again.

Max shuffled down the stairs. "We're going back to the Coliseum again? So soon?"

Something horrible and sad crossed Lila's face. "It's what your father wants."

"Do you know what he wants us to do there?"

Her strange grey eyes darted away. "We're supposed to pack for a couple days."

"*What?*"

She shrugged. Something was wrong.

"I'm serious, Lila. A couple days? How long are we talking?"

"It's just an overnight bag," Lila said.

It wasn't. It wasn't just an overnight bag.

Max had never slept outside of this house. Not since the end of the world. His father wouldn't have allowed it. Not ever.

Except, apparently, now all the rules were being thrown out the window.

"I don't-"

Max's words died in his mouth. Pilot had appeared in the doorway to the study, a smile on his face that turned all thought into a brick in his stomach.

"Is there a problem?" Pilot asked, nothing but polite curiosity in his voice.

But Max would die by the steel in his eyes.

"No."

There was a moment. Max hesitated at the foot of the stairs, waiting for his father's expression to cool. For one, awful second, it didn't look like it would. It looked like Max had been too late and his father was about to explode. But then the moment passed. Pilot smiled his careful smile and Max was released.

He went up to his room and packed an overnight bag. He was thorough and quick. He made no sudden movements.

Even though Lila followed him upstairs, they didn't speak. She just stood behind him, leaning against the wall by his closet, and watched. He turned, once, to get something from the bottom shelf. Their eyes met, and she offered him a sympathetic smile.

Behind the smile, there was something else. Something that was hurting her—just a little bit more than all the other things that were always hurting Lila.

Something was *very* wrong, then.

But Max decided that he didn't care what she was keeping from him. It didn't matter. So long as she kept smiling that hopeful, apologetic smile.

Let her keep her secrets.

As long as it kept her alive.

Max smiled back.

On the car ride, he and Lila argued about the ending of *The Iliad.* And when Lila lost the fight, Max reached over and squeezed her hand. She smirked at him. Pilot didn't say anything. Pilot didn't care.

Why should he?

Max was just a boy. He'd barely survived the end of the world. He spent all of his days carefully locked up in the big, empty house. He was afraid of everything. He was petty with his hatred and better at holding a grudge than he was at taking care of himself. He was lonely. He was angry. And sometimes, he was brilliant. Loyal. Brave. Strong.

But he was still Pilot's son. He could not hurt him, because he loved him.

He was Pilot's *son.* And he didn't know any other way.

This was Pilot's first mistake.

***

When Max saw Lieutenant Davis, they were both alone. Max was sorting papers in his father's office, trying to figure out the most efficient way to get a tax-tribute of rations from Lincoln Park to the stadium. Davis was apparently just returning from a visit to the arena, if the way he blinked in the sudden darkness was any indication.

"I thought you were going to give me a proper tour before I left?" he said.

Max glanced up. His politician's smile followed a beat behind. "Are you leaving us so soon?"

"Tomorrow morning. I've got about fifty miles to go before I catch the route that the jeeps run. But I was hoping-"

"The jeeps?"

Davis chuckled. "You and I really haven't talked, have we?"

"Since when does the army have jeeps?"

Again that low, throaty laugh. "Since always. But if you mean since when has there been an army to drive the jeeps around, that's pretty recent."

"I thought the Lieutenant thing was—old, I guess. Like from before."

Davis gave a thin smile. "Most people do. But there's a base…" He paused, expression darkening. "I've told your dad all of this, I'm surprised he didn't mention it."

Max shrugged. "My father doesn't tell me much."

"I get the impression that Pilot doesn't tell anyone very much."

An awkward silence.

Davis sighed and ran a hand through his hair. "I'm sorry. I shouldn't have said that."

Glancing down at the papers on the desk, Max finally dropped his pen. "It's true," he said quietly.

The lieutenant weighed something in his head, then crossed the room and sat abruptly in the seat across from Max.

"Can I ask you a question?"

"Shoot."

Davis rubbed his hands together. "Are the boys here happy?"

"I don't know. I guess. Why?"

The older man's face hardened. He leaned in, and all at once, Max was sorry he'd asked. The atmosphere had shifted. This was not just a conversation. This was a rebellion. This was something that Max wanted nothing to do with.

"Because it doesn't seem like they are. It seems like they're scared and angry." Davis glanced over his shoulder, then back to Max's face. "But none of them will leave."

"How do you know?"

The lieutenant sighed. "It's my job, Max. The army's opened a military base south of here. Just outside of Norfolk. We've got vehicles to move populations. We have resources. And the boys here are definitely interested. But they won't leave."

Max worked his way around this. Landed on the only thing that mattered to him.

"You've got a military base?"

Davis flashed a smile. "Most of our housing blocks have electricity."

"*Electricity?*"

"Not all of the engineers died in the war. We've got ways to make power. Wind and solar. Most of the farms out there were running on their own grids anyway. It's local, and there isn't a lot as far as heating and cooling go, but it's electricity."

And then, finally, other things started to register.

"You've been walking around, telling people about your electricity and your food and your cars, and nobody wants to *come*?"

The lieutenant just looked at him.

It was perhaps because Max was Pilot's son that it took him so long to realize it.

"You think my father is holding them hostage?"

"No," Davis said hastily. His eyes searched Max's face. He sighed. "Yes."

Max bridled. "Well you're wrong. It's all voluntary."

"That's what they keep telling me," Davis replied, but he kept looking at Max. Like he was saying something else.

"Well, that's it then."

The lieutenant got to his feet. "I guess it is."

Max watched him turn away. He watched him pause in the doorway.

"Thanks for talking to me, anyway."

Pilot's son said nothing to that.

***

"God, I hate it here," Lila said, interrupting Max for the second time from his work in Pilot's office.

He groaned, thinking of Lieutenant Davis. "No kidding."

"Everywhere I go, people are looking at me."

Lila was a blur of fury and fire. She didn't pace, exactly, but she didn't stop moving. First her hands went through her hair, then to the back of the chair, gripping tightly, then smoothing the cloth of her pants.

"I don't even say anything. I just walk down the hall, and they're talking. At first I thought it was because I was with Pilot, but he went off to meet his Council or whatever, and they still stare. And when they aren't staring, they're yelling at me. Do you know how many times I've gotten some sort of glare and then heard some guy say how he'd rip me apart if I ever went back into the arena? It's so—*infuriating*. If they had any idea what I could do-"

Suddenly she stopped. Her grey eyes flickered to Max's face, as if seeing him for the first time, and she abruptly twirled around. She pulled her hair out of her face. The sharp angles of her cheeks were echoed by her shadow, made bigger than life by the strange lighting in Pilot's office.

Her voice was quieter. "You should have heard what they said, Max. About me."

Max froze.

"What do you mean?"

Lila examined her shadow. "It wasn't just about the arena. When they talked about me-" She stopped. Exhaled. "You know, it wasn't just about what they would do to me in a fight."

Oh.

Max stood up. He wanted to pull her close to him, to hide her. She sometimes let him. She sometimes didn't.

And he couldn't figure out if this was one of those times.

How often could you hurt a girl, before she finally broke down and *destroyed* you?

"I'm sorry," Lila said suddenly. Her back was still to him. "I didn't mean to make you uncomfortable."

This was so far from what Max was thinking that it took him a second to think of what to say.

"Do you think they'll actually-"

"No. They wouldn't dare."

Of course they wouldn't. She was Pilot's hero.

It didn't seem like enough.

"Lila-"

"You know what," she interrupted, turning back to face him. "I don't want to talk about this anymore. It's fine."

Her expression was stone.

Max shrugged.

"Your turn," Lila prompted.

Max raised his eyebrows and Lila crossed the room, gesturing to the door. "When I came in, you were pissed about something. What's going on?"

"I'm not *mad,* exactly."

Lila picked up the forms Max had been filing and started reorganizing them. She leaned around him, their arms touching, to write a new address as his pick-up location. "It'll be easier if you avoid the northern overpass. People don't like walking that trek because of the looters."

Max nodded.

"So, if you aren't mad, what are you?"

He grabbed a handful of sheets back from her and laid them out on the table. With his pinkie, Max outlined a new route along the map. He nudged Lila, looking for confirmation, and she spared it a careful search before nodding.

“Better,” she said.

Max dropped the whole mess, settled back into his seat, and scrubbed his face with both hands. “It’s Lieutenant Davis.”

Lila was standing at his elbow, still working with the papers. “You saw him again?”

“Just now. Did you know there’s a settlement south of here?” Max glowered. “It’s not like Antipas’ Cleveland thing, either. Davis says it’s an actual city. Electricity. Running water. The whole nine yards.”

“Like a military thing?”

Max sighed. “There’s a whole goddamned world out there, and my father doesn’t tell me anything at all.”

“And Davis is doing what? Recruiting?”

Max shrugged.

He felt her stiffen. “Hard thing to manage in a place like this.”

Max couldn’t tell if that was supposed to be a question or not. He glanced sidelong at Lila, but she wasn’t looking at him. Her eyes were on the door, body tense, expression utterly unreadable.

“Tell me what you’re thinking.”

Lila flinched. When she looked at him, her face was masked. “Nothing. Did he get many volunteers?”

Max narrowed his eyes. “No, no one. I guess they don’t want to go.”

He didn’t repeat what Davis had said, about being scared.

But Lila must have known.

Her colorless eyes turned on him, intrusive and calculating. “Maybe. Or maybe it was something else.”

It was like they were having a conversation. Except they weren’t talking.

Lila was just changing, in front of him, into someone Max didn’t entirely recognize.

She gave him a sharp, distracted smile, and shook her head. “I’ve got to go. I’ll be a few hours.”

Something was sliding, slipping, rushing right out of control.

Max wanted to tell her not to go. He wanted to stop her from racing off whatever cliff they were standing at the edge of. But he had no idea what cataclysm they were facing.

He wasn’t even sure how’d they come to be standing there.

And then Lila was gone, and it didn’t really matter anyway.

Chapter 21

She woke him in the middle of the night with her hand over his mouth, whispering in his ear.

"Don't make too much noise," she said. "You'll wake your father."

Max sat up. He'd fallen asleep on the couch in the office. Pilot was in the adjoining room, on a makeshift bed. Lila hadn't been back since that afternoon.

"I need your help."

Max, still half asleep, crawled to his feet. He followed her into the hall, where it was cool and damp and dirty. The chill under his skin woke him more completely.

He rubbed his arms. "What's going on?"

Lila didn't say anything. She headed for the archway beyond Entrance C and Max reached out to stop her. She felt him and spun, pulling away from his touch. They stood facing each other, Max looking at Lila. She was looking at the floor. The silence between them was a wall.

Then she raised her eyes to his face, all fire and glass, and Max's heart dropped like a stone.

"There's something I have to tell you, after this is over," Lila said quietly. "Something that you won't like."

Max could have cried.

He wasn't even surprised.

And the worst part was that he'd known. He'd known and he'd done nothing. *Nothing*. He'd been foolish enough—loved her enough—to let it go and hope that her secrets wouldn't destroy them both.

Max sighed. "Fine. What do you need me to do now?"

For a second, Lila looked sorry. But then she smiled.

"Thank you."

***

It was easy. All Lila needed was the key to the box office where Pilot kept the rations. Most of them were stored away in the back room, which was locked by a second key for good measure. But both were kept in the same drawer in Pilot's desk.

Max had spent all day at that desk. He knew.

Lila took the keys and went to the box office. She was quiet, absolutely, and it silenced Max in her wake. He just followed her. When she opened the box office door, he didn't ask questions. He didn't even ask questions when several boys—all of which he recognized as Coliseum fighters—appeared to help her carry boxes of rations out.

It did occur to him, though, that all of these boys were new to the Coliseum. Most had only been in a fight or two. All looked worse for the wear.

Pilot had told him that all the fighters volunteered. He'd told him that living in the Coliseum was better than living on the streets. Infinitely better. So much better, in fact, that no one—not a single fighter—had ever left the Coliseum.

How was it that Max had never thought to ask why?

Two of the boys started ripping boxes open. They packed the supplies into backpacks. Six in total. One for each member of the group.

Max watched. He looked at Lila, her eyes bright and feral in the darkness.

"It's not against the rules to leave," he said quietly.

She smiled thinly. "But no one ever does."

"Are we stealing these?"

Lila shot him a look that he didn't quite understand, but she didn't have a chance to reply. Her eyes refocused behind him and he turned.

Lieutenant Davis emerged from the corridor.

"Fancy meeting you here," Davis said, grinning.

Max blinked. "What the hell is going on?"

Davis barked a laugh, glancing at Lila. "Didn't you tell the boy what you were getting him into?"

Lila didn't answer. She probably hadn't heard. Already on her knees next to one of the boys, she was carefully tearing apart packaging and reassembling them, separating the necessities—taking what they would need to survive.

"Lila cornered me a couple of hours ago with this half-concocted, crazy idea about stealing winner's rations," Davis explained. He leaned low so that his voice would not carry.

Max watched the boys pack up supplies as Davis continued, quietly, at his side. "She had a theory, see, that if someone could get their hands on the basic necessities, the boys would leap at the chance to get out of here."

Max looked at the boys around him. Not fighters, it turned out. Not really. They were just trying to survive.

Bound by a man that used food as a weapon.

How much more was there, that his father would never tell him?

Then there was a noise in the corridor and Max was spared from the terrible things he didn't really want to know.

Alec emerged from the darkness. Max recognized his slack, bruised jaw from the day he'd dragged Lila off the arena. Not that it mattered. He would have known Alec in an instant, on Lila's reaction alone.

Apology. Sorrow. Remorse. Scribbled all over her face. Why was it so easy to know what she was thinking sometimes?

And so impossible at others?

It was not lost on Alec, either. His expression matched hers—overflowing.

"My God," he whispered. "You didn't have to-"

"I'm sorry," she interrupted, low and quick and heartfelt. "For everything. And I'm so glad you…it was the only thing I could think of to do. To make it up to you."

Max had no idea what was going on.

But Alec laughed. "Lila. I forgave you the moment I saw the rations."

Max looked at the bag on Alec's shoulder. His eyes darted around to the other bags, the boxes half-empty on the ground.

"Wait. Those were your winner's rations?"

Lila gave a sly smile. "Well, mine from the hero fight and then the double rations that—that we were promised before that."

She'd been about to say Red. Max was sure that was the name on her lips. But he had no idea what she was talking about.

"Pilot owed you rations?"

Lila hesitated. "Like I said, that was before. He didn't expect it to be me who won."

Because Pilot's hero was never supposed to be Lila. It was supposed to be Red.

She didn't say *or did you forget what your father did?* but she didn't look at him either.

Max shut up after that.

The group emptied the boxes. Each boy took a backpack on his back and a weapon of some kind on his person. They walked through the dark corridor and out into the lobby of Entrance B.

Lila led them out.

At first, there was just the breath of fresh air. The moon was brighter outside, and it cascade light like a path into the countryside. Somewhere out there, Max knew, was Red's grave.

He didn't know what else was out there. Apparently, there might have been a whole world.

Lila turned. "This is where we go our separate ways."

Lieutenant Davis grinned. He shook her hand. "Thank you for everything," he said. He looked at Max, nodded. "We'll be about a day and a half on our own. The jeeps make the run along the I-80 pretty often. It's not far. So if you ever want to follow…"

Lila inclined her head. "Then we know where to find you."

Davis left it at that.

Several of the other boys thanked Lila, each in a shy, non-confrontational way. They only nodded in Max's direction.

And then it was just Alec, still in the shadow of the Coliseum, expression a mess of sadness and urgency.

He stepped up to Lila, voice low. "Come with us."

Max almost missed the flicker of her eyes. But there was no mistaking it. She didn't look at Alec. She looked at him.

"I can't," she said. Then her eyes were back on Alec.

They had a whole conversation just in that glance, and Max understood none of it. Then Alec sighed.

He shouldered his bag. "I'll see you around."

Lila smiled affectionately.

Before Alec joined his group, he tossed a sidelong glance at Max. "Take care of her," he said.

Max just nodded.

With a grunt, Alec turned away from them. He didn't look back again.

Lila kept her eyes on the distance, but when Max came up behind her, she reached back and squeezed his hand. They watched, together, as the small party picked their way up the hill. Neither of them said anything.

Lila waited until she couldn't even see their shadows against the horizon before she pulled away. When she turned around, her too bright eyes were trained on the ground.

The smile she gave him was an apology.

“I’m going back into the arena,” she said.

And then she left him in the darkness, alone, to choke on her words.

Chapter 22

Checkmate.

It was the only thing he could think, as he watched Lila walk away.

In his head, he was screaming. She was going back. *She was going back*? Lila, the girl with the alien eyes and the savage sadness, the girl he'd brought back to life, was going back to the Coliseum. She was going to be the hero. His father's hero. *Pilot's.*

Max had lost her. It was unthinkable and impossible and it roared and tumbled and warred and hammered inside his head, until there was just noise. Everywhere.

It was all slipping away.

And she was *leaving* him.

But all that came out was, "Why?"

Lila didn't stop. She was already gone.

And oh God, how it hurt his heart.

***

In the morning, Pilot explained to Max that they were going to stay at the Coliseum for the foreseeable future. Lila was going to sleep in the spare bedroom and Max was going to stay in one of the empty bunks in the fighters' dorm. He said that things were going to change. Max was expected to devote all his energies to getting to know the mechanics of Pilot's New Chicago. He was supposed to get to know the fighters, the governors, the movers and shakers in the new world.

In other words, Max was not going to be spending much time with Pilot's hero anymore. The Coliseum would groom her, and Pilot would groom Max. It was time. For both of them.

Lila, for her part, was not there to give her opinion one way or the other.

Pilot said other things too, of course. He mentioned a new wardrobe for Max, complete with new shirts and a bright, shiny watch that made Max feel itchy and overexposed. He even said something about the missing rations.

"I'm afraid we'll have to be even more careful about our supplies. There was an unfortunate accident. Some people just don't appreciate what they've been given."

Max was pretty sure that Pilot knew what he'd done.

For some reason, that made Max less nervous. Pilot knew everything. It was over. He'd been caught red-handed, so that was that. It made it even easier to shed that uncomfortable burden—the lingering feeling that there was something he had to do. For Lila.

Because no one else would.

Obviously, he'd been wrong. Every day since he'd met her, Max had been trying to make up for the things his father had done. Max had always thought that he had to make up for the things that Pilot had done.

But he didn't. Because Lila didn't need his help. She didn't *want* his help. She wanted to be whatever Pilot made her.

Of course, Pilot had plans for his son too.

Lila had just thrown in her white flag. Why shouldn't Max?

He didn't even flinch when Pilot rested a heavy hand on his shoulder.

Chapter 23

Lila found Max at the box office, resorting the rations that they'd left behind. He was sitting cross-legged on the floor across from another boy who was about his age with lemon-colored eyes. They were talking about Edgar Allan Poe, and they did not see her.

"I must have finished the *House of Usher* like a day before that fight, you know?" the other boy was saying. "And I haven't been able to look at it the same."

Max used both hands to drag another box to him, pulling out canned carrots one after another. "So you remember it? The day he…"

"Died?" the other boy finished. Casually.

Lila felt lightheaded.

"Everyone around here does," he went on. "It was a big surprise, you know? I mean, it was Red. The guy was practically a god. But we all saw—or heard, at least—

what happened in the arena. And at first-" The boy hedged. "Well, you know. Nobody was really sure why he'd saved her."

"You mean Lila."

As if it needed to be said. As if Lila really needed to hear her name, laid bare next to his. As if she could take it.

The boy nodded. "Yeah, the girl. At first, we were all a little unconvinced—and I guess some of the guys still are—but you just have to look at her to know. She must be lethal in a fight."

"Come on, Peter, you can tell that just by looking?"

Lila hated how gently Max said it.

She hated even more that the other boy—Peter—laughed. "Can't you? God, it's even in the way she walks. I've never seen anyone more alert. And I heard that Red actually trained her. Let me tell you, she's not a girl I'd want to cross, and I've been in the arena for almost six months."

Is that what Red had done, when he'd run drill after drill in the hot afternoons? Had he made her *lethal*?

Max's voice was benevolent. "She's going back into the Coliseum."

"Everybody knows. Her name's on the list for the fight this weekend."

This time there was something in his voice. Lila could hear it, just under the surface—how much she'd hurt him. "That soon?" he asked.

"Not soon enough," Peter said. "You wouldn't believe how crazy the fighters are getting. Practically gnawing at the bit to see what she's made of."

Max wrote something on the clipboard. He didn't look up. "I wonder if the guy she's supposed to fight is scared."

Peter snorted.

"Saul? Hardly." His face screwed up, examining Max's downturned head. "You know the girl pretty well though, right? What kind of fight are we in for? Is she scared?"

Yes.

Max curled his fingers into a fist in his lap absentmindedly. He sighed. "I don't know," he said.

Yes, you do. You know me.

***

The word spread. By the time the morning of her fight arrived, there was what looked to be an entire nation piled into the bleachers. The stadium was nearly half full—a record high, one unreached since before the war.

Pilot asked, in his reasonable, neutral voice, if Lila wanted company while she waited.

She'd only looked up at him, darkly, from her seat on the couch.

Pointing to a small pile of clothes on the desk, he said, "That's what you'll wear in the arena. Be ready in an hour."

Then he was gone.

The clothes turned out to be a pair of white gauchos and an off-white tank top that was just a little bit small around her hips. There were no shoes, of course. Lila would fight barefoot.

It was the only way she knew how.

Pilot hadn't said anything about her hair, so Lila left it down. She washed her face with one of the small, pre-packaged wet napkins that Pilot had left. Then she curled up on the broken futon in his office, knees pulled up to her chin, and waited.

Max never came, of course. Lila convinced herself that she was glad that he didn't. She'd seen the look on his face—then and every time she'd closed her eyes since—and she did not want to see it ever again. That night, after Alec left, Max had held her hand and held her together, like always. He'd saved her. And she had betrayed him.

He knew it. She knew it.

So of course Max never appeared.

Why did he have to be your son?

But he was. And she would not hurt him.

Pilot came back and smiled his careful smile when he saw her.

"You look like a hero," he said.

Lila felt like nothing.

***

The day was cloudy. It wasn't a good afternoon for a fight. It wasn't the right moment to introduce a hero.

But the crowd had gathered—so big that Lila could hear them, grumbling, growing, even from within the tunnel where she waited—and Pilot would not have been the man he was if he could not make the most of it.

"Ladies and gentleman, are you ready for the fight of your lives?"

All that time, all those fights, and this was the first round that Pilot had ever been the one to say those words. To make it his.

The mob roared.

"Out of the east gate, Saul Slater!"

Lila closed her eyes. The flood of sound rolled over her, impossible and loud, and then it was hushed. Saul had made his entrance. The crowd was excited.

But that was nothing compared to how much they wanted to see the hero.

Pilot carried her name like a prayer over the loudspeaker. "The girl you've all been waiting for, Lila Sinclair. The hero of our Coliseum."

It was like an earthquake. There was so much sound that the stadium literally shook.

Lila thought, suddenly, that she couldn't do it. She couldn't walk into that arena and face all those people. It was *too much*—too much sound, too much light, too much pressure—and it would bury her. Pure and simple.

But where else was there to go?

So Lila pretended she was fearless. Limitless.

She pretended she was Red.

And she stepped into the light.

***

The arena wasn't like the last time.

For one thing, there was the dust. It hadn't been so windy before, and Lila wasn't quite prepared for it. Strands of her hair got caught against her lips, collecting crystals of dirt that made the air feel clouded and heavy. In the sudden silence after her introduction, Lila could practically hear the dust rolling along the arena floor. It sounded like a desert.

Across the field, Saul stood. He was watching her, taller than she expected. His eyes were narrowed in the wind. Lila let her hair cascade across her vision. She raised her face to Saul. For a second, they just looked at each other. He wasn't close enough for her to see the expression on his face, but she could tell by the way he was standing that Saul wasn't sure. She was a girl, sure, but—

Well, he'd heard what Pilot said.

The girl they'd all been waiting for.

She smiled at him. A devil's smile.

Someone in the crowd screamed and the call was taken up, moving like a wave across the stadium. Saul burst into action. He ran the length of the arena—no hesitation, no plan, just a straightforward sprint—to meet Lila where she stood.

She didn't move.

It wasn't like they had weapons. He was going to have to meet her eventually.

Then she was just outside of his grasp, but he reached anyway. Lila took a half step backwards, cocking her head. The red in her hair must have caught the sun, because she saw his eyes dilate—

what was it with men that made lust so much a part of the fight?

—and he misjudged his center of gravity. It wasn't by much.

But when he leaned forward, tucked low to swing at her solar plexus, Lila spun and hit his left shoulder with her elbow. Saul, already off balance, stumbled.

He fumbled his way through a sort of grapevine maneuver with his feet and then he was back, using the full force of his body to hit Lila square across the jaw. Or it would have, if she'd still been standing there.

Saul had been in the arena eleven times. He'd lived in the Coliseum for almost eight months. Undefeated. But he'd never fought a girl before, at least not like this.

He had no idea how fast she could be.

When he threw his arm into his second punch, Lila ducked and twirled. She slammed him in his unprotected sternum, almost dislocating her own shoulder.

Saul crumbled. Lila used his body to push herself past him, then behind him, and caught his chin firmly in one hand as he fell.

He must have felt her fingers bracing his right shoulder. He must have known that she could have killed him then.

She didn't.

This was the fight that was supposed to make her career. Pilot would expect a show.

Lila let her hand slide down his back, met the place where her knee served as a crutch to keep him from falling backwards, and then yanked him towards her. She broke a rib and dislocated his shoulder at the same time. When she released him and he slumped forward, scrambling out of reach on hands-and-knees, Lila wondered if Saul understood what had just happened.

Probably he wasn't really thinking about it, considering the rib and the shoulder.

But then he got to his feet. He looked at her and Lila knew that he *did* understand. The fight was hers. It was over when she said it was.

There was a certain amount of power in that.

Lila circled.

Saul kept his eyes on her. He didn't move.

Another rustle of wind kicked up the dust. The mob mimicked the sound, rolling a low, anxious groan around the stadium. Every noise they made was amplified in the arena. It echoed and grew, transforming into something that was alive. Squirming. It itched under Lila's skin.

Was this how Red had felt?

Was she alive enough now?

Lila pounced.

Saul reacted, tumbling on his weak shoulder and then turning wildly to face her again. His face was burning. Lila measured his swing and decided at the last minute to take it, absorbing the punch in her gut—lower than Saul had intended—so that she could grab his head with both her hands.

It was like the crowd was two steps behind.

They saw her get hit. She heard them cry.

Then the aching silence.

It must have been the look on Saul's face that clued them in. Because she already had his head in her hands by then. It was over.

The mob, for some reason, didn't realize it until they saw it in Saul's eyes.

They screamed—both in fear and in thrill—and it was crucial seconds too late.

Lila had already yanked his head down. Saul was dead. She never even heard his neck snap. But she knew, because at first he'd fought her.

He wasn't fighting anymore.

She looked at the ground. The mob looked at her. In the silence, the wind picked up again. Lila raised her face to the crowded stadium.

And the mob stood, crying, and worshiped.

Lila was not a hero. She was a god.

***

It had been complicated before.

There'd been the problem of love. Lila had loved her mother. Even after she was sold and Pilot locked her up in the box. She'd loved Red. Even after he'd made all his beautiful promises and kept her safe in the darkness, and then left her. She'd loved him even after they killed him. And she loved Max. Even though he was Pilot's son. Even though he'd been too late.

So much that could hurt her.

She used the wet wipes to scrub her hands clean.

Life had been so complicated before. Now, finally, it was simple again.

Chapter 24

One by one, the dominos fell.

Max was sitting on floor in his father's office, pouring over the reports from Hyde Park, when Peter ran up.

His face was flush. "The governors sent me for Pilot. Something's happened."

Max thinned his lips. "The governors are here?"

"I guess," Peter said. He wet his lips, bright eyes eager. "It's not just the governors. All the districts' councils are here, the secretaries. Everyone. I've never seen anything like it. You should hear them. Something—something big must have happened."

"Did you-"

"Thank you," Pilot interrupted.

Both Max and Peter's heads jerked up. Pilot nodded. "You can go."

"Sorry," Peter replied. He barely looked at Max as he hurried away.

"What is it?" Max asked, getting to his feet. His father was already sweeping past him, into the hallway and towards the stairs. "Where are we going?"

Pilot did not smile. But his lips were upturned and his eyes bright. Everything about him was animal. Feral.

"We're going to meet the Council. An emergency meeting was just called. Jonathan Haze is dead."

***

They elected Pilot as the new leader of the Chicago Council by a unanimous vote. Since Jonathan Haze's daughter was dead and his son by all accounts missing, Pilot got the Yard too. It would be assumed into his duties as governor of the Coliseum.

His first decision as acting president was to reduce general resources to allocate more to the Coliseum. His second was to declare his intentions to expand.

"It's time to put all of our efforts where the real profit is riding. We have the opportunity here to make Chicago the beginning of a new age. We were lucky enough not only to have the idea first, but to have the resources to make it happen, and we don't want to squander that. The only reasonable thing to do is to encourage more people to join the Coliseum."

One of the governors looked uncomfortable. "We barely have the resources to feed and clothe the fighters as it is. How will we pay for new recruits?"

But he was in the minority. Several of the others, governors and councilors alike, actually laughed.

"I take it you didn't see the fight yesterday."

The governor shook his head. Max swallowed hard, trying to subdue the sick feeling in his stomach. He hadn't watched the fight, of course, but he'd seen the lines at the gate.

Pilot had told him there'd been thousands.

Max recognized the governor from Hyde Park. "Do you think she'll draw in the same size crowd every time?"

Another, older man shook his head. “Won’t matter,” he said quietly. Several heads turned his way. “Even if she only makes one more sale like that, we’d still be able to feed the fighters—hell, we’d be able to ration back out the donations into the surrounding communities—for at least a year. Maybe two.”

A surprised whistle.

“Cleveland doesn’t have a chance of catching up.”

The governor of Lincoln Park grinned toothily. “Antipas can take his copycat Coliseum and go straight back to hell.”

There was a chorus of dry laughter.

“That girl is going to save us.”

Of course.

Max didn’t have to see his father’s smug smile to know that this was what he’d meant, all those months ago, when he said that he was going to show Max a hero. It wasn’t that she could fight. It wasn’t even that she would survive.

It was simply that Pilot could sell her—the way he could sell anything—and she would buy him time.

She would buy him enough food to feed his new nation.

***

Peter wasn’t at the box office.

It made sorting the rations a lonely job.

Then Max felt her.

Lila passed him, just a shadow in the dark lobby, while he worked. She stopped. He could feel her strange, colorless eyes on him, but he refused to look up. He didn’t even look at her.

He just ducked his head, a dutiful son keeping to his work.

In his head, he willed her to say something. Anything.

But eventually Lila just went away.

Max waited until she was gone before he threw the box of expired fettuccine at the wall. It burst open with a satisfying thud, echoing in the tiny room. Masking whatever swallowed sob that had escaped Max's lips.

Chapter 25

There were benefits to being Pilot's hero. He rewarded Lila for her fight by taking them back to the house for a few days, where she wouldn't have to deal with the other Coliseum fighters.

"It'll be better for you now," he'd promised. "This is where you belong."

Max wouldn't even look at her the whole ride home.

Pilot, on the other hand, was as good as his word. He smiled tightly whenever Lila looked over at him. He kept his mouth closed and his opinions to himself. And he never asked Lila for anything.

But the best part was that he didn't care where she went anymore.

"I want to go over a schedule with you tonight," he said when she told him she was going out. Lila hesitated at the door, one hand on the frame. She didn't look back. "So don't be late—it's dangerous out there after dark anyway."

Lila kept her head down. "Okay."

It wasn't like she'd been planning to disappear. She just needed a little distance, space, air. *Something*.

"It won't take long," she said.

Pilot didn't say anything.

Neither did Max. He was standing at the top of the stairs, a ghost in his doorway. She could feel his eyes on her back. She could feel him hating her.

But Max's anger just made her tired now, so Lila left him there. She closed the door behind her.

She walked almost all the way back to the Coliseum, following Lake Shore Drive as it meandered in and out of view of the receding shoreline of Lake Michigan. She walked until her feet ached and her mind cleared and she forgot that she was running away.

Like always.

It didn't take long.

Life outside the Coliseum was largely the same as it had always been. Soldier Field could have been a relic, not even a single column damaged in the war—but whatever had been across the street was gone now. City blocks leveled, cars piled up, abandoned, the skyline crumbling. Even the road that trekked towards the lakeshore was in disrepair, shattered asphalt and dirt where there'd once been street lamps and trees and park benches. Something *more*.

But it was not all gone.

Lila followed the fork in the road until she came to the remains of the Red Cross tents. They'd expanded out of the stadium after it became apparent that the evacuation center would have to be moved. Too many wounded, no national support in sight. The tents out here still stood, empty of supplies. There was a thin layer of snow on the ground, settling on the abandoned tent poles and unstable roofing. A ghostly reminder of what had once been.

Beyond that was the Field Museum.

Or at least, beyond that should have been the Field Museum. Lila walked instead past a half-standing lot of renovated houses. The museum itself was completely destroyed, except for the rectangular entryway. At the end of the street—if that's what it could be called—the aquarium had been transformed.

It might have been housing.

It seemed like it was actually some sort of church.

But there were people there. Several dozen, all collected under the shaded atrium. Lila stuffed her hands into the pockets of her coat, head ducked down, and stepped carefully inside.

The sound amplified immediately. Men, women, and children were all talking at once. They stood at what looked like booths—some made of broken planks from houses, some actual folding tables—and passed goods between them. They laughed. They argued. They bartered.

It was a *market*.

Now, Lila had lived in post-war Chicago. She'd been there when the food was rationed and the panic begun. She was there when the electricity went out and never came back on. She'd seen them board up the windows of the shops. She remembered the city as it had been in those first months—desperate, afraid, and uncooperative.

But a long year had passed since then.

Things had changed.

The market was booming. Whole families had come to see what they could get their hands on. The women congregated at empty tables, swapping food and stories. Across the room, most of the men did the same. Shy smiles flickered between them. Friends waved. And always, between the adult efficiencies, the young voices rose up.

The noise, alone, was astounding.

But it was the idea of family that stopped Lila cold. She'd almost forgotten what the word meant.

"Can I do something for you, sweetheart?" a woman asked. She was squatting on what appeared to be a tablecloth that she'd spread out like a blanket on the floor. Splayed in front of her was a slew of second-hand clothing. There were hats, gloves, coats, and even comforters, carefully folded and set aside.

"I-"

A high pitched scream interrupted Lila. She looked up, but none of the kids looked particularly upset. Two of the older boys and one of the girls were sitting cross-legged in the center of the marketplace, leaning over some kind of board game that held their full attention. Others, younger, raced around them. Chaotic. Frantic.

Happy.

Lila cleared her throat. "I didn't know anyone was over here."

The woman smiled toothily. "Where you from, dear?"

"Kenwood," Lila said automatically. It was only after she said it that Lila realized she didn't want to tell them she lived at the Coliseum.

Not that it meant anything.

The woman was nodding, "I know the place. You've heard of the fights then, at Soldier Field?"

Lila acknowledged that she did know the place. She didn't elaborate.

"Well, to be honest, most of our business comes from that," the woman explained. She gestured to the others. "We all lived downtown, before the war, and afterwards, there wasn't enough left standing to get by. If that Coliseum hadn't gotten started, we'd probably have gone our separate ways. But it turns out that the people that go to see the fights are required to bring certain items, and if we get our hands on them, we can trade for things we can't get our hands on. You know—coats and gloves for the winter, paper to burn in the fireplaces—there are so many things in other parts of the country that they don't need. And we desperately do."

"Not giving your sales pitch again, are you?" a man interrupted.

The woman looked up and smiled at him. "This is my husband, Ralph." She glowered. "And no, I wasn't pitching anything. You can see that the girl doesn't have much. Besides-"

Here she turned back to Lila.

"-you weren't planning on trying to get in to see a fight any time soon, were you?"

Both husband and wife chuckled at that. Lila ducked her head, feeling her face flush. She wasn't sure what to make of this satisfied, easy banter. Should she have been offended?

Should she be *ashamed*?

The man sighed. “To be honest, I wouldn’t mind a bit of that cotton you’ve got. That shirt looks almost new.”

Lila’s fingers strayed to the hem of her white T-shirt. It *was* new. Pilot had gifted a whole new wardrobe to both her and Max. Hers was white shirts and jackets, yoga pants. Max’s was suits. Jackets. Vests. Too hot even for winter in New Chicago and much too well-dressed for the end of the world.

She hadn’t seen much of Max himself, though. It was probably for the better. He’d look small, buried in all those clothes.

Ralph was still looking at her, so Lila shrugged.

He grinned. “You have no idea what my son would give to have a nice clean shirt like that.”

“Your son?”

Ralph gestured absently towards the boys pouring over the board game. “He’s over there. Turning ten next week and hell if I know what I’m going to get him.”

“Don’t say that,” the woman chided. She was pressing a glove flat between her fingers. “He’ll be glad for the coat we picked out for him.”

Lila wondered at the ten-year-old boy that would be happy with a coat for his birthday.

Especially a coat picked out of a pile of coats that his mother sold for their living.

She didn’t have to think of anything to say, though, because another woman waved, walking carefully over with one hand on her belly—steadying.

“I don’t want to interrupt, but I thought I saw a red scarf in your pile.”

Ralph’s wife chuckled. “I thought of you the moment I saw it. Tell me you’ve got a couple jars of that jam left. Ralph won’t leave me alone if we go another month without something that isn’t peanut butter to spread on everything.”

The other woman laughed.

The sound made Lila want to laugh too. It was that beautiful.

She felt a tug on her jeans and moved, swiftly, just out of reach. There was a surprised gasp.

“Sorry,” a little voice said.

It was a girl, no more than five, with round hazel eyes and a big, frightened 'o'-shape on her lips. She giggled, her surprise melting into a shy smile.

"You have really pretty hair."

Lila's eyebrows furrowed. "Thank you."

The girl rolled onto the balls of her feet and clasped her hands behind her back. "I want to make my hair long like that, but mommy says it's too much shampoo. So she makes me cut it like this."

One little hand tugged at a short curl. "See."

"That's too bad. Your hair would be pretty long."

The girl grinned. This time, when she reached out and intertwined their fingers, Lila didn't pull away.

"I saw you talking to Ralphy's mommy and daddy. Did they give you this belt? I like it. It's pretty like you."

Lila squeezed the girl's hand. "What's your name?"

"Mia."

"Do you want my belt, Mia?"

The girl squealed, rounding on Lila with doe-eyes. "Really? Are you sure? Mommy says it's not good to give presents."

Of course it wasn't. Only a fool gave what little they had away.

"I don't need it."

Mia grabbed Lila's other hand, forming a circle of their arms, and leaned back. "Then why do you have it?"

That emotion stirred again, making Lila burn. But it wasn't shame yet.

It wasn't shame until after she'd tugged the belt out from its loops and wrapped it up in her palm. Mia snatched it from her hand, professing her love and thanks, and stretching it out again to look at the pattern.

Lila was surprised by the veracity of Mia's fingers. She was disarmed by the earnestness of her thanks. It felt good to be wanted. It felt good to be needed. Loved.

For one, beautiful moment, simple was good. It was gentle and earnest and loving.

Then, in the next, Mia's arm was ripped back. The girl stumbled several steps, dropping the belt. She cried out.

But the woman who'd grabbed her was louder. "What do you think you're doing?"

"The girl with the pretty red hair said-"

"Didn't I tell you about talking to strangers?" her mother interrupted. She gripped Mia firmly on the shoulders, pulling her flush against her legs. The little girl was crying now. "You don't take things-"

"It's okay," Lila said quietly. "I gave it to her."

And then the woman's eyes flickered up to her, full of surprise and concern and—

And hatred?

Fear?

"I am so sorry. I had no idea she was over here, making a mess of everything. And I'm sure she interrupted you. Mia has no idea when she's being a pest. She didn't mean any harm. Little girls will do what they will, no matter what you tell them."

Lila wrapped her arms around herself.

The woman's grip tightened on her daughter. "It's an honor, of course, to see Pilot's hero here-"

Pilot's hero.

The words fell like a brick.

"-and if there is anything I can do for you, please don't hesitate."

Mia started to say something, but her mother shoved her quickly shoved her away. "Go run along. Let the adults talk."

Disappointment was scribbled on Mia's face, but she did as she was told. Lila watched her go. Then she turned to the girl's mother, intending to explain that it was all a mistake. Mia could have her belt.

The look on the woman's face stopped her dead.

Relief. *Relief.*

Lila thought, suddenly, that they could have her whole goddamned wardrobe.

If only this woman would take it back.

And Lila wouldn't have to feel so ashamed.

Chapter 26

Max had not forgiven Lila. He found her in her room, sitting on her knees, piling object after object into bags. She was nearly surrounded by them—trash bags, duffel bags, it didn't seem to matter—and she filled each of them. He stood in the doorway, watching her, and as the minutes passed, Lila only got more frenzied.

She must have heard him. She must have known he was standing there.

But she didn't care. She pulled a cup of pens off the desk and dumped them in a bag. She pulled out the ripped piece of cloth she'd been using to tie back her hair. When the razor straight strands cascaded down around her face, she started.

Then, abruptly, she turned to him.

"What do you want, Max?"

Raging. Burning.

He'd almost forgotten what it looked like, when Lila was on fire.

His voice was quiet, frightened. "What are you doing?"

Her too-bright eyes searched the room, considering. She shoved a bag away from her, grabbed another. "I'm giving it away. All of it. I don't want any of this stuff. I don't *want* it."

A beat of silence.

And Max could swear she was almost crying.

But her voice was steady. She said it again, more quietly this time, not looking at him. "I don't want it."

Max didn't stop to think.

He went back to his room and dragged his suitcase across the hall. He rolled it to her feet and settled down beside her. He felt her watching him as he grabbed a suit jacket from his suitcase and folded it carefully on top of her pile. Then he looked at her.

Lila smiled.

Together, they ravaged everything they owned—everything they had that they didn't want, everything they'd been given that they didn't need, everything that had been forced upon them that they hated –and they carried it away.

Max followed Lila down a haphazard road after dark.They didn't say anything, because Max hadn't forgiven her for the things she'd done, but he followed her anyway.

Even after she turned and said, "Pilot won't like it, you know."

He met her alien, burning eyes and shrugged.

"I don't care."

A split-second's smile. "Me either."

They left the clothes and books and pens and shoes on the front steps of the old aquarium. Max didn't ask. He didn't want to know.

It was enough to feel as light as he did walking home again—in the dark, empty-handed.

***

They hesitated at the bottom of the stairs outside the house. The moonlight struck the pale sheen on the paint oddly and it seemed to glow. Even the dark could not shadow the light pouring out onto the porch from the thin space beneath the front door. The lantern was still burning on the kitchen table, which meant Pilot was waiting for them.

Lila didn't look at Max. Her expression was lost in the dark, but Max could feel her fading at the foot of his father's house. Her hair cut across her face in strands, casting blood-colored shadows across her face.

"What are you going to say to him?" Max asked.

Lila's colorless eyes flickered to his face, then away. "Nothing."

Nothing.

Max exhaled. He waited for her to say something else—*anything* else—but she didn't. She just stood there.

Shutting him out.

He wrapped his empty arms around himself. "So that's all?" His voice broke over the last word. He wished it hadn't.

Lila looked at him. "What?"

"Nothing? Really? Is that all I get?" Max spread his hands out in the dark, palms up. He wasn't sure if he was reaching out or pushing her away, but his voice was rising and something in his tone was turning from hurt to fury. "What happened to you, Lila? I thought we were friends."

"Max-"

"It's fine," he cut her off.

The silence rang out between them.

Max turned away, sweeping past Lila up the stairs to the door. "*Nothing* is more than enough."

It was such a lie that Max could have laughed when the words finally came out.

Or cry.

Lila didn't fight him. She didn't say anything at all. Max went into the house and slammed the door shut behind him.

His father was sitting at the kitchen table and their eyes met in the sudden light. Max blinked.

Pilot didn't say anything either.

So Max walked passed him to the stairs. "If you want to talk to her," he said over his shoulder, "You'd better do it in the study."

His father made a noise—surprised, angry, maybe even hurt. Max didn't care. He spun around, catching himself on the banister, and his voice came out low and wrecked.

"I don't want to hear anything that either of you have to say."

Pilot closed his eyes.

The front door opened and Lila came in, her features a series of contrasts. The red of her hair, the sheer whites of her eyes, the ashen shade of her skin. She looked sad and sick and haunted. And beautiful. Always beautiful.

A tragedy.

She found Max with her eyes before she'd even stepped inside.

He shook his head, turned, and ran up the stairs.

Their voices rose from below him. "Is this what you consider acceptable behavior for a hero?" Pilot said quietly. They hadn't gone to the study.

Max didn't close his door. He sat, curled up with his back against the wall, just out of sight.

He heard Lila sigh. "I didn't think being the hero amounted to much more than killing people in the arena."

Pilot barked a laugh.

"You and I both know that's bullshit." Pilot's voice hardened. "And you didn't have to bring my son into it."

Max rubbed his face with his hands. On the other side of the door, Lila turned to stone. He could hear it in her voice.

"Is there something in particular you needed from me?"

A clock counted off the seconds. Then Pilot sighed.

"There's going to be a ceremony tomorrow afternoon. You'll go. It's a celebration of New Chicago, a dedication ceremony of sorts."

"They're dedicating the city to me?"

Pilot chuckled dryly. "*I'm* dedicating the city to you, Lila. And I'll need you to be on your best behavior."

There was a moment of silence.

"Why?" Lila asked.

Between the banister rods along the landing, Max could only see his father's back, but Pilot's shoulders stiffened. "The people need to remember who is supporting them."

Lila looked bewildered.

Pilot ran a hand through his hair, dropping unceremoniously back into his seat at the kitchen table. He looked tired.

Max hadn't noticed before.

"There's still trouble in the suburbs," Pilot confessed. "Your presence in the Coliseum boosted confidence, of course, but it isn't enough. Not with Antipas and his big plans for Cleveland. Did you know he's after Toledo? There was a colony there, and he just came in a declared himself their leader. He's inching closer to us every day, and the people aren't convinced that they will be safe. There's been some fighting on the outskirts of town. There've been disappearances and the citizen police don't have enough force to intervene. It'll be chaos soon. If we don't show them what the Coliseum is for, what New Chicago is for, right now, than we might lose control. All the progress we've made—gone."

"All the progress *you've* made," Lila corrected. But there wasn't much fight in her voice.

Pilot shrugged. "Progress is progress. And you'll feel the same as I do if fighting breaks out on the streets again. But this ceremony could prevent that. If we let them see you, up close and personal, it might make the difference. It might be enough."

There was another long, weighted silence.

"I just want peace, Lila. The same as you."

Max willed Lila to fight, to be brave and strong. He willed her to be like she was in the arena. *Invincible*. But it wasn't Lila who fought in the arena. That was the hero.

Lila was just a girl. A girl who was giving up.

"Fine," she said.

Max stayed where he was when Lila swept past him. They didn't look at each other. Maybe she thought he would be angry.

But he wasn't. He was just disappointed.

Lila had already hurt him as much as he would let her.

***

Did Pilot know that she was having another nightmare? Could he hear them?

Max shuffled in the dark, scrambling for the doorknob and then the bed, groping for Lila's hand. Her gasping whimper turned suddenly into a short scream.

Then she woke. She sat up, wrapping the blanket up around her shoulders. Her face was pale and sheen in the dark. She didn't look at him.

"You-you can go. I'm awake."

Max settled back onto his heels. At first he thought he wouldn't be able to find his voice, but he was wrong.

The darkness made it easy.

"Why are you doing this?" he asked.

Her hesitation could have meant anything.

Then, "What do you mean?"

Max hissed. "Don't. Don't be like that."

She turned away from him, but not before he saw her expression. Not that he knew what it meant.

She withdrew to the other side of the bed. "Go to sleep, Max."

But he couldn't.

"I thought you said you wouldn't give up," he accused quietly.

Lila flinched. He saw it.

"Is that what I'm doing?"

Max wished he could see her face. He wanted to make her look him in the eyes when she lied to him.

Again.

"How *could* you?" Because Max was hurting too. And he needed to know.

Nothing.

Max got up abruptly. "Fine. Whatever."

Then a choked sob.

For a second, he hated her. He hated her for making him care about her—when she didn't care about anything at all.

And then, in the next second, he felt sorry for her. Because she didn't care about anything at all. And she'd given so much.

For nothing.

"How could you go back into the arena after you saw Red die there?"

This time it wasn't malicious. It was just a question. The only question that Max had to know the answer to.

"How else am I supposed to survive it?"

Oh God, he needed to see her face.

Max whispered. "Did it work?"

Do you feel better?

Lila didn't respond. The silence screamed her answer.

They were both hurting.

Lila was always hurting. And Lila still hurting was killing Max.

"Then why?"

Lila sighed. She closed her eyes.

It was just darkness now. Max glared. "I mean it, Lila. Why go back? How could you let him win?"

Even as he said it, Max wasn't sure what he meant. Was that how it was—Lila losing was Pilot winning?

But then, finally, Lila reacted. She turned to him, her face flooded with light from the other room. Her skin was fire. Her expression was wild.

And something had shattered behind her eyes.

"My God, Max, because he's your *father*. What am I supposed to do?"

The words came tumbling out.

Then there was just silence.

A whispered, “Oh. Oh God. Max…”

But he was already gone.

Chapter 27

Pilot helped Lila get dressed for the dedication ceremony. She didn't know where he got the clothes from, but he handed her a clean white sweatshirt and a pair of clean jeans. White boots.

Where the hell did you find white boots in the new world?

They didn't talk about Max. He'd been quiet in the car that morning and after Pilot parked it in the lot behind Entrance C, Max had just climbed out and walked away.

"Are you coming to the ceremony?" Pilot had asked. His voice was softer than Lila expected.

Max didn't even turn around.

Neither of them had gone after him.

Lila put on the outfit that Pilot had waiting for her in the office. She brushed her hair. She stood quietly and went where Pilot told her too. When he told her that there was a fight at the Coliseum today, as the part of the opening celebration, she barely looked at him.

Twice as many new recruits had shown up in the past week, thanks to Lila's reappearance in the arena. Pilot was offering more rations to anyone willing to join the Coliseum's ranks. The food was incentive, of course, but Pilot was smiling his predator's smile when he told her.

"I think it's you, mostly," he said, gesturing for her to follow him around to the lobby in front of Entrance A. "There's nothing like a challenge to peak interest."

Lila's colorless eyes flickered to his face. Void.

Who was she to judge Pilot?

He only had to look at what she'd done to his son to know that she was a monster.

***

"Show time."

It was unreal. The moment Lila emerged into the sunlight, the crowd went wild. There were people everywhere. They lined the shattered asphalt street, throwing shredded pieces of paper and stray trash and glitter.

She didn't smile. She barely even looked at them. There were so many people, and they were all pressing closer and closer—trying to touch her, trying to talk to her, trying to share in whatever it was that made her so special—that Lila could barely hold herself together, let alone hold herself apart.

They cried. They screamed. They loved her. They coveted her. They wanted her. Whether it was her luck or her strength or her beauty or her title, they wanted her. Now. Everything. Always.

It was horrible, how much they wanted her.

But there was gentle love in the crowd too. As Pilot led her on, grinning and waving and touching hands and cheeks, Lila noticed the softer ones. They had wide eyes and hopeful expressions. Their fingers on her skin were almost a comfort, because they didn't seem to want anything. Instead, they wanted to give it.

They loved her.

They *loved* her.

Heaven knew why, but there were people in this crowd that believed that she was truly the hero. She could save them. They thought she *would* save them.

And they reached out their hands to kiss her, to touch her, to show that they loved her because she was going to take care of them.

Except that she wasn't. Not really. They didn't seem to understand that. She wasn't their hero.

She was Pilot's hero.

But Lila let them touch her anyway, because it was nice to be loved. Even if she didn't deserve it.

But there was a third kind of people there too.

Lila didn't realize what was happening right away. She saw Pilot paying special care to some. The younger boys. The stronger girls. The teenagers without parents. The healthy men. She saw the way they looked at her. She saw the way that Pilot looked at them.

But still she didn't get it.

Not until one of the boys grabbed her hand. Lila half turned, nodding to him.

He didn't let go. "I'm gonna be just like you," he gushed.

Lila hesitated.

The boy grinned, easy and in love. He shrugged bashfully. "I just wanted to tell you, look out for me. Pilot says that anyone can join, and I'm almost old enough. I'm gonna be a hero too."

"Just like me?"

The boy nodded urgently.

And Lila's stomach dropped.

She knelt down.

The crowd shuddered, leaning in to accommodate for the sudden change. She was their whole world, and she was going to speak to them. Silence rushed, unbidden, across the watching audience.

Even Pilot hesitated. He couldn't go on without her.

They all waited for Lila.

She touched the boy's chin. "You can't be like me," she said quietly.

The boy thinned his lips.

"Because no one else is allowed to be a hero."

"Why?" the boy asked petulantly. "I could be a better fighter than you."

It shouldn't have mattered. It shouldn't have mattered what this little boy—not even half her height, barely half her age—did. It shouldn't have mattered what he said, or dreamed, or wanted. Even if what he wanted was to be just like her. She shouldn't have cared.

But she did.

Too much.

It was all she had left.

Lila didn't even think. It just happened. She stepped into it. Her mask, her second skin. The hero.

"You think you could be stronger than me?"

The boy shrank.

"You think you could win?"

His eyes watered.

Lila didn't care. Let it frighten him. Let it hurt him.

Let it *bury* him.

"If you ever set foot in the arena, I will kill you." Her voice was a whip. Her laughter was foreign, dark. "And I'll be sure that it hurts."

The boy flinched, cowering into his mother's arms, but he never took his eyes off of her. Lila saw his expression, his wide, earnest eyes. And she was not ashamed.

Today, she was many things. She was a figurehead. She was a possession. She was a weapon. She was a hero.

She was a monster.

But she wasn't Lila. This had nothing to do with Lila.

Let them be afraid.

Let them hate her.

So long as not a single one of these kids followed in her footsteps.

Abruptly, Lila turned and strode away. The crowd parted for her. Every pair of eyes followed her graceful movement.

She didn't know what they were feeling anymore. All Lila knew was that they watched her. It took her another minute to realize what it was—their fascination with who she was, who she wasn't, and what she would or wouldn't do.

They were *obsessed* with her.

And she owned them.

***

Pilot was not happy.

"What the hell were you thinking?"

She leveled him with a look. "I was thinking that I don't want any more recruits in your Coliseum."

"Since when do you have an opinion on this?"

"You made me the hero."

Pilot glared. "I thought we'd gotten past this! I know that you're still grieving, but for God's sake, can't you see reason? The Coliseum saves lives, Lila. It teaches people how to survive. These boys are strong. They eat, they sleep safe, they thrive."

"Right up until the part where it kills them."

And then suddenly Pilot was there, inches from her, and he slapped her hard across the face.

"I will not let you ruin this," he whispered.

Lila raised her eyes to his.

She dropped her arms over his shoulders and kneed him in the gut. Pilot was not a fighter. He was surprised, then sick, doubling over. Lila used her weight to spin them both around, so that it was Pilot pinned against the wall and Lila's forearm forcing his chin up.

Lila leaned in. "Touch me again, and see how fast it all falls apart."

His eyes were glassy and wide. She could feel his heartbeat under her hand.

He hissed it out. "Are you threatening me?"

Lila smiled coldly. "Of course not."

She let him go.

Then, cocking her head and fitting the image of Pilot's hero on like a second skin, she chuckled. "What could you possibly do to me?"

The question of what Lila, on the other hand, could do to Pilot hung in the air long after she'd gone.

He should have taken it more seriously. He should have considered exactly what Lila could do—and what it would take for her to do it.

But he didn't.

This was Pilot's second mistake.

Chapter 28

A fight had broken out in the dormitory.

No one seemed to know what to do. The boys at the Coliseum weren't allowed to fight outside of the arena and, for several horrible minutes, there was the distinct possibility that no one would intervene.

But then Lila found them.

She was seething—the red mark that Pilot had left on her cheek still stung—and at first she didn't realize what she was hearing. She pushed the door open.

Most of the boys were still on their bunks, but several had circled around the two guys on the floor. They didn't see her come in, and they certainly didn't turn away from the fight. Conflict was abnormal, to say the least.

It was attractive.

The one with the dark hair was on his feet, dragging the blonde up with him and tossing him against the wall. The other boy tried to move, but he was caught by surprise by a punch in the nose.

At least nothing broke.

The blonde guy slid down the wall, both hands cupped over his nose. He didn't fight back.

It took a minute for Lila to notice that the blonde never fought back.

Which only served to piss off the other guy even more.

He swore and kicked him, hard, just above the temple.

The second boy—younger, Lila suddenly realized—flinched. Made a noise like a plea.

It was another long minute before Lila realized that it was Max on the floor.

She threw herself into the fight, grabbing the attacker from behind and swinging him roughly backwards.

A surprised whistle came from the onlookers.

He stumbled, tripped over her knee and hit the wall violently. His head jolted painfully forward.

Lila blocked his wild, ill-formed punch towards her head with an arm. She used her own weight to pin his arm across his chest, gripping the other forcefully over his head.

"Do you want to tell me what the hell is going on?"

The boy growled. "Get off me."

Lila didn't move.

"Get off me."

He surprised her. She'd forgotten he was a Coliseum fighter. He shoved suddenly off the wall, using his own head to slam into her. She caught the full force of the blow at her temple.

For a second, there was just darkness and stars.

Then she felt him shove roughly past her and she simply reacted, swinging out half-blind but well trained. The punch landed his solar plexus and, when he crumbled, she grabbed his arms—blinking back tears—and twisted his wrist until he arched towards her.

But he was crying now.

"I'm sorry. I'm sorry."

He wasn't talking to her.

His body sagged. She felt the anger rush out of him.

Lila fumbled with his arm, letting him loose. He slumped forward onto his hands and knees. Drained. Done.

She turned away, pushing through the circle of boys and back to Max.

He was alone now, where he'd been left.

Sitting up, back of his hand pressed to his mouth, a black-eye forming that stretched all the way across the left side of his face, he looked pitiful. She reached out, but he turned away. He wouldn't look at her.

"Max-"

"Not here," he interrupted, trying to get up. Lila touched his arm and he flinched. "Not here."

She followed him out of the dorm and down the hall. They didn't speak, but limped along in silence. Max leading, Lila behind. So much distance between them that Lila thought it might swallow her whole.

When he went into the bathroom, she hesitated. A minute passed. Another. And then Lila couldn't wait anymore. She went after him.

He hadn't even tried to clean up his face.

He was just standing at the sink that didn't work, staring at himself in the mirror. His eyes refocused over his shoulder, meeting hers in the reflection. There was a hardness in his face, a hatred that turned his wide, gentle eyes to knives.

She hadn't known that he could do that with his expression, like he did it to his words.

But then he shattered.

And when he opened his mouth, it was like listening to someone crying so hard they can't speak, except that he wasn't crying. He was just staring at her in the mirror, holding on as tightly as he could to whatever was holding him up.

"Can you see it?" he whispered. "That I'm his son? Is it branded on me somewhere?"

Lila said his name, but he wasn't listening.

He dropped his eyes, looking at the tile floor, leaning down and using the countertop as a support. “Peter’s brother is dead. Apparently he had his first fight this morning. Didn’t survive it.”

Max swayed. He chuckled. Manic.

“He was too young to be in the arena, and Peter didn’t want him to go. But with my father’s new benefits for fighters, it’s hard to argue with a kid that wants to bring home food for his parents. The new rations would feed a whole family. And no one pays much attention to the age limit thing. So he went ahead and joined.”

Max steadied. He searched the floor with narrowed eyes and then suddenly looked up, raised a fist, and smashed it into the glass.

Lila reached for him.

He rounded on her. “Did you go back into the arena because of me?”

Lila groped for words.

“*Did you?*”

She shouldn’t have hesitated, but he’d surprised her. There was that thing again—that thing she’d promised to never say aloud.

“Max-”

His big, gentle eyes went wild. “Oh.”

It wasn’t fair. He was putting words in her mouth.

But he was still going, rushed and desperate. “All of it, then? You—what was it?—did you just decide you had to save me too?”

He searched the room frantically. Grasping for something. When he looked at her again, his expression was too full. Tearing. Coming undone. And she couldn’t help him.

Then, almost too quiet for her to hear, he asked it again. That thing he’d asked the night Alec left.

“Why?”

Lila didn’t have an answer for that. She pulled him into her arms, and this time he didn’t fight her.

Chapter 29

The worst part of seeing his father again was the compassion. Pilot took one look at him and dropped what he was doing. His thumb was gentle on Max's bruised face. He sighed.

"Who did this?"

Max didn't say anything. He turned away.

He hated that Pilot loved him.

Because how was he supposed to love a man who didn't love anyone else?

"I want to go home," Max said.

It was so much worse in the car.

Max sat in the passenger seat, Lila in the back. Pilot drove and he asked his quiet, probing questions. Max never answered. He didn't say anything. He just sat with his head against the window. He winced against the chill on his cheek, but was unwilling to risk it swelling more than it already had.

Pilot even asked Lila, once, what had happened.

Her eyes flickered up to meet his in the rearview mirror, and Max could only imagine her expression, because his father's face turned to ash.

He turned back to Max. "I want to help you," he said.

Max closed his eyes.

"I don't understand. You know that, whatever happened, it wasn't your fault, don't you?"

Max almost laughed.

How could Pilot not know? How did he not see it—in everything Max did?

The fault was entirely his.

There was a knife in his bedroom that had once belonged to Red Ferris which proved it.

When they pulled into the driveway, Max started to get out.

"Wait," Pilot said.

Max stopped with his fingers still on the door handle, his eyes on the floor.

His father shook his head. "I know we've had our problems lately, but I hope you know that I'm always here for you. I love you, Max. I want to help you. I hope, when you're ready, that you'll talk to me."

Max continued to look at the floor. His hands shook.

"You've been through a lot, and I know that you're strong because of it. We'll make it through this too. I just want you to know that you aren't alone."

For all Max could tell, Pilot meant it. He sounded sincere.

But then again, he always sounded sincere.

It had been a long time since Max could tell the difference between what Pilot wanted and what Pilot was. He pushed his car door open.

His father reached over and squeezed his shoulder. "When you're ready to talk, I'll be here."

But of course, in the morning, he was gone.

Chapter 30

"He left." Max said, deadpan. His back was to Lila.

There was a beat of silence.

Then, abruptly, Max hurled the pitcher off the kitchen counter.

***

When Pilot came back, he didn't actually want to see Max.

"It isn't that," he told Lila quietly, looking towards Max's closed bedroom door. She didn't tell him that Max was sitting in the study. She figured that if he didn't make his presence known, he didn't want to be found.

"It's just that I've been with the governors all day," Pilot continued. "And they've heard about the incident in the fighters' dormitory."

"What about it?"

"Well, it's just brought some negative attention to Max, that's all. And it's getting worse in the suburbs. Antipas is officially expanding his stadium to be even larger than mine, and that means he'll need to get his hands on more fighters. The governors are afraid that he'll think of trying to acquisition us next. He's got an army, apparently. The Council thinks we should have one too. They're considering other options. They look at Max and say that clearly some people aren't equipped to be fighters. Or worse, that the economy that New Chicago is built on, my Coliseum, is causing more harm than good. It's making the suburbs unstable."

Lila bent to pick up the dishes from the lunch she and Max had just finished. "Is it?"

"Is it what?"

"Is it making the suburbs unstable?"

Pilot made a noise that caused Lila to glance back up at him. "Don't be like that," he said. "I know what you think about the Coliseum, but that doesn't change anything. It's a good cause. It's the best bet we have right now to survive—hell, to make something good out of all the horrible things that have happened in the last two years."

That depended on your definition of good, apparently.

Lila didn't say anything.

Pilot ran a hand through his hair. "But the problem is that the governors don't trust it anymore. I'm going to have to prove to them that it will work. That's all. If the people in the suburbs see that anyone can become a fighter, I could get them back on board."

Alarms in the back of Lila's head.

Her eyes flickered to his face.

But it was Max, in the other room, that asked the question she was thinking. He appeared in the doorway, almost as quiet as Lila these days. His face was tired. "What are you going to do?"

If Pilot was surprised, he didn't show it. He only shrugged. "I don't think I have a choice. I'm going to have to make the decision—everyone goes into the arena."

"*What?*" Lila exclaimed.

Max just stared at his father.

Pilot rounded on her. "What else do you propose I do? I believe in the Coliseum, whether or not you do. It works. It's the best option for anyone. For everyone."

Max didn't say it immediately.

But eventually, in the silence that followed, it just slipped out.

"Even me?" he asked.

Quietly. Frightened.

Pilot looked up. "Of course," he said. "If it's good enough for the whole world, why shouldn't it be good enough for you?"

And just like that, it all fell apart.

Max looked away. He blinked, wrapping his arms around himself, and then turned and fled the room.

Lila called after him, but he didn't even pause.

He ran.

"How could you?" Lila snapped, rounding on Pilot.

He was surprised. "What are you talking about?"

Lila stared at him.

"My God, how could you *do* this to him? He *loves* you. Do you have any idea how much he loves you?"

"This is bigger than us."

"No. It's not."

Pilot sighed. "Let's not do this right now. I have bigger things to worry about. I'm going to make the announcement today. I need you there with me."

"What makes you think I'd do that?"

Pilot, who'd started preparing already, hesitated. He glanced at her. "Why wouldn't you? After everything—this is where you draw the line? For God's sake, you're already in the arena, what do you care where the fighters come from? Or how many there are? This isn't your battle. Don't pretend you give a shit about the fate of the world-"

He narrowed his eyes.

"-because you and I both know that if you ever cared about anyone but yourself, it was a long time ago."

Lila looked away.

Pilot gave a grim smile. "That's what I thought. Let's go."

They were at the door when Lila heard it. She glanced back and saw Max on the stairs, watching her. His eyes were wide and gentle and hurting.

But he didn't say anything because he'd promised, in another life, that he would never hurt her.

And look at how she'd repaid him.

"I care about what happens to Max," Lila said quietly, turning away.

She hoped he knew that. She hoped he knew that she loved him. *Tell me what to do.*

He didn't. He just let her leave.

Pilot stiffened, giving her a mean smile. "Not enough."

More than you.

But she didn't say it. Because she knew that Max was listening, and she'd already hurt him enough.

Chapter 31

Max sat at the top of the stairs. He sat and stared at the door, even though Lila and Pilot were already gone. He sat as the cold settled in. He sat as his hands went numb, as his heart turned to steel, as everything that he thought he understood just slipped through his fingers.

He sat there and wondered if he was going to let his father do this.

Destroy the whole world.

His whole world.

Lila.

Again.

And he decided not.

***

It only took an hour to walk to the Coliseum. He walked the same route Lila had shown him that night when they trekked through the dark to the foot of the aquarium. He walked through New Chicago, wearing his coat and the backpack he'd stolen from the study on his back, Pilot's maps and supplies inside. No one stopped him. No one noticed.

No one cared what Pilot's son did.

Lila was being made into a hero.

Max left the letter for her on his father's desk.

***

Later, when people started telling the story, they always said that Pilot found the letter. Several hours before Lila did. They said he read it and knew what his son had decided to do, but made no attempt to stop it. He believed that Lila didn't care enough to truly betray him.

If it was true, then it was Pilot's third mistake.

It would be his last.

Chapter 32

Lila stood motionless, erect, hooded by her dark cloak and glass eyes. Her face was stone. Her body was diamond.

Beautiful.

Terrible.

The governors had seen Max before. They knew Pilot. But they'd never seen Lila. Not like this. Not when she was the hero.

She made them nervous.

Pilot used that.

He talked about parents protecting their children and how girls in particular were at risk after the war ended. He mentioned that Lila's mother was selling her when they'd met.

He didn't say he'd been the one to buy her.

But maybe that was implied.

He talked about the future. It sounded beautiful and safe. He told them how everyone would be like Lila—perfect, strong, unafraid. A new breed of indestructible people.

Exactly what this volatile planet desperately needed.

At least, that was what Pilot told them. His governors did not disagree.

And Lila watched. She looked at them with her blank, burning expression and thought about Max.

He'd left her a letter.

He'd left a letter saying goodbye.

Leaving was the word he'd used. Because he simply couldn't stay anymore. Even though Pilot was his father. Even though he wanted what was best for Lila and was so sorry for what Pilot had done to Red. Even though he had nowhere to go.

Still, he left. Because he had to.

And with Max, it had always been that simple.

Pilot was still talking.

"The important thing, though, is to figure out how best to make that future happen. And I think, right now, that the most valuable effort would be in getting every able-bodied person into the Coliseum. Training for the future should begin today, right now. As soon as possible."

His eyes flickered to Lila.

She knew that there would be nothing in her expression for him to read.

He finished with his eyes still on her. "Which is why I've decided that, from this point forward, any healthy man or woman between 16 and 30 that doesn't enlist in the Coliseum will have to move."

He paused.

There was a murmur of hushed concerns.

"Do you think that's wise? Forcing people's hands?"

Then Pilot smiled coldly.

Checkmate.

"I'm stepping into the future, gentleman, and I intend to bring the whole of New Chicago with me."

The governors looked at each other, but no one objected. Maybe they didn't agree, but they didn't disagree either. Once upon a time, when the world was still freshly ended, they'd all agreed that something had to be done.

The only man who'd known what that something should be, the only one who'd *ever* known what it should be, was Pilot Archer. More than two years ago, with his son sick and dying in a hospital tent, he'd told them to build a Coliseum. He'd told them that they would make a New Chicago, one that would stand the test of time and save them all.

Now, abandoned by the son he'd saved and all alone, he was telling them that the Coliseum was still the way. He still had all the answers. He could—and would—still save them.

Nothing had changed in all that time. Pilot Archer was still the only one who knew what had to be done. So they would do as he said. And they would follow him.

Just like that, it was over. There was nothing left to say.

Except that there was.

Because Max hadn't just left Lila a letter.

Pilot had no chance to react. One minute Lila was nothing, just a doll with strange, hollow, glass eyes, and the next she was alive.

The knife slipped from the waist of her jeans to find the mold in her palm. She moved, inches, feet, it didn't matter except that one moment she was a dead thing—*Pilot's*—and the next she had slit his throat. One soft, muted stroke.

He dropped like a stone.

She looked up, Red's knife flush against her thigh, and all at once she was not Lila.

She was the *hero*.

The hero that Pilot had made. The hero that had killed him.

And Lila was free. For the first time since the world had ended, she was not afraid. Pilot was dead. His Coliseum could not hurt her, the nightmares would not reach her, and all of those kids who wanted to be just like her could not follow in her footsteps anymore. No more death, no more hurt, no more sorrow. Nothing.

Finally.

"I am closing Pilot's Coliseum. There will be no more of this."

The governors of the Chicago Council agreed. If they did not understand, well, the knife at her side spoke volumes. They must have seen the blood. They must have known that Lila had been made for this. She had destroyed the king—the devil—of New Chicago, and she would destroy every one of his governors, if she had to.

They only had to ensure that today she wouldn't have to.

Lila smiled her devil's smile.

"Consider this your final warning."

Epilogue

The governors worked quickly. They shut down all the roads leading in and out of New Chicago. They paid people, in rations and fuel, to patrol neighborhoods. They increased the resources to supply a new, city-wide police force. All the dividends from the Coliseum were split equally between the governors and they went to work, conquering and dividing. The idea was that, if they got a tight enough leash on the city, it wouldn't slip right through their fingers.

It became almost impossible to move between districts. Everything was contained—the people, the resources, and, at least as far as the governors were concerned, the future.

But they couldn't stop the news. After Pilot's Coliseum closed, the panic swept like wildfire. Most of the fighters left within the day, but by the time the last, lingering boys had finally packed up their bags and headed for the road, everyone already knew. Pilot was dead. New Chicago, such as it was, had finished.

The governors promised that nothing would change, of course. They upheld the old laws. Curfews stayed in place. Rations were traded at the neighborhood markets as always. Citizen patrols made their rounds and were paid. Life went on.

Except that it didn't. Without the added income of the Coliseum, New Chicago couldn't support the full size of its population anymore. Rations dwindled. The governors bickered. One by one, the districts closed their borders, defending their resources. With fewer people, they could survive for longer. Tensions rose.

And the people, the citizens, understood. Nothing would be as it was. Just as they had in those long, awful days after the bombs had finally stopped falling, they would move on. They would walk out of New Chicago and away from that past. They would find a new future. And Pilot's city—Pilot's great, beautiful, shining beacon of hope—would die. Maybe the people had come to terms with that. Maybe it didn't frighten them. Maybe they were ready.

The governors of New Chicago were not.

So they closed their borders and locked their doors. They created district armies to defend their resources. They built walls. And then they settled in and waited for war. Because, if New Chicago was going to die, it was going to go out the same way it had come—

In flames.

It would have been different, maybe, if the governors had ever caught the hero. But they didn't.

Pilot's hero had vanished.

They never found Pilot's son either, but at least that was forgivable. They weren't looking for him.

They should have been.

No one knew Lila like Max did.

And he found her where he expected to find her.

She was sitting cross-legged in front of Red's grave. The grass was coming back around it, just bits and pieces, mostly buried in weeds. Winter had barely come, but it was already on its way out. The dirt almost looked healthy against Lila's pale skin.

Her hair was tucked away inside the hood of her sweatshirt, pulled up to hide her face. It was grey, blood stained. Too big for her.

She'd have looked like any other Coliseum fighter, homeless, to anyone else.

But Max knew.

He came and crouched down beside her. They didn't look at each other.

"It's beautiful," he said. He meant the grave. And it was. Beautiful and horrible.

Lila still didn't look at him.

Max sighed, scrubbed his face. "I heard what you did."

Finally, a reaction. Lila choked. She turned her bright eyes on him, mouth working words that wouldn't quite come out.

"I'm so sorry."

There were a lot of things he could have said to that. He'd known, after all, that she would do it. He'd practically asked her to. Put the knife in her hands.

Literally.

And it had to be done.

But there was the other part. The part that hurt to think about. The part that made him sick with sorrow. Grief. Guilt.

Pilot was his father.

Was.

Max shook his head. He tried to smile. "I thought we'd agreed not to be sorry."

For a second, Lila just looked at him. Then she gave a sad, startled laugh and turned away. "We agreed not to apologize, we never said anything about not being sorry."

Max settled into the grass next to her.

The minutes rolled by.

"We'll have to leave New Chicago," Lila said.

"I know. There was talk in Lincoln Park already about starting a manhunt for you. We can't stay."

He felt her eyes on him. "Where will we go?"

She must have known.

They both looked east.

If only the governors could have seen it. Pilot's son and Pilot's hero, sitting side by side in the grass, tearing everything he'd built apart.

"It'll have to be Antipas next, won't it?" Lila said.

She said it like it was simple. She said it like they were almost done, and it was almost over. The end. *Finished.*

It wasn't.

Max could already see it all, in his head. The governors, the districts, the future. New Chicago—what it was and what it would never be. And Antipas, on the other side, just waiting.

For there to be nothing.

"If he doesn't find us first."

CPSIA information can be obtained at www.ICGtesting.com
Printed in the USA
BVOW07s2037230114

342789BV00002B/10/P